DOMESTIC
DYSFUNCTION

Domestic Dysfunction

Contents

Fields
3501 Elevation Lane

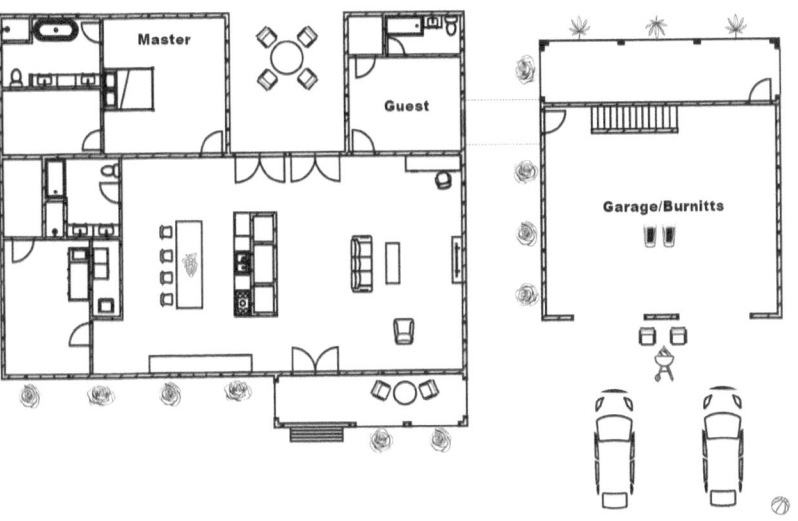

Master

Guest

Garage/Burnitts

Intro

My name is Marty Fields. Lucky for you, you are not me. I'm a different kind of loser. You might have to look closely to see it, but my spineless existence has been worse than a waste. I'm 42 years old and have yet to consistently enjoy my depleting, so-called life in ways that I imagine. The ominous outlook that I have developed has made me passive and hopeless on the inside. With that, I grew weak and unable to stand up for myself on the outside. This world has molded me into an aggravated but submissive man with long-lost ambitions and desires. There has never been any living on cloud-9 for me. My reality has better resembled the lowest levels of gloomy fog. I have been lost in a depressing haze and fading faster with every shitty moment.

As the bright side continued to dull for me, my life quickly diminishing to dark seemed inevitable. In recognizing just how easy that has been for me to accept, I've been compelled to dig deeper and realize what I'm truly capable of. Fuck it if I'm disregarded, only existing in the blurry background of other people's lives. Acting on certain impulses will be easier to get away with if no one's paying attention.

There's a lot of my life that I can't recall but assume bad memories are best forgotten. For the most part, my marriage has been anything but memorable. It was inseparable love at first but soon became constant loneliness and growing animosity. Despite that, I've never stopped craving love and will still do just about anything for a high-quality experience. It's a drug for me. Unfortunately, it's a powerful and unpredictable drug that my sanity's dependent on. Lately, the unwanted side effects of it have become increasingly difficult to tolerate, and my desire to get a grip on the disease has intensified. My drug is Jane, and I'm addicted.

Chapter One — Friday

Out of nowhere, I began to accept that I was conscious and that I must have been sleeping. Since it's still dark out, I probably haven't had the most beneficial amount of sensory suspension. My first thoughts emerge as unknowns of the night before. I think Jane might have been mad at me for something. Yesterday got away from me at some point, and now I'm left confused. The sound I inadvertently make through a long exhale and barely tolerable stretch is a crude vocal representation of how I feel. My body hurts, and this shitty couch that I always find myself trying to sleep on is likely half the reason. I've hated it just about every night for years now. It's upholstered in fine Italian silk and has contemporary lines, which means it functions perfectly for Jane, but it's no sleeper by any means. However, even with its discomfort and lack of length, getting up and moving won't be the easiest thing this morning.

Just as I was about to make an effort to sit up, I noticed the half-full glass of wine on the table distorting the TV's firework screensaver behind it, and my mouth was lacking moisture to the point of concern. Despite it taking a couple of thoughts to convince my arm muscles to reach for it, I drank it in two swallows still lying down, careful not to spill any on her precious fixture. Thankfully, the cheap fix managed to hold up to its description and allowed me to move my tongue again. I probably knew that I would wake up thirsty. After all, every morning is the same. However, I like to think that in the past, my present self thought about my future self like that. At the time, I was only thinking about myself. At the same time, that was pretty selfless of me.

My lack of recollection is a born strength. Some might go out on a limb and assert that it's all the drugs and alcohol that I consume that are to blame. I disagree. There's evidence to suggest some possible exceptions, but I tend to believe that it's mostly my resilient brain protecting itself as it should. It's a defense mechanism that I need when dealing with Jane. The drugs simply complement the strategy. Jane often accuses me of being out-of-my-mind drunk, but she struggles with bad habits such as being oblivious like that.

Admittedly, I have been drinking even more than I used to the last few years and often find nights like last night difficult to fully remember. How I continue trusting myself getting that drunk, I couldn't tell you. For me, other side-effects of the home hooch hobby include periodic feelings of anxiety, remorse, and social awkwardness. Complications also include sleep deprivation and the inability to maintain healthy relationships. Despite the potential problems, I do my best to ignore them all. Alcohol helps. After drinking my way through reality and into the twilight zone, things are usually better blacked out anyway. Whether it's my own buzz-inspired, bizarre behavior or Jane's relentless dissatisfaction with me, the alcohol-induced Alzheimer's can prove convenient for sanity's sake. More often than not, I prefer to forget altogether rather than have out-of-context, unreliable fragments of memory to make sense of.

Over time, as nights have become less and less clear, I often wake up needing answers and assurance. That's why I developed a routine of morning checks. Investigating my clothing situation is typically the first thing I do once I become aware enough. For me, the overwhelming desire to be naked is another one of those drinking drawbacks, so how much fun I wanted to have the night before is always in question. Waking up fully clothed reduces the likelihood that I exposed myself around the neighborhood looking for something to do. Despite never knowing for sure, it's always a relief when the evidence suggests I stayed decent. Maybe I didn't make a scene the night before in full solute to curious onlookers and fucking passersby.

Thankfully, I woke up in my pajamas this morning, so I don't think I let anything overly disgraceful happen. I get worried when I'm naked and have to find my clothes. Finding them in random places worries me more. What's even worse than that is when I wake up naked in random places. Luckily, I don't think that's happened in a while. Most of the time, I find myself on the couch where I should be with my clothes within reach. From there, it's usually whether or not I closed the blinds that I become most concerned about.

These days, I'm drunk at nightfall, so remembering the window coverings is a necessity. I don't want people looking in. Typically, there's a variety of questionable and disturbing behavior happening behind my blinds. From my experience, it's domestic dysfunction at its best. Drinking as much as I do is always a gamble. With blacking out, anything could have happened. The who, what, where, when, and why's are always unknown. Who did I call? What did I do? Where's Jane? When did I pass out? Why don't I have clothes on? Pleading to myself out loud is something I often do—*please everything be good*.

It's just after five, and after a quick comb through the house, I find nothing too out of place. The kitchen light was left on, but at least all the blinds were shut. Jane and the dog were sleeping in the bedroom, the two of them dominating the California king. I noticed that Jane had two empty glasses on the nightstand beside her which suggests she was drinking water. We don't use real wine glasses around here anymore because full glasses tend to be a little too top-heavy with compromised abilities. For her, one glass means wine, and two glasses mean wine with water on the side. Since there's no distinction between them aside from contents, I just refer to them as her "winter" (wine/water) glasses.

With everything inside appearing more/less in order, my initial worries lessen. So far, it seems that I was able to keep it together despite my blemished brain. However, I still feel like Jane was enraged for some reason. Something in my head hints at her being excessively expressive. These days, her being pissed off and yelling at me is more common than not. Just me being myself gets under her skin. I'm sure she was snappy at me for her usual reasons, and as usual, I eventually said something about it. That's what usually happens. Jane doesn't like it when I do that. My potential reactions to her outbursts are what worry me most. She doesn't have a filter and says some legitimately hateful shit. Luckily, I don't remember anything about me yelling or being heated, but I'm not sure how much I should be trusting myself.

Jane's repulsed by me always wanting to party with her and get laid. Her constant pushback has been inappropriate and careless. She's a difficult person to deal with most days. Alcohol helps. I've learned that silence is best, but that's always been challenging for me. Trying to keep my mouth shut is one of those rare exceptions in which alcohol doesn't help. I don't want to be quiet anyway. The truth is, all the silence has been insufferably lonely. And my loneliness is reason enough for the questionable behavior I've been exhibiting.

Lately, I've become increasingly aware of just how short life is. It's hard to believe so much past is gone already and so little future lies ahead. With those thoughts, I had somewhat of a revelation that I can't stop thinking about. Regardless of what I do and any consequences of those actions, it'll all be over soon. There's no reason I should ever be silent.

Jane acts as if she has the right to lose her shit and express how appalled she is by me anytime she's not in the right mind. It's not the special treatment I imagined getting as a husband. The wasted time and constant reminder of how she feels about me causes me significant stress, and it's likely dome-damaging. I've advised her to stop shitting on me, but she continues to flirt with the limits of my self-control. Jane has been reckless about how grave she's forcing me to be. Whether I accept her rejection or not, I'm losing my fucking mind. And things are destined to end badly if I don't do something about it soon.

What seems to bother Jane most about me is essentially everything. We've grown divided in what each of us thinks is important in life. It's the simple things that I value most and choose to focus on. Jane, on the other hand, has a professional image to uphold. Her career has become everything about who she is, and it's made her uptight and high-strung. She's a living advertisement for her employer. I work for a paycheck and go home in hopes to live my real life. I've become a serious problem for Jane. She chooses to be serious all the time and can't stand how easygoing I am. If I'm on the spectrum, as she often claims, I couldn't be farther away from her.

Over time, I haven't changed much at my core. All I've ever lived for is celebration and consummation. That said, I manage the responsibilities that I have and the different roles that I assume as well as anyone. However, I'm not proud of how well I can adapt to the shit I despise. That's a skill only people with no backbone can develop. My career and marriage are perfect examples of my ability. What disturbs me most is how intolerable I am to Jane when I'm at home and get to be myself. It's like she's forgotten the reasons for wanting all of this in the first place.

My frivolous conversations and constant jokes are intentional. It's often blamed on the booze, but I tend to think that the alcohol only enhances the humor. Jane's halfhearted at best with my personality. She's better than me, and her actions speak even louder than her words. That's saying something considering how loud she gets. I keep suggesting her mouth could be used in more productive and seductive ways if she ever wanted to try something different—like shutting the fuck up, for instance.

There has been an ongoing lack of affection and growing frustration between Jane and I that's driving us farther apart. I never would have expected her to develop into such a passive prude all the time. She puts her pussy on a pedestal but doesn't even know how to use it. There was a time when I thought our aspirations were along the same path, but it's since been proven that our individual routes were just crossing each other when Jane and I first met. Unknowingly, we were headed in different directions but connected perfectly back then. Mathematically, our perpendicular, straight-line life tracks are likely to never cross again.

Jane and I having genuine fun together is something that happens sporadically and is always brief at best. We have to try to get along. Lately, it doesn't seem worth the effort anymore. The way I see it, Jane decided a long time ago that our relationship peaked and there would be no further reason to exert herself. I miss the better days with Jane and how good I felt. Unfortunately, they were relatively short-lived compared to the many years that followed.

Sensuality came naturally when Jane and I first met. She had my full attention from the moment I noticed her. Right away, my attraction to her overwhelmed my thoughts. Her long dark hair and perfect teenage body had me crushing hard. More important than that, she was attracted to me. That's what has always turned me on most. These days, she's distant. Her hair's always in a bun, and she never wants to show off her body unless she's going out. Jane used to want to have as much fun as possible and fuck just as much. A lot has changed with her since those days. The only thing that's changed with me is that I don't give a shit anymore. I did spend a lot of years trying despite her increasingly inconsistent interest in me. These days, I think we're both over it but can't find enough logic or motivation to move on. I'm amazed that divorce isn't a line that's been crossed. That line must be wider than the world. Even though we haven't exactly passed it yet, we have been on that edge for too long.

Chapter Two

Water is essential for me at this point. Apparently, Jane's on to something having two glasses. Maybe I should be as prepared, knowing that I always wake up more thirsty than I thought I'd be. Either way, it can only be avoided for so long. My lips are chapped, my eyes are dry, and I'm unable to consciously perform the normally simple subconscious task of swallowing. Heading into the kitchen, details of last night continue to be redacted. The light being left on happens every so often, but since I prefer it to be dimly lit by the various appliance and gadget lights, Jane probably neglected that. After all, those two glasses of hers were probably refilled multiple times throughout the night. The water out of the fridge is too cold for the amount that I need to consume, so I opt for the tap. After almost three glasses, I had to stop. But I'm aware that my body probably requires much more.

With it being so early, I still have three hours before I have to leave for work. Despite my lack of sleep and hangover, I won't be going back to bed. What husband could without a reasonably comfortable couch to sleep on? Instead, I decided that a morning cup of wine wouldn't be overly inappropriate with so much time available. Ironically, it would be good for the uneasiness I'm feeling about my lack of memory, which is often escalated with cups of wine. Even so, it would be perfect on the porch being washed down with a morning smoke. Not to mention, it's customary on a Friday. Tonight will be the worthwhile celebration that comes but once a week, and I'll happily drink to that—out of a coffee mug for appearance reasons.

Drinking before work isn't something that I do every day, but today's not going to be the exception. I'll try to consume just enough so that I can come down to the legal limit by the time I hit the highway(ish). Before heading out, I put a fresh pot of coffee on knowing that if Jane got up and there wasn't any, she would know exactly what I was sipping on. Knowing her, she would have something to say about it too. If Jane's not minding her own business, she's minding mine.

As mentioned, I've been on a bit of a binge. Multiple days in a row are known to get away from me occasionally, but an entire month or two is taking it to a new level. It's not a new level up, so it must be a new low. Everything around me seems confusing to some degree. It's like I've been operating on autopilot. Sometimes I get the impression that my autopilot doesn't always have the best intentions for me, but since I'm drunk, I just go along for the ride. Maybe I shouldn't be so faithful, but I trust myself to take me where I need to go.

I woke up naked on the bathroom floor the other day with two 3-liter boxes of wine (one empty), the dog toy, my cookbook next to me opened up to beef wellingtons, and a nut in the toilet. I don't know what the fuck went down that night and probably don't want to. Regardless, I think that I stayed home and out of trouble despite being blackout drunk and active. So even without memory, I think that my autopilot's guiding me well enough. I have fun being drunk but recognize that the lifestyle can't be sustained. I need to make a change much sooner than later but know that now's not the time. If I stop now, I'll never get through the weekend. It's going to be one of those super rare weekends, one that I'm not entirely looking forward to.

I wish that I could say that Jane and I are celebrating our anniversary on Sunday, but that would be misleading. Sunday's our anniversary. Unfortunately, there's nothing worth celebrating. In these times, the day is just a shitty reminder that another year has passed since the last shitty reminder. When a relationship's at its worst, an anniversary only evokes thoughts of disappointing days. I've learned my lesson. This anniversary's a sham as far as I'm concerned. I should just call out of work and get an early start on drinking my way through it. Too bad that I have a ton of unimportant work to finish or else I would.

Jane wasn't the only thing flooding my thoughts this morning. Always in the back of my mind is having to go to work and sit at that fucking desk. Asset management, it's such a bullshit, mind-numbing, suck corporation dick and fuck the end-user type of environment. I'm the glorified middleman in this threesome. As nice as a good suck and fuck sounds, not with those cocks.

Although I had a knack for business in my early days, having wheeled and dealed everything from music and movies to electronics and weed throughout high school, I always liked shooting video. I even studied media production before spontaneously deciding on pursuing a finance degree. It would allow me a good-paying, steady career is what I casually thought, not knowing it would lead to this daily dose of pride I'd have to swallow.

My life feels like it's been reduced to two things. Work and marriage now define me. All the fun has been boiled away. It's those two things alone that dictate the vast majority of my unoriginal existence. My career has never once brought joy to me, and my marriage has become joyless. I don't know if I'd be happier if I never changed majors or married Jane, and I don't necessarily regret making those choices. I am, however, disappointed with allowing myself to be this unhappy for so long. I have become increasingly curious if I could spend what's left of my life with more satisfaction. It's too often that I want to tell both the job and the wife to fuck off.

Today's my favorite day of the week despite having to show up to the daily grind. It's more like the daily grinder with all those cocksuckers. I have a better mindset on Fridays knowing that the workweek is so close to being over. I like Saturdays too, but the problem with Saturdays is, by then, one carefree night is already over. And it's difficult for me to fully enjoy Sundays knowing that with every tick of the clock, I'm that much closer to the miseries of the week to come. Sundays feel like that last day of a vacation when I'm left having to accept that it's over. Most people would do just about anything for it to be the first day again. That first day is what Friday evening feels like.

I finished my drink lost in deep thought but wasn't ready to switch over to coffee. It's too early, so I went in for another cup of the grape goods, confident that I'll feel better once I get it in. Turning from the fridge, the empty water glass on the counter caught my attention. It alerted me that I could be making better choices. I compromise with the better me and drink another half glass before returning to the porch. Earlier, I was too lost in forgotten thoughts to enjoy my smoke, so I lit another one and walked around the house to complete the outside portion of my morning checks. It's always a relief finding the garage locked up and the cars parked where I remember last. Since I dislike road driving so much and am reluctant every time I have to do it, I never leave too intoxicated. However, I always fear that I might if I let Jane get the best of me. It's dangerous dealing with her. Considering the wife I have, the job I have, and the habits I have, it's clear that I have become well-versed in flirting with my limits of tolerance.

Nothing outside seemed out of place, so I went back in

and headed to the spare bedroom's bathroom after topping off my "coffee." I've only had a few drinks out of it but generally like to keep it full. It's better to have more than enough in my case. I don't sleep in the guest room, but I've essentially taken over the closet and the bathroom. Jane and the dog get the master. I've been considering setting up the space so that it functions better for me, but I haven't decided what I want most. Rather than it being a dedicated bedroom, maybe it would be best to make it a proper living room because the rest of the house is anything but. Either way, I just need to sleep better. From here, it'll be an attempt to shit followed by a shower and bath. First, a shower to brush my teeth and wash all my pits, then a bubble bath to relax and refresh—lavender to be specific. I'll spend the next forty-five minutes sipping my wine in candlelight and cigarette smoke trying to convince myself that I can make it through the bullshit to come.

Jane works random hours, so I don't know if I'll see her this morning. Part of me wants to know if something went down last night, but most of me doesn't even want to think about what could have. She's so hateful that I often imagine different ways to shut her mouth. Sometimes I give her the verbal lashing she deserves, sometimes I do more. One thing's for sure, my imagination spares no details. With Jane's sporadic real estate career and refusal to communicate normally, I never know when she's working. She works with her mom, Karla, who's known around here as the property "Queen." Jane has a broker's license herself, but she seems happy enough being Karla's daily sidekick with choice clients. With ABRE, Jane has the exact opposite type of job as me. While she goes out to lunch, I pack a lunch and sit in my parked car. While she's mobile all day, I sit stagnate at my desk. Her work is flexible and delegable, mine is required. As far as I'm concerned, the only thing our jobs have in common is that both our bosses are cunts.

In all honesty, that's not entirely true. My boss is a cunt

but Karla's not. Despite being materialistic and somewhat annoying, Karla's all right. For the most part, she seems to mind her own business. She's never directly given me shit for anything, so I can't say anything too bad about her. That said, she is best friends with Jane and probably gets earfuls of one-sided mistruths from her.

It's hard to say with complete confidence what Karla thinks about me. Again, most of what she knows of me comes through Jane. With that, I'm surprised she doesn't openly despise me. Over the years, I've come to believe Karla's more in touch with the reality of modern life and relationships than Jane. She's twice married and gives the impression of knowing men well. She's had an affair with the same man in both of her marriages and is with that guy now. Karla's not an innocent woman by any means, but she owns it. From what I know, she's confident, well off, happy, living her own life, and nonjudgemental when it comes to other people living theirs.

After thinking about it more, I hope that I can get out of the house without seeing Jane. It would probably be best for my mindset this morning. With it being Friday, she's probably not a risk worth taking. As usual, when it comes to her, I don't know what I want. When everything's good, she leaves me wanting more. Unfortunately, that's been the exception for too long. Waiting around for it has become a bad habit of mine that I'd like to kick.

With only an hour to go before I have to leave, I drink my last bit of wine in one big gulp, rinse my cup, and wisely move on to coffee. Going outside to get the paper, I notice the day looking, smelling, and feeling like the mid-summer Friday morning it is. Earth as a whole seems more joyful on the weekend. I guess when there are millions of happier people in the world, you can sense that collective positivity in the air. Jane doesn't contribute.

The classifieds are about the only thing I'll read in the

paper. Although I continue to receive it, I've been refusing current events for twenty years. The shit out there has absolutely nothing to do with me. Plus, I feel strongly about how the news media instigates negativity and depression. They're like wives in that way. Popular news coverage is good entertainment for many, but for me, it's a disgusting reflection of what's wrong with us as a species. As with my home, the world would be a better place if everyone just focused more on fucking and partying.

Before heading in, I watered the flowers and plants as I do most mornings. If I didn't, they'd be dead. With it just being the usual miserable Jane and myself, enjoying the results of affection and nurturing fills a void for me. The plants out back in the special patch will do more. With that said, my newspaper subscription isn't a complete waste. It's always saved and used a few times a year to hold back any of the unwanted garden weed.

By eight-o-clock, I'm as ready for work as I'm allowed to be. It was a tough morning in terms of energy, but I crossed that hurdle and probably feel about as good as I can on an early work day. A couple of cups of "coffee" can do wonders. Before leaving, I glanced in the bedroom, only to see Jane still sleeping. Her being so pretty and quiet makes me want to turn my back on the world and join her, but she wouldn't see it as the romantic gesture I'd intend it to be.

The dog is all the company Jane prefers. He has essentially claimed possession of her since she brought him home as a pup. He's a dick about it too, but I can't blame him for acting the same way I would if she would allow me to. I'm sure he heard me opening the door but didn't bother to move since she didn't. Jane insisted on getting the dog. I was openly and strongly against it. It didn't seem like the right time to be taking on obligations. I thought that focusing on our relationship should be the priority. Of course, there was nothing I could do about it. Jane brought him home within days of first mentioning it. Even so, I insisted on naming him Warden. It was the first thing that came to mind. I just knew he would be the dog dictator he is, and this so-called home of mine would be the prison he governs. I'm around three years into my sentence.

With the weekend and my anniversary in mind, I thought a note would be the best that I could do in terms of trying to start neutral with Jane, especially since my mouth might have gotten away from me. It took a few minutes to come up with something just right to write. Of course, I had to say hi and acknowledge her, but it had to be in a calculated way because I can't quite decipher my broken memory. I'm certain she was bitchy and angry before the night's end. I'm just not sure if I instigated or perpetuated it, and if so, to what degree. *Good morning. Happy Friday. -Marty*, is what I settled with. I started with *Good morning beautiful. Happy anniversary weekend! Love, Marty*, thinking it would give the impression of excitement for our anniversary. It's also sounded good in case I was at fault for something. Maybe it would suggest being sorry if I should be. I couldn't stick with it though, it felt too deceitful. No need for me to kiss any ass these days. Jane detests me regardless—even if I use tongue. With that, it's just one more smoke out in the garage before packing up and pushing through the fucking day.

The fact that I can actually get myself to work is a testament to the power of body over mind. Every day, every part of my mind is telling me to eject with such convincing reasons, but somehow my body can go about the motions of getting me there anyway. It doesn't happen like that every time, but more times than I'd like to think about. At work, I have to put on face. But I find it easy to perform my so-called responsibilities as convincingly as possible in my condition. I figure that I'm performing well enough considering I continue to have a job. I fucking hate it though—more than anything. Jane's hate for me doesn't compare to my hate for work. The only thing good about a desk job is not having to hide the hard-on that I have all day watching the skirts walk by. I don't want to be there though.

Alcohol helps. That's why I carry a fifth of vodka in the center console of my car. Every morning upon arrival, I down a drink, finish a smoke at the entrance ashtray, and check my dignity and self-worth at the door.

Five out of seven days, the reliance on money dominates, and they couldn't go by fast enough. To me, time is the most bizarre but predictable phenomenon. It's as if it knows that I watch it, and it never gives me what I want, moving either agonizingly slow or cruelly fast when all I want is the opposite. On Fridays during work, I use that experience to my advantage. With my typical procrastination during the week, the work needing to be finished has built up; so much work, that I put myself on the border of needing more time. By having to rush and telling myself throughout the day that I don't have enough, the hours seem to go by a little faster. Friday's are agonizingly long, but they don't compare to Mondays. I've always heard the expression that time is money. For me, it's the opposite and not worth it.

Chapter Three

The highlight of most days for me is the final few miles of the drive home from work. The exit off the highway is the long-awaited entrance to the "high" way. For the less than four miles of pavement from there to the house, I'll be in what I refer to as the taint of my life. It's the little time that I get in-between the ass of a job and cunt of a marriage that makes up the rest of my existence. It can be a little harry at times, but that comes with the territory. It's during that short drive, when I'm out of work, out of traffic, and out of house, that I get the most consistent enjoyment. In the context of my day-to-day, this is when I get a break from the piss and shit.

Once I hit that exit, I'm more than ready to be me again. All day I've been immersed in a blackhole reality that I don't want to be a part of, and this will only be a short intermission. A proper beer and buzz have been a long time coming. By the time I get off, one beer has been retrieved from the rolled-up sweater under the seat and opened—my first guzzle always slightly messy (likely caused by excitement or road conditions, rather than sloppy can engineering). Either way, the satisfaction I get from wiping the beer off my face with the sleeve of my work shirt is always justified. It's sort of like cumming on Jane's toothbrush after a weekend of her belittling me. I drink an IPA from a local brewery called ShackBrew. Bottles are what we keep in the kitchen fridge, but I secretly buy cans for the road. Those beers are never cold. I hide them in the garage and "pack up" before work, chipping away two at a time throughout the week. I try to get one more in on Fridays.

Unless I absolutely need to be home, Lookout Corner is where I park to get that second or third beer in. Jane knows nothing of my routine. It's a scenic overlook with some picnic tables and enough parking to avoid the occasional police officer stopped there. Given the hillside corner and people's inability to drive safely, I assume that they sit out there to be seen. It's a relatively frequent spot for accidents, and their presence tends to slow people down. However, it's also likely that they don't give a shit and are doing the same thing as me, taking a break from whatever they're supposed to be doing. In all these years, they have never bothered me, so I'm never bothered by them. Today I chose to enjoy beers two and three at the corner. From what little I have to choose from, this is where I want to be.

Lately, I've been bothered a lot by my approaching anniversary. I wish it was another weekend. For not having any fun this year, the time sure has moved surprisingly fast. In a dysfunctional marriage, the last thing that a couple needs is any type of added expectation of romance. It produces a different kind of pressure that can be difficult to cope with. Jane and I can't be happy with each other, and this weekend will just be another significant reminder. If we can't have a great time together most of the time, especially when we reasonably should be, the relationship is clearly shit. There's no pride in just surviving another year. The love hasn't grown stronger, it's not even there. The thought of it all was too fucked for a Friday. I needed to not think about it until I had to. All I should be doing right now is concentrating on the tasks in hand, my much-deserved beer and joint.

I leave Lookout with enough distance remaining to

smoke another cigarette. Similar to a last meal on death row, it's one last enjoyment before Hell and a lifetime of torture. I always wish that I had another beer to drink with it, but disposing of the cans before I get home helps keep this operation going without being compromised. Jane's probably doing the same thing as I am, but she would jump at the opportunity to paint a broken picture of me no matter how functional I am. As usual, I end the cigarette just in time to flick the butt at The Neighbors' mailbox before pulling into what is supposed to be my American dream.

Driving over the exaggerated road swale at the start of the driveway is the all-to-familiar reminder that I've arrived. I'm turning myself in and will have to do the time. Joint out, beers gone, music off, living … over. Getting out, it's hard not to sigh at the suburban facade within the HighBlue housing community. I think of it as the feeling high but feeling blue community. Other people seem to like it though. Within it, there are repeatable patterns with everything: houses, mailboxes, plants, professions, hot wives, hot rods, asshole dogs, assholes, newly divorced, and newborns every first, second, or sixth fucking door. It can be kind of trippy at times. I don't fit in and have never desired to. If it wasn't for Karla securing so much house at such a great price, I wouldn't be here.

It feels like unnecessary competition all around me. I don't compete. I drive a thirteen-year-old hatchback and landscape like I manscape. I'm not constantly trimming, I just cut it when it gets too high. Everywhere, people are vying for the greener grass with generic material possessions of varying calibers. It's just people overcompensating for the lack of sexual satisfaction in their own dysfunctional homes. Simple men like myself surrender to the neighbors shorter, greener grass contest, though there remains plenty of dissatisfaction here.

Seeing Jane's car at home was the kind of a buzzkill that I don't need right now, but I know that I have cold beer in the fridge that can help with that. The events of last night never came to me, but it's probably better that way. If she's pissed off, it's time to find out. As I was about to walk in, I could see her sitting out back on the phone. She looked great. I love seeing her being herself when I'm not around. There's surviving passion in me that's hard to contain when I admire her from afar. She's different. She doesn't look like a person that could hate anyone. Maybe I am special. After standing there for several seconds watching her through the French doors, I turned back around and picked a few fully-bloomed roses from out front. Seeing Jane immediately made me feel different about being home. I suddenly had hope and excitement for the weekend. Maybe we should try to celebrate. While on the phone, she looks happy. It's the look I miss most. I can't remember the last time it was directed at me, but just seeing it reminds me of her beauty.

Deciding to meet Jane out back, I first went to the fridge and cracked open a couple of cold ones. Despite my high hopes, I was met with a look that turned to relative disappointment the moment she saw me.

"Hey," she said, briefly rotating the phone away from her mouth. She gave nothing away with that greeting. Jane didn't seem overly excited to see me, but it's a normal-enough welcoming from her. "Did you pick my flowers?" Her displeasure in me was suddenly much more obvious. "Why did you do that?" she annoyedly asked. With that, she didn't even bother to rotate the phone away. It's fucked-up that she demands answers before even allowing me an opportunity to say hi back to her. Not to mention, it felt like she wanted the person on the other line to hear her disappointment in me.

She stopped me in my tracks. "Just a few," I said as I stood there for a moment holding the three roses in one hand and beers in the other. It felt like a fight-or-flight situation. Technically, Jane was right. They are her plants. They were given to her, by me, as a birthday gift many years ago. I grew about two dozen clippings that I cut from her parent's house—

her childhood home—and rooted and nurtured them in secret for months. I'm the one that planted them, and ninety-nine percent of the time I water and take care of them. She wouldn't have the flowers if it wasn't for me, let alone clones from the plants that her mom has loved for as long as I can remember. Her dad even enjoyed the roses. I didn't know what else to say. "Happy anniversary weekend. I grabbed you a beer too." I went in for the emotionless, quick kiss that we still share on occasion. She returned it.

"Thanks, but I have wine." She glanced at it quickly as if pointing to it with her face. It didn't take thirty seconds for me to be repulsed by her demeanor after just picturing her so inviting. Within five minutes, I went from being reluctant to come home, to excited to be home, to not wanting to be here again. Whatever her problem is, she doesn't seem interested in trying to get over it. Without saying another word, I dropped the flowers in her now vase of a winter glass and walked back in with both beers. I'll be drinking the two of them myself, in the bathroom that accurately describes how I feel—like a guest.

Prior to washing, I spend a minute standing nude in front of the bathroom mirror blowing smoke rings at myself. Watching them hit the glass and slowly spread evenly outward until dissipating has become somewhat of a pre-shower ritual as I look myself over. I've always been satisfied with the way that I look, more so from the neck down. I'm no ten-inch fitness and diet freak, but I've kept up physically and like my dick good enough. I'm not hung like a horse but proud to be very much able and willing to work like one. Neck up, I can't remember the last time I admired what I saw. Looking myself in the eyes gives me a deeper reflection that I prefer not to face.

I finished the first beer and a cigarette sitting naked on the toilet. I was too constipated to shit, too dehydrated to piss, too depressed to jerk off, and damn near too lazy to shower. If I didn't have a second beer and the ability to sit down while doing so, I doubt it would be happening at all. A broken and dejected, grown-ass man wallowing hopelessly about in the shower—no wonder we fucking hate me.

Getting dressed, I could smell food and hear the sounds of Jane in the kitchen. She's somewhat belligerent as if having to cook was so difficult. Her effort's exaggerated with everything but me. We still make dinner for each other most times, even when not getting along enough to actually enjoy the meal together. My submissive stomach instantly expressed a loud hollow plea for food without me even seeing any. I don't think that I've had a bite to eat since yesterday. The only thing that I had for lunch today was a couple of parking lot shots and a cigarette. After that, I went right back to work so that I could get out on time. After so long, fluid calories just aren't enough. Getting out of the house without running into Jane was my initial plan, but I quickly surrendered to my appetite without a fight—hopefully. Regardless, I needed another drink.

I haven't specifically mentioned it yet, but Jane's an alcoholic. To me, she's intoxicating in more ways than one. It became a regular thing for her starting in college. I think as a way to incorporate some fun into her new and unfamiliar busy life. It wasn't long before I enjoyed having a few with her from time to time. Back then it was fun. For the most part, she remained in a good head space with it. Early on, Jane's drinking created a window of opportunity for me. She loosened up, and it felt like we were able to enjoy each other's company again. It was like before, when we weren't so caught up in life.

Drinking was introduced and taught to me as an exciting way to change things up and keep it interesting for Jane. For me, it was always about sex. After some drinks, fucking around was pretty much a given at first. It was never exceptional with her, but at least it felt like we were finally starting to go in the right direction again. In the beginning, enjoying each other while we drank together was the standard. We were always in a good mood and looking forward to it. If nothing else, we celebrated not having anything else to do. It was always a proper alcohol-inspired, two-person party when we got shit-faced. I figured out later that, by that point, drinking was already becoming an out for Jane. Before long, the drinking continued and became an out for both of us. Though it's still all about the sex for me.

The inexperience I had with Jane in my younger days left me optimistic about a fun life with her. Everything was new, and there was excitement for what was to come. Back then, I used to imagine having our own home, more money, and more time together. I thought things would be great. With that, there would be no sexual limit. Unfortunately for me, good things never last as long as I hope. The sex that used to happen every time we drank together died down relatively quickly, and things only got worse. This pattern of me getting less and less affection as I get older couldn't be more opposite of what I expected. I only get older, and the idea alone is making me crazy. Looking back, outside of some early dating, things have never been consistently right with Jane and me. It infuriates me knowing that most people have become so much more sexually open these days, and I'm stuck with this girl that acts like her pussy's her private part. I'm just normal. Jane thinks I'm exceptional.

We should have been having the best time of our lives back then, making the memories that fuel love. Instead, Jane regressed. She can't handle the amount of alcohol that she's able to consume, and she always seems to have something that she's dealing with that prevents her from joy. Her threshold is outside of her tolerance. Drinking herself miserable and tired soon became the norm when with me. She became distant and unapproachable more times than not. Jane didn't want to drink and fuck anymore. She wanted to drink but then be left alone at any instant she desired. If I persisted, she would rage. At first, it was occasionally. Soon enough, it became as predictable as death. A trip with Jane can turn bad at any moment. It's one of her side effects.

I've always known that by keeping it together at work, Jane justifies falling apart at home. Between the two, she's made it clear what's worth her time. However, even though work is where she would prefer to be, Jane continues to be home as much as she can. I suspect that's because she can't get as smashed in-office or at property meetings, so it loses its appeal in comparison. Despite having predictable toxic mannerisms, drinking is what Jane's most concerned with; it's not sex, not work (unless it's from home, then she multitasks), not me, not anything. She's responsible for how I've become. More and more, I think she shouldn't be getting away with it.

With Jane, my emotions can sway unpredictably in reaction to her. It takes effort to not act them out, but it's probably best that I try to avoid all conflict. Maybe I've just grown to be a candy-ass coward. I'm not proud of it. Right now, I don't care what day it is or her fucking attitude. I won't let her get to me this weekend. And she won't be able to as long as I have no relationship or anniversary expectations. Maybe she'll give me the best gift ever, the gift of leaving me the fuck alone.

Chapter Four

As I entered the kitchen, I could immediately tell tacos were on the menu. It's one of my favorite meals, especially with a cold Cerveza.

"Hey," Jane said. She had a little more interest in her voice now. Even her body language was different. She seemed kind of friendly to my surprise. With her bitterness before, I was sure she was holding something I did last night against me. She does this though. After so many drinks, I just never know how she's going to feel about me. She's confusing, but I try to go with it as much as possible. Alcohol helps.

Right away, I want to tell Jane to shove her food simply out of spite. It might address my munchies but does nothing for my underlying hunger. She knows that I can't resist a good taco, but compared to what she brings to the table, maybe I'd be just as satisfied, or more, with a warmed-up bratwurst. I'm sure that Jane making food that I love is friendly at most. I can't expect anything else. If there's any indication from me that I would like more, it'll be as if I'm insulting her. She'll turn savage the moment I express interest. I want and try to be around Jane until I don't. It's at those times when I'm capable of going off. She knows that I don't want to just be friendly with her.

I was just successfully convincing myself that I needed

to keep my distance, but Jane's cooking is making me change my mind again. It's likely my fault that she takes advantage. Her being bitchy and expecting me to forget about it is a learned behavior resulting from years of me being more mouse than man. That's the kind of loser I am.

The tacos rendered me unable to just grab a beer and walk on by. I was helpless. Before replying, I noticed she put the roses in a small vase and showcased them perfectly in the middle of the island bar. The winter glass was more fitting, but at least she was taking care of them. I'd like to think she was suddenly all-in for a great weekend, but I know her better than that. Soon enough, she'll flip face for something stupid and brush me aside again, but not without some of her finest poetic psychobabble first."Hi," I said, somewhat reluctantly. "Need a drink?" I asked. My head was already in the fridge as I reached for a cold one.

"No thanks, I have one. I made us tacos. They're pretty much done."

"Yeah? They smell delicious."

"Help yourself." She had a dialed-down version of that irresistible smile that used to captivate me. Nowadays, I don't trust it as much, but it's always nice to see what I can of it.

"Sorry, did you just say help myself with your taco?" I quickly said "just kidding" before she could respond with whatever disgust she could come up with. "Thank you, after you." Just with those few words and that little smile, I think that I might have been missing Jane. Underneath it all, maybe I've been hoping we could make up for some lost time this weekend. There's no reason we shouldn't be able to get along on our anniversary. Why not enjoy some good food and drinks together at the very least? Both of us deserve that at a minimum. Either way, losers like me take what they can get. Opportunities and options don't present themselves as often as they used to. Jane will be Jane, but I'm easily intrigued by her change of tone and cautiously decide to go with it.

In all honesty, with Jane serving up good food on a Friday night celebratory weekend, she's in the process of converting me again. But I know that I have to keep in mind that she's familiar with how susceptible I am to her. In regards to Jane putting me first tonight, my experience disciplined me into knowing that it's no sure thing. As soon as she feels content, she'll be back to being her cunt self. Being notoriously vulnerable to her is something that I've become less proud of these days. That's probably because my pride is in my dick, and she doesn't give a fuck.

Regardless of what happens with Jane and me this weekend, our life together will never be a classic love story. By now, I think Jane's done too much harm. There is a foundation of love between us, but the structure seems to be crumbling and possibly irreparable. It's a type of love that I'm very familiar with but never understood. I recognize it as the same dysfunctional love our parents shared. That kind of love has more of a resemblance to Stockholms Syndrome than some fairytale of passion. Somehow, various stresses and pressures are able to dictate choices and produce incredible feelings. Marriage is misery poorly disguised as contentment. However, I'm far from being content with simple small talk, quick meaningless kisses, and empty love ya's. Simple gestures are for friendly strangers. Playing along is how Jane and I make an effort at being friendly. However, we're far from being in the same realm of love and life expectations. Worse than that, the underlying true friendship has been compromised by the marriage. Alcohol helps with contentment efforts, me keeping quiet and giving her space would help more.

With it being just Jane and me, our living room functions as a multi-use space. It's essentially our all-in-one media/gaming room, entertainment space, dining area, and office. It's also a bedroom for me most nights. I guess that it could be considered the dog house too, though Warden gets the master suite. We'll be eating tacos at our dining table, which is the coffee table that I typically refer to as the wine table. Turning on Netflix, I see the uncensored version of Hell's Kitchen first in the 'Continue Watching' row. That must have been what I fell asleep to. I got lucky. I forgot that I forgot to look this morning. It could have easily been porn of any variety. It's not uncommon for me given my constant frustration with Jane's stagnate sexual evolution.

"This has been funny," I say as if I remembered. I hit play and went straight to the tacos. "Yum." I practically swallowed the first few bites whole. The overstuffed spicy beef and cheese soft shells, topped with pickled onions, tomatoes, and hot sauce win me over right away. "These are great."

Just as Jane was about to respond, our attention quickly turned to the TV. "Fuckin hell" was yelled with such an angry frustration that we couldn't help but look. Chef was red and growing veins in all the wrong areas. Something about an under-seasoned and mushy risotto was pissing him off. With that, we shared our first genuine laugh in weeks, if not months. There's something about a pissed-off, cussing accent that's always such fun to hear. Maybe I should have married a foreigner. After two tacos each, we were both done. It was a fantastic dinner, and I felt happy to be home. I didn't want to sit around and watch TV though. Once my food settled and my beer was finished, I was ready to move on to something else.

"Wow. That was awesome, Jane. Thank you so much."

"You're welcome. Can I take your plate?"

"Nope, I got it. You cooked, I'll clean up everything." I don't think she planned on getting up anyway.

What a fucking mess I walked into. I didn't notice it earlier. Must be I had my food goggles on. Now I feel like I just volunteered myself to be Jane's bitch. She knew I'd clean if I ate. That means she had no incentive to keep up. None of the banging around I heard earlier had anything to do with cleaning up. When Jane wasn't tending to food, she must have been tending to drink. It looks like there was a five-course meal prepared by a child here. Never does she rinse things off, keep the counter clean, or empty/fill the dishwasher as she cooks. Don't get me wrong, I would have paid for those tacos. However, I could have just as easily eaten tortillas and salsa and been left as satisfied without any kitchen duties. I certainly wouldn't be feeling like her desperate fucking servant right now. Only beer can help with this mess, Jane won't.

After packing up the food and handling the dishes, I wiped down the counters and swept the floor. Jane came in just in time for it all to be finished. Right away, I can tell she's different now. That last glass of wine and food clearly caught up with her. It's only a matter of time before she has that all-too-familiar, drag-ass, try-not demeanor about her.

"Hey. How are you doing?"

"Ugh, I ate too much," she said with a look on her face that already said it all. She turned to the fridge and attempted to recover what was left of wine box number one today. I know that because I had to open a new one this morning before work. I reached around her for a beer as she continued to drain every last available drop without a bag squeeze. Once convinced that no more could be retrieved with that approach, she began working on it at the counter. Without hesitation, she ripped the plastic bag out by its tap—clearly well seasoned with the move—then managed to extract, at best, a sip more wine by bladder-milking the fuck out of this thing. After taking that desperate drink, Jane tossed the garbage in the bin and swiftly retrieved a new box from the pantry. I'm standing there watching her like it's paid entertainment as she swiftly punched through the box and pulled out the tap with confident expertise. She then replaced the drink she just had, stuck the box in the fridge, and came back for another large swig of the Grigio. It's then that I can tell that she's starting to buzz in the wrong direction, just as I am in the right.

That's the predictable behavior I expect of Jane. She feels like shit with everything but booze. We'll be having a decent time up until she begins to not feel good in whatever way her excuse will be. If she didn't eat too much, it'll be that she's tired, not feeling well in some way, or suddenly just not in the mood to have anything to do with me. Drinking makes her sluggish and wretched, and she couldn't care less about how condescending her excuses are. Just when I'm convinced that we're going to have a fun time, she'll all of a sudden, and without shame, want nothing to do with me.

In a way, it feels like I'm allowing myself to be stood up by the same person over and over again—but it's worse. It's more like I continue to wine and dine her despite her always getting up and leaving before dessert and without warning—but it's worse. It's more like I continue to wine and dine her despite her always getting up and leaving before dessert and without warning—but not before angrily expressing how much of a piece of shit I am for looking forward to and talking about dessert. A slap in the face and kick to the balls on her way out would make it an even better analogy.

Jane sat at the bar two chairs from where I was standing and looked up at me. She doesn't realize how bad her poker face is. She needed to sit, the wine was weighing her down. I'd bring it up and make a little fun but I know any humor could very well be the death of our evening together. Maybe now's not the time, but it won't be long before I can't avoid having a laugh at my expense. Alcohol helps me see the value of a good chuckle even though it pisses her off.

"Cheers. Happy anniversary weekend." I tilted my beer forward so Jane would have to reach over to meet it if interested.

"Cheers. Happy anniversary weekend," she said, matching my dying excitement with each word. Her response meant nothing to me, but her meeting me more than halfway did.

"Is there anything that you would like to do?" I know

that there isn't but ask anyway.

"No, probably just hang out."

After about fifteen seconds of me just standing there in silence as Jane sat looking defeated, the situation already seemed pathetic to me. She should feel lucky to be full. The weekend just started and she's already coming off sorrowful. "Sorry that you ate too much. Want to smoke with me? It might make you feel better."

"No, I'm fine. I just need to give it some time." *Give me some fucking time.*

"Okay. A hit or two should help take your mind off of it." Even though I know that no means no with Jane, I didn't think it would hurt to offer again.

"NO!" she exclaimed, responding to me as if I offended her or was trying to pressure her. Now I want to start poking at her. There's no reason for her to snap other than she wants to and thinks she can get away with it.

"Okay. No need to get mad, my wife. When was the last time you took your heart medicine? It is our anniversary. Come to think of it, now would be the perfect time to hit the vape. It's a celebration, let's do something different together." I put my hands on her shoulders, realizing I haven't reached out to her in a while. Neither of us seemed entirely comfortable with it.

It's no surprise that Jane doesn't feel well and is now miserable. She does that shit to herself every day. And it's like she expects a hug or some empathy because she's fucking full and drunk. I have no interest in babying her. She deserves to be laughed at. She has it so bad. "C'mon, let's get high, my friend. It's Friday!"

"I said no. Stop! Just leave me alone, Marty." She didn't need to yell. Jane got up and began her retreat back to the couch. She's been triggered, and my brief hopes of this evening being different fade back to this groundhog day of a marriage that I'm doomed to. Jane's just full of shit and constantly fucking rancid if you ask me. She knows just what to do to bring on my aggravation.

I persisted with Jane nonetheless. "How about sitting on the porch with me for a few minutes? It's a nice out. Join me while I smoke, then we'll come back in." I said it with an increasingly louder voice so that it sounded the same to her as she walked farther off. "Where are you going? Thanks again for dinner. Happy anniversary." I was being obnoxious and sarcastic but technically didn't say anything offensive. It didn't matter to Jane. She feels too shitty to smile but can yell well enough.

"I told you that I don't feel good. Leave me alone." The only thing she's full of is hate now. There she is. There's the Jane that I knew I would see again before the evening was up. But at least I got cold beer and good tacos out of it.

Heading to the bathroom, I passed Jane without even looking at her. There's no point. Suddenly Hell's Kitchen took precedence for her. After rolling one up and witnessing my piss-poor dehydration, I found myself stalled at the bedroom door, hesitant to cross Jane again. I felt trapped and wished I had a safe way out. The window was a tempting option until I remembered the wine in the kitchen. That said, I have no choice. It's not all bad though. In thinking about it, I decided that regardless of what this room ends up being, it will definitely have a fridge.

Jane wasn't as interested in the TV as I initially assumed. She was on her phone, and she definitely didn't seem as ill in the company of it as she does with me. It's funny how phones have become the perfect companion for so many people. It's the one thing more constant in Jane's life than drinking. As in her case, phones have replaced spouses in a way. Unfortunately, they're difficult to compete with. A phone can meet most, if not all, expectations and provide an endless supply of knowledge and entertainment. Phones also offer social interaction options practically unmatched by bars, clubs, or universities. What hits home for me is, more times than not, they don't make you mad or act unpredictably. That's not all. I can even shut my phone off when I don't want to fucking deal with it. Not that Jane ever would. I don't even have to turn it on for fuck's sake. It'll turn me on with all that ass available with simple swipes.

"Hey, real quick," I said to Jane with importance. She lifted her eyes off the phone without any head movement. "Seriously, you wanna get high, girl!" I said it with a purposeful smirk, knowing damn well she could lose her lid. Thankfully, she didn't respond. Her attitude is childish. We were just eating and laughing together, and now she can't even smile. It's our anniversary weekend, and just like all others, Jane impulsively decides to switch gears on me. Now she's full speed, no head. It's not okay, but I have to go back to the mindset of not giving a shit. She can sit there entertained and full of tacos, I'll leave alone, full of deserving self-pity.

Removing myself from Jane's hostile environment has its pros and cons. Not having to hear her anger is a valuable pro for sure. Also, unpredictable retaliation is impossible if I'm not around. That one carries a lot of weight too. The most significant con is that it doesn't result in the intended behavior I expect. Jane hasn't learned to keep her cool. The only thing she's learned is how to get me away from her.

"How is it that after a decent dinner and drink, you can be agitated to the point of telling me to leave you alone? You just walk off and can't even look at me when I'm talking to you. You're all pissy because I'm inviting you to the porch with me. You won't even consider it."

"I told you that I don't want to get high, Marty." I knew from experience to start walking away. "And I told you that I don't feel good, so leave me alone before I get fucking pissed. Fuck you."

"You don't," I asserted. I was glad to be past her. Jane

can't get along with me. That's how we end up sleeping in different rooms. She'll be in the Master's bedroom, and I'll be in the dog house.

From the kitchen, I went straight outside without saying anything more to Jane. If I don't tread lightly, things might go sour grapes around here. Fucking with Jane too much has its consequences. Her outbursts will get considerably worse. There's no real limit. I have a lot that I would like to say to her, especially regarding her selfishness, but I'm not drunk enough to want to deal with her flare-ups. I'm plenty happy just not being at work. Divorcing myself from Jane is the best thing for me.

I could sit on my porch getting fucked-up all day and night. It's one of my favorite things to do. I spend more time out there by myself than with Jane anywhere. She's always invited but rarely comes out. The last time she joined me was around this time last year. It took some convincing as usual. She eventually gave in but couldn't show up without the dog and her phone. I smoked a cigarette as she sat out there going back and forth between them, evidently enjoying herself but not saying a word to me. It wasn't quite what I envisioned thinking of her company. I would prefer that she didn't come out at all if it's just going to be a fucking dog and phony show. I've been trying to convince myself to stop inviting her. Jane acts like that with drinking too. We both have a daily routine of partaking, we just don't do it together. It's kind of sad knowing we're drinking the same thing, at the same time, under the same roof as husband and wife, but we're not doing it together. So even when we're together, we're not doing things together. It's far from the type of interaction that I yearn for.

Chapter Five

Looking back, I've been waiting to get to this point all fucking day, all week for that matter. Thinking back to this morning, I was close to spending my entire day on this porch. I grabbed two cold beers from the fridge to come out with and foresee myself opting for some warm ones out of the garage next. I wanted wine but would need the whole box to avoid Jane for as long as I intend to. Not that she would make my presence known anyway. As usual, a drunken, fun, fuck-fest with my wife would be nice, but I'll unhappily settle for warm beers and a large helping of loneliness and regret. Since it's a celebration, I'll take what I can get.

With it being as dark as it is now, it's the perfect time to sit out front. My garage sits back a little farther than the front of the house, so I get no direct light on me when my porch lights are off. The house is positioned perfectly between a couple of streetlights that are on the other side of the road, but they're spaced far enough away from my property that it can be pretty dark in the shadows here. I prefer it like that. It's better that people can't see everything.

At this time of night, I can see The Neighbors far better than they can see me. They're not directly across from me, instead they're closer to the left streetlight and on the same side.

They always keep their outside lights on as if they're inviting spectators. Their house is the first and last house that I see pulling out of and into mine. It's the one with the mailbox that I flick my cigarette butts at. We might have introduced ourselves when they first moved in, but if so, I don't remember their names or care enough to. Maybe I was drunk at the time. With her, it's better that I keep my distance anyway. I'm always looking out for Neighbor and see her most days. From here, she's become a temptation that I'm aware could get increasingly overwhelming as the proximity between us decreases.

Neighbor has an erotic aura about her that resonates so much of what I've been missing. She's hard not to watch. Every day I find myself wanting more of what she has to offer. With Jane having a constant aversion to me and my desires, impulses that I keep imagining myself acting out have been spawning more intensely. My thoughts about it go back and forth. I often wonder how much of what I think will turn out to be a premeditated reality. It's an interesting thought.

The Neighbors being somewhat younger than Jane and I reminds me of how much I've missed out on over the years. Not that Jane could ever compete with Neighbor's persona and vibrancy. They moved into HighBlue about a year ago and have been setting the standard for my relationship ideology ever since. Before Neighbor, a girl able to offer so much was nothing more than fantasy. It's hard to believe that she's only a window away. Because of her, I've remembered who I am and what I want. I don't want to be this man that I have become. The suppression has done nothing for me. All that it has been is a drawn-out, unsuccessful attempt to satisfy Jane. I have believed for too long that something's wrong with me, and her constant reminders haven't helped. Jane's managed to brainwash me in a way, but I'm no longer as convinced as I once was.

The Neighbors don't hide the good time they like to have together, especially on weekends. I'm not sure to what extent they take it, but I've been curious and like to imagine. Neighbor would be something totally different for me. From what I remember, they weren't made like that when I could have been an honest contender.

Thankfully for me, The Neighbors like to chill out front too, so I always get a good look. They're regularly out there grilling and listening to music. I see them playing basketball and doing yard work and projects all the time. They often sit out there well into the night, and I can tell that they at least get to drinking quite a bit sometimes. Often, when hearing and seeing them, I imagine what it would be like if my wife sounded as impressed with me as Neighbor does with her husband. Lately, however, I mostly imagine what it would be like if The Neighbor's wife was as impressed with me as she is with him.

At times, I do find myself getting a little annoyed with the constant fun that I'm always hearing across the street. Like right now, The Neighbors are having a blast together. Whatever they're cooking smells amazing—probably something as exotic as she is. They're messing around, playing 90's alternative rock, and sitting by the grill like friends are supposed to be doing on a Friday evening. I'm guessing that it's probably not even their anniversary weekend. Neighbor looks good in her tight blue shorts and scrappy white tank top. It's a little outfit that I could easily wash thirty of in a single load. She's a five-foot-nothing, hundred-pound slab of energy that likes to have a simple good time with her husband. It's not jealousy, envy, or even them as neighbors that vexes me. Spectating them enjoying life only makes me more irritated with Jane. Maybe it's my tampered cognitive abilities that are to blame, but I can't seem to understand her.

Only able to take so much wishful thinking, I decided to distract myself. It's making me depressed not having an ass like that to smash my balls against this weekend. I could watch her all night, but I'm afraid if I continue much longer, my dick'll come out to join me. After finishing my second beer and joint in possibly near record time, probably due to the failed expectation that Jane would have a change of interest and decide to hang out a bit, I'm starting to be drug by the drugs. Through the door window, I could see Jane still awake. Her face is so concentrated on and close to her phone screen that it looks like she could be browsing a dating app with scratch-n-sniff capabilities. Swipe-n-sniff dating apps, I just thought of it. I considered ringing and running before I went to the garage, but can relate to being caught up in fantasy. To whatever extent, we all prefer it.

The upstairs of my garage is where I house my warm beers. I'm too frugal to keep the fridge on when I'm the only one that uses it. There, I custom-built a nice bar/game room with all the proper frolicking fixings. Though they are always welcome, I didn't build the space with big parties in mind. I built it for Jane. It was an attempt to create something that would allow us a fun time together without leaving the house, meaning without compromising alcohol consumption. I put a lot of good thought and work into the project. Despite that, we've only been up there together maybe a handful of times in the past seven or eight years. Jane hasn't been thankful or interested. She refuses to come up and claims that I built the bar for selfish reasons. I did envision some benefits, so I never argued.

I can't help but grin coming up the stairs when the sign "Burnitts" reveals itself. I named the bar and custom-made the sign as a gift for Jane. Burnitt was her name before she took mine, but it's meant to be a tribute to her dad. It means a lot to me too. Weston was easily the coolest guy that I've ever met. My time knowing him before his death was short, but the way his simple mind presented itself has been something I've increasingly admired as I've aged and understood more. He had his life figured out and had a straightforward way of living out his priorities. Though she was ignorant and resistant to it at the time, Jane was always at the top. I can relate to Weston in that way.

My routine at Burnitts is pretty much always the same. I show up alone, turn the music on, grab a beer, rack 'em up, roll one up, throw some darts, and lift some weights. Sometimes I turn the music up loud enough to let Jane know that I'm up here, thinking she might bring that ass of hers up to join me. Unsurprisingly, she never shows. She's been close though. Her screaming up to me to turn it down happens occasionally. In her defense, she probably had to work some of those next days. Regardless, I don't want to deal with the fucking killjoy, so I'll keep it down and possibly spare my ass tonight.

As I sit around smoking the night away, I'm lost in thought. I'm thinking about Neighbor more than I probably should be. In terms of relative looks, I used to consider myself lucky with Jane, she's prettier than I am. But nowadays, I'm not as easily spellbound by her facade. Turns out that beauty doesn't have the same effect when it repetitively causes pain. It's different with Neighbor though. Her allure hasn't been blemished by her complacent commitment or stifled sexuality. What I see is what I want to get, and I think plenty about getting what I want.

I often imagine what it would be like if Neighbor came over and partied with me here at Burnitts. That's what this place needs, a nice ass appreciating all the fun the bar has to offer. Without a doubt, that's what's been missing up here all of these years. I haven't even broken in the pool table yet for fuck's sake. In fact, I'm the only one that has ever gotten me off up here. Neighbor's what I need. A pretty girl genuinely appreciating what this dick has to offer without disgust and complaint. Someone that just wants to have a great time as often as possible.

After being lost in thought for a couple of beers and a few laps around Burnitts' favorite pastime options, I was finally bored with my own company. Typically, I have a high tolerance for being alone which not a lot of people can claim. Without something to be occupied by, difficult thoughts tend to get the best of most. Loneliness forces a person to face themselves, and most prefer not to compromise their self-ignorance. I haven't been able to avoid myself ever. There's no pride in that. It's been self-torture this entire time, and it's no wonder my depression runs so deep. Being alone isn't easy for anyone. Just because I have to be, and can take the beating a little more than most, doesn't mean I can always handle it. As with Jane and work, I just have to put on face and suck it up for now. However, I'm ready to find something other than these contaminated constants to live for. I'm aware that my conscience doesn't keep me in line as much these days, but I'm starting to accept who I am. I want what I want despite any potential outcomes.

If I don't find something to do soon, my thoughts will probably steer me in the wrong direction sooner than later. Bad things can happen when I'm bored, lonely, and drunk. There should be shot glasses that say that for those like me that drink alone—Bored. Lonely. Drunk. With that thought, maybe my mind's already skewed considering I decide not to leave Burnitts without doing a shot first. All the liquor choices make it a difficult but humble commitment. It's the vodka that I ultimately choose. It's nasty shit, but in taste, they all pretty much are. I drink it without a toast or company, but immediately felt the jump start I needed to get on track. The next one might even get me going.

Before I get too far ahead of myself, I have to shut down Burnitts. It's not uncommon for me to just stumble away after drinking too much. I've been trying to engrain in my habits cleaning and closing up the right way. It's similar to morning checks but the opposite. Doing so limits the who, what, when, where, and whys that I likely won't remember. If everything's how it should be, there'll be fewer questions about my control. Maybe I didn't walk around outside naked and aroused yelling at

Neighbor to come party. With the way my mindset has been recently, I acknowledge the potential of something like that happening alarmingly high.

Chapter Six

There are only a couple of hours remaining of this long-awaited Friday, which means my long-dreaded anniversary will be only a short day away. Monday would have been a more fitting day for it. It's officially the final countdown to another regrettable year in the bag—the trash bag. Anniversaries for me are like birthdays. Men that are my age don't celebrate being older, just as husbands like me don't celebrate another shitty year with their shitty wives. The evening's been nothing worth remembering either, but at least the buzz has been good to me.

While locking up, my thoughts stayed on Neighbor. I began to think that maybe if I could make myself seen, there's a chance she might invite me over for a drink. Convincing myself of its plausibility was easy. After all, it is the neighborly thing to do. Maybe my thoughts are turning somewhat obnoxious, but I can't help thinking about how much my night would improve if I was able to see Neighbor's ass up close. It was a far-fetched idea that I knew was vodka-inspired, but now the seed was planted and I was curious. I worked myself up about it and was expecting to see her outside when I looked but had no such luck. That seems to be the theme of my life. They're probably fucking more than Jane's fucking me right now.

Back at the porch, I glanced inside through the door and

noticed Jane now lying on the couch. I was practically fingers crossed and pleading that she was sleeping. She would have to be drunk to get any sleep on that fucking thing. Choosing not to chance it too soon, I took a seat and lit a cigarette. Maybe it was the shots kicking in, but I felt myself getting anxious. My thoughts were dictating my blood pressure. Jane makes that happen for all the wrong reasons. Thankfully, I calmed down after a couple of minutes. I always wonder how much my heart can take.

After about ten minutes with no sign of Neighbor, I'm too drunkenly ambitious at this point to give up. Judging by what I typically see, there's no way she's done for the night. Right now, she's probably putting The Neighbor to bed the proper way. I might just be optimistically inebriated, but there's still a chance that she'll be back out alone and bored before long. My mind started wandering as random scenarios played out in my head. I convinced myself that it was urgent to have a plan in case she reappeared. There has to be a way for me to be closer to her.

My desire to be close to Neighbor has become something I think about daily. All I want is a better look, one that would flood me with fantasy. If the opportunity presents itself, I'll take advantage. After some thought about it, an idea came to me that would be a sure thing if she's susceptible. Calling in reinforcements isn't ideal for me, but with this plan I have no other choice.

I needed to see what Jane was up to. Going in casually for a glass of wine shouldn't raise any suspicion. From there, I figure that I could instigate the dog in some way that would give her the impression that he has to go out. I'll sneak the leash, let him out, and then just take him down the road. We could walk by Neighbor's without Jane even knowing. I rarely take Warden for a walk, but if she ends up saying something about it, I was just bored. She doesn't feel well anyway. I picture Neighbor feeling a lot better. With the dog, she would have the perfect reason to address me as we walked past.

"Hi," she would say, once noticing us.

"Hey, how are ya?"

"Ooh! Can I pet your dog, he's so cute?" *Fuck yeah, you can. You make me wad my shorts all the time. You can do whatever you want.*

"Of course," I'd say. She would bend down as far as her nylon threads would allow, defining everything about her. Her focus would be mostly on the dog but she would occasionally look up at me smiling. My dick would be practically head-butting her face. I imagine her bra bending away as she moves about, exposing her little titties behind it. I think of how tantalizing it would be to see her overcompensated, puffy nipples peek out as I become unavoidably bigger.

Even this drunk, I know that's an outlandish thought. But a man in my position needs something to imagine. It's all I have these days. With that, all I can think about is having a real-life closer look at Neighbor. The far-fetched opportunity is worth dealing with the dog. If we're lucky, we'll take these nightly walks more often. These are the deprived and drunken thoughts that lead to the forgotten shit that I fear in the mornings.

I walked in quietly and went straight for the kitchen, focused primarily on the wine part of the plan. The vodka taste in my throat still needed to be washed away. After filling my glass, I sat at the bar thinking that Jane might come in for a drink or something. Not likely, but maybe. These days, I spend about as much time alone in here as I do on the porch and at Burnitts. The kitchen had an island before it had a bar. Nothing about the cabinets or countertop has changed, only the function of it all. We used to at least enjoy occasional conversation and food here. Farther back, the kitchen felt like the heart of the home it was expected to be. There used to be so much more enjoyment here. It's sort of sad that a big, beautiful, modern kitchen like this is essentially a waste of space not having a traditional family to appreciate it.

For the most part, Jane and I only cross paths in the kitchen when one of us comes in for a drink while the other's already in there, likely drinking. For me, alcohol is on the short list of things even worth a run-in with her. I'm sure she feels the same about me. Ironically, nothing brings us together more than wine. I like to think we built this home one box at a time.

With the exception of the problems that it most certainly creates, boxed wine is the best. It's a practical and economical solution for the drunks. Three liters of thirteen percent alcohol will get you there quickly, and at a reasonable taste and price. I like the tap too. I often drink right from it. It's mostly when I'm too lazy to get my glass, but a lot of times, I'm just trying to sneak some without leaving any evidence. It can be fun as well. Drinking from the tap is similar to a keg stand but the opposite. Instead of it being beer below an upside-down drinker, it's wine above an upright drinker. The same goal applies nonetheless, don't stop drinking until you can't anymore.

After half my glass, I gave up on thinking that Jane might come in. She's probably not even sleeping, just not giving a shit that I'm here always alone. I'm agitated but have other interests in mind, so it's for the better anyway. I snuck into the living room and discovered both her and the dog with their eyes closed and mouths open. Even when Jane's passed out she looks angry. She has the same look when I have sex with her, so who knows what the fuck? Ramsey's still on the TV cussing like a shit-faced sailor. Something about overcooked scallops is pissing him way off. It's interesting how all the anger's able to soothe Jane right to sleep. I guess that's her type of bedtime story. For so many others, it's more tranquil sounds that are preferred to fall asleep to.

Moving on with the plan, I decided to clean myself up before heading out. Best case scenario, Neighbor wants to pet my dog. But if she's not around, maybe something else is happening in the neighborhood. Either way, I assume that I should get myself smelling better. After throwing on some khakis, I put on deodorant and rinsed my mouth. I spit most of it out but left some to swallow for longer-lasting freshness. Then I sprayed some cologne above and away from me and waved a little back over my body for extra light and even coverage. From the room, I grabbed a shirt, backpack, pocket knife, headlamp, smokes, and weed to roll a couple up with. No wallet or phone needed, just the way I prefer.

Back at the fridge, I first fill my sixteen-ounce wine bottle with Grigio. It was advertised as a reusable water bottle, but it works just as well with the wine. I also grab a couple of ShackBrews, a bottle of water, a plastic bowl, a chunk of aged cheddar cheese and salami, and a couple of dog treats to pack up. After spinning the joints, I went back to the living room and gently waved a slice of sandwich meat over Warden's nose. It was quick to get his attention. He instantly woke, and without hesitation, followed me to the kitchen after a simple confirmation nod. From there, it's just the leash for him. For me, it's backpack on, wine in hand, joint in ear, cigarette in mouth, and dog in tow.

Even though I didn't see Neighbor outside, I crossed the street for a closer look. Maybe she'll come out as I walk by. I notice that the grill's been put away and the garage doors are down, convincing me I'm too late. The lights are still on in the house, so I'll stay hopeful for when I pass back through. However, as I approach, I began to think that it would be better to see her through the windows. I'd rather catch her being herself behind closed doors. Jane's better that way too. Now thinking about it more, talking to her isn't something I want to do at all, especially about anything to do with my fuck-head dog. My mind quickly imagines her dancing around in her living room in tiny pink panties like nobody's watching. Better yet, like I'm watching. Her simple sensuality couldn't be mimicked by Jane with effort. I would love to see her doing anything at this point. I'm mad lonely, and she's more than capable of lifting my spirits. Unfortunately, despite everything I let myself think, I had an unsuspecting glance with no such luck. My imagination didn't skip a beat though. It moved on and went right to picturing all the things she might be doing to herself in bed right now.

I was able to ignore the part of me that considered stopping. It's a tempting thought to hide in the shadows and just wait for her. I figure it's only a matter of time before an opportunity will present itself. Even with Warden, I can't be backpacking down the street at this time of night taking breaks behind bushes, not in this community. There's guaranteed to be some asshole with prying eyes paying constant attention around here, intentionally trying to stick his dick in other people's business.

I started thinking about Neighbor's backyard probably having a lot more to offer in terms of visible opportunities. I know they're backed against a patch of woods that separates them from HighView Golf Course, and I'm pretty sure that they have a pool too. That's probably where she is now. I don't think I can get away with any late-night golfing this evening, but I have a feeling that I'll be fading left and busting some balls in those woods soon enough.

These random, particular, and perverse run-ins that I imagine with Neighbor all the time might indicate obsessive tendencies and dark motives, but I don't actually see myself acting them out. I can visualize all my thoughts in detail. However, at the same time, I always have several tabs open at once. My mind stays busy, but I feel like I'm in control of what ends up presenting itself. Whatever my actions, I'll know that I gave them a lot of thought.

Regardless of my drunken daydreams, I know the reality of my situation. There isn't anything out here for me. Being sidetracked by Neighbor's invite would have been nice, but I had a backup plan all along. Even though the last thing I picture myself doing on a Friday night is volunteering to please Warden, the notion of getting out and walking him sort of appealed to me. With that, I thought it would be cool to take a trip down to Lookout. It'll be about a mile walk to get there if we make it. Company from the dog is better than none, but definitely not the asshole I prefer.

With The Neighbors house behind us, I turned my headlamp on and proceeded down the road. It didn't take long before I had to remove it and wrap it around my wrist. It was giving too much of an indication of where I was looking. The curiously long, inconspicuous peeks that I couldn't avoid wanting were too obvious. I pictured people wondering who was shining a light through their windows. The last things that I want are cops and accusations. It's hard not to look though. The things that happen behind domestic doors and closed blinds could be written about. Sometimes I wonder how some homes can even function.

Admittedly, Warden's a good walker. I should probably take him out more often. He doesn't pull, which means I can smoke and drink at leisure. He doesn't bark, allowing us to creep by without attention and at leisure if desired. And he doesn't want to stop to piss on everything vertical that crosses his path, so I don't feel like I'm tending to his dick the whole way. Warden has no desire to be the alpha dog with anything but Jane. I was a lot like him at one time. Sometimes I wonder if he thinks I'm neutered too. With Jane, he's able to pull rank on me, but we're both submissive to her. I'm actually surprised that he was willing to leave her side. Maybe he's starting to take a liking to me or starting to appreciate the benefits of moderation. I doubt it though. Warden's a hard read, but for all I know, he's been looking forward to me walking him. Jane usually takes him up the hill to the park, but I think he likes this different way.

We managed to make it to Lookout without incident. I probably wouldn't have made it at all without Warden's instinctual forward guidance. He nosed us to my usual picnic table without hesitation. After tying him off, I went straight to laying on it—fuck Italian silk. The bowed wooden planks with popped nails and splinters are an upgrade compared to Jane's couch. I don't even have to worry about spilling my refreshment. I'm at peace here, and could easily get caught up in the universe staring off into the depths of space. Knowing that, I managed to sit up before I lost myself trying to ponder reality.

Even with the ominous nature sounds coming from everywhere, Warden's eyes remained fixated on me. It could easily be mistaken for a look of appreciation or loyalty, but I knew he could smell the food that I packed. After lighting my joint, I threw him a bone and poured him some water. Even though I tried to stay hydrated, we were both thirsty after that walk. Lookout's a lot different with no other people around or cars on the road. I like it better this way. I'd be able to enjoy it a lot more if I started walking Warden here every weekend that Jane dismissed herself from me. During daylight, the view beyond the parking ledge goes on for many miles in spots. At night, the view of the sky goes on forever. Looking out, everything feels so distant. I can only dream of my anniversary being that far away. As I thought back to work earlier and being here already today, it registered to me just how long the day has been. Come tomorrow, it'll seem like it never happened.

We were spending what seemed to be quite a lot of time at Lookout. I'm able to roughly calculate knowing that I have smoked a couple of cigarettes and enjoyed a good portion of my wine. I wasn't in a hurry to get walking back. It'll be a daunting, uphill task with me being stoned and sideways. That being said, and with nothing to go home to, I wasn't in any rush.

After eating through the snacks, Warden found himself a comfortable spot in the grass to lay in. I, being enticed to do the same, had to fight through it as I attempted motivation. The thought of finding a spot over in the woods to spend a few hours crossed my mind. Thankfully, my autopilot kicked in before I risked getting discovered here by the police passed out in public with my short-haired pointer hanging out. Making the effort to get going will be easy compared to the actual walk. That said, I threw the garbage away, packed up the wine and bowl, popped open a beer, untethered the dog, and slowly headed in the general direction of home.

We made it more than halfway there before the temptation to take a break became more than I could resist. On the curb next to a random mailbox is where I found myself next. I lit a cigarette and fell back into the grass to rest my back, pleased to discover that it was even more comfortable than the table. Two miles of hill is a lot of sloped walking for an office guy.

It's difficult to say how much time passed, but suddenly everything was white bright. My first thought was that I was seeing the light of death, but I must have put my hand near my face allowing my headlamp to practically blind me through my eyelids. My fingers still grasped the remains of a well-spent cigarette that I don't remember smoking. It took me a minute to realize where I was and that the dog was with me. He managed to make himself comfortable too. Although, if his leash wasn't still around my wrist, I'm sure he would have abandoned me and found his way back to Jane.

I flicked the cigarette butt in the road and then used the mailbox post next to me to get my stance. Looking around, I see my half-empty ShackBrew safely sitting curbside. Despite being barely able to bend down without falling, I managed to swoop it up without spillage. After finishing it, and for no reason other than thinking that it was appropriate, I decided to leave the empty bottle on top of the mailbox post. It looks like it belongs there. From there, I lit the remains of my joint and took a long inhale. Warden was already up and shitting on the sidewalk as assholes do. After a few pulls, I raised the outgoing mail flag and put my roach inside. I guess I looked at it as both a "sorry" and "thank you" gesture. Here's some pot, sorry for the shit and the bottle—thanks for handling it. It was intended for the owner, but I realized afterward that the mailman would likely find the roach first. First come, first served, I suppose. After that, I retrieved my last beer, lit another cigarette, laughed at Warden, and let him put us back on the home track. My walk turned into a bit of a stumble at times. Out loud, I would just tell the dog to stop pulling. Blaming him for the erratic slog seemed convenient. In my mind, I pictured all the neighborhood nosies watching this dog and fucking lonely show, so I was trying to hide my drunk.

I noticed that Neighbor's lights were out as I walked up the hill. It's too bad that there'd be nothing for me to see. It's probably best that I go straight home anyway. My cigarette wasn't quite gone as I was walking past, but I flicked it at the mailbox anyway. Finally at my driveway, I chugged the rest of my ShackBrew and set the bottle on the post of my mailbox. I liked the way it looked, and why not adorn it for the occasion? Even Warden was dragging ass by the time we reached the house. Despite his exhaustion, he must have remembered Jane and managed to break free of my hold. He quickly leaped up to the door wanting nothing else to do with me. He wouldn't go anywhere now. He's as addicted as I am. Stepping in, I see it's no longer Friday. It's always too long of a wait for such a short go.

Jane woke up at some point while we were gone and found her way to her mistress mattress. As soon as he walked in, Warden sniffed her out to claim his side of the bed. *Fucking traitor*. I noticed that Jane made sure to bring wine and water in with her as usual. The glasses were empty now. Her waking up and making the short trip from the living room to the bedroom without wine would be absurd. I've never met such a dedicated, thirsty girl. Wine is always Jane's priority. More than likely, she didn't even notice us gone. Even if she did, I'm sure she didn't question where I was or what I might be doing. She doesn't give a shit.

At this point, I'm well drunk, but fill a cup of wine anyway. It's just common practice these days. On my way to the TV, I gave the couch a dirty look and chose to sit in the chair instead. Other than in my bathroom, I don't normally smoke inside but decided to light one anyway. With no actual ashtray, the house plant soil functions as a good substitute. Before long, I recognize that I'm alone again and think about how life might be if I wasn't so often.

Having something to do other than myself every once in a while would be nice. Maybe I just need to sleep, but it's hard to want to when all I want is so much more. I'd like to be having a good time right now. At my age, there's no telling how many Friday nights I have left. Why should I keep sulking in silence because of Jane? It's a torturous way to live, and nothing makes me feel more like the fucking loser I am.

Luckily, thoughts of Neighbor helped get me out of the rut. A girl like her, I can only imagine for now. So many things would be better for me if my happiness wasn't confined to Jane's condescending clutches. We should have plans together. This should be a completely booked weekend of flirt and fuck sessions. Things could be much different with a girl like Neighbor. At the very least, we'd be cuddling comfortably on our standard, inexpensive, microfiber sectional.

My thoughts about Neighbor quickly go from a temporary solution to being bored, to full-on mind stimulation. I want to be able to see her body, not just imagine it. Fantasizing about her makes me want to get my dick out, though I'm aware of the trouble it could lead to. Despite any potential ramifications, my thoughts get out of control and I start to wonder if there might be a way for me to incite some action.

After convincing myself that there is, I head Jane's way, drunk and without concern. Now that she's been sleeping a while, there's a chance that she would like to catch up. Maybe she would appreciate the interest and spontaneity. There's nothing wrong in my mind being woken up by someone unable to help themselves. It's a compliment like no other. The selfless me thought it was worth a go. Call it desperation, but I don't even care if she participates. If she prefers, I won't be offended if she doesn't make a sound or move. From what I can remember, she seems to enjoy it more that way.

After navigating my way in, I first had to tell Warden to fuck off. He growled with resistance but slowly obeyed. He usually does, but still, what a dick. I just took him for a walk for tit's sake. Jane was sleeping well, her breathing indicated that. It sounds similar to what I imagine a ventilator sounding like. Maybe that's a good thing, I might actually have an opportunity. I spoke her name somewhat sternly at first, thinking I'd soften it up once I start seeing signs of life.

"Jane?" She didn't move. "Jane?" I thought she might be coming to. "Hey, Jane, you've been sleeping for a while. Do you want to wake up and party?" I gave her a few light kisses around her face. I wanted more but had to test for signs of life first. "Hey, Jane, do want to get up and have a drink with me?" She would move, moan, or mumble something at best, but I kept trying. I couldn't have been more turned on. Her not having anything to say about what I wanted made her seem perfect. "Hey, beautiful? Do you want to fuck around a little?" And just like that, as if I woke her with a blistering smack to the face, she abruptly awakened with nothing short of unreserved anger.

"What are you doing? Get the fuck off of me. What is wrong with you, Marty? Fucking asshole."

"I was just seeing if you wanted to hang out."

"Leave me alone. I have to fucking work in the morning. You won't even let me get any fucking sleep."

"I'm sorry."

"You're a dick, leave me alone."

With a response like that, fucking around with Jane probably isn't in my foreseeable future. It was a bit of a long shot anyway. There was no point in asking her not to cuss at me. Other than drinking and working, I think that it's her favorite thing to do. I did as I was told. When she acts like that, I lose interest anyway. Warden must have heard the whole thing. I barely made it out of the room before he scuffled by on his way back to bed, confident in his entitlement. I shut the door behind him, not so confident in mine.

With little choice, I made my way back to the porch. It looked like shit out there. The overflowing ashtray and empty beer bottles were reminiscent of my evening alone. Jane has turned me into a junkie. I wanted to stop thinking about her. My mind was starting to be influenced by "Janger," a term derived from Jane's anger. Janger affects the feel-good area of the brain. Side effects include the inability to have fun and get laid. It's brought on by Jane and her anger.

In my defense, I didn't know Jane had to work in the morning. As much as she drank, most would assume she didn't. What reason did she have to be so angry about it anyway? Why not just appreciate the effort and politely decline? Suddenly, I felt the need to pick up, stay in control, and keep my shit together before I lose myself. I went in to get rid of the bottles and empty the ashtray, then brought my wine and broom back out with me. With late-night Janger, I tend to drink and clean a lot. I start picking up my pieces in an attempt to put myself back together again. Of course, I'll also appreciate things being somewhat in order when I wake up in a few hours confused.

Chapter Seven — Saturday

Out of nowhere, I began to accept that I was conscious and that I must have been sleeping. It's still dark out, so I probably haven't been resting for as long as I needed to be. My first thoughts materialize as uncertainties of the night before. I think that Jane was mad at me for something. Maybe I just dreamt it though. After all, she's often what nightmares are made of. Yesterday must have gotten away from me. The first thing my eyes bring into focus is my half-filled glass of wine on the table distorting the TV's screensaver. The colorful firework reflections make it look like an inviting party that I'll attend to right away, without reservation. I'm noticeably dehydrated, and it's the only thing I want. Just attempting to reach for it is painful. I hate this fucking couch with every muscle in my body. In doing so, I realize that I'm only half dressed. Lucky for me, I still have my pants on, so there's no need to assume the worst right away. It's always somewhat reassuring waking up with my dick behind a zip. Maybe I didn't take a blacked-out, balls-out, moonlit stroll down Elevation Lane.

As I turned and reached for the glass, I unknowingly rolled over the controller disabling the TV's rest mode. Despite being as sore as I am, I flew off the couch as quickly as possible to find it and change the channel. Once I got it under control and looked around, I was relieved to find that the blinds were shut and Jane was nowhere near. It was pretty clear at that point what most likely happened last, the night before. Evidently, I fell asleep still watching the porn that presumably led me to cum in my shirt, which I now see bunched up on the floor. More specifically, "fitness" porn from the looks of things. It's a new genre for me, I think, but clearly stimulated by thoughts of Neighbor.

Sixty-five inches of 8k porn in the morning rendered me incapable not to pick up where I might have left off, especially with having easy clean-up still available. After turning it back on, I can't help myself. Within thirty seconds, I came hard into my shirt like it had been weeks, not hours, since the last time. Maybe last night I stayed on edge or passed out before finishing. More than likely, I'm just that backed up.

With that out of the way and my blood pressure now under control, I snap back to reality and realize that I have to start figuring shit out. It's tough getting up, but I badly need a drink just thinking about what could have gone down last night. Plus, I should get rid of the shirt before I forget and find it in Warden's mouth later. He's a sick fuck like that. It wasn't until I tossed it in the hamper that it registered to me that I had changed at some point. I'm not sure why I'm wearing my khakis and need to figure out if I should be worried or not.

With no other choice but to deal with what I have got myself into, I nervously begin the investigation. Once confirming that Jane was home and peacefully passed out, I moved on to the kitchen part of the walk-through. The overhead light was turned off, but I can see plenty enough with the appliance lighting. The bar had a bunch of random shit on it. Things like beer bottles, wine, garbage, and dishes aren't anything new to come across in the mornings, but the knife and headlamp left me with some questions. At that point, I was without explanation, but I couldn't help opening the knife for any evidence of use. It looks like I might have murdered some cheese and salami last night.

Being that it was only just after five, I did the only thing that I could do—fill my "coffee" cup. Nothing else inside seemed too mysterious, so I headed to the porch for a smoke. Walking out, I kept an ear out for any music and peeked around the corner making sure the garage doors were down and the lights were off. Since the cars are still in the driveway where they should be, it's my change of clothes and the shit on the bar that are the unknowns at this point. Also, I'm not sure if Jane's mad at me. I zoned out trying to jumpstart my memory by repeatedly starting from when I came home from work. What I can remember goes from home, to tacos, to Jane bitchy, to Burnitts, to… potential possibilities.

Before long, Jane having to work crossed my mind. I'm pretty sure that she mentioned having to. She often works Saturdays, but I expected this one to be different. If she has to go in, that would say a lot about how much consideration that she's put into the weekend. I would take the whole week off if I could. Groceries would be bought, automated email responses would be generated, and I wouldn't get dressed for seven fucking days. I guess it's different for me though, I want to have fun. Knowing Jane, she's going to take the weekend off from me.

Maybe Jane will be in a better mood today. Maybe she'll even loosen up a little. Typically, that would be far-fetched, hopeful thinking with her. However, with it being our anniversary, she might make an exception. I just can't piss her off. Although, that's essentially impossible anytime that I try standing up for myself. She really shouldn't be putting me in the position to have to. Regardless, I'll do everything I can not to instigate her today. I'll have to be kind but keep to myself. I also have to be sure not to provoke her or entertain any drama she starts. Most importantly, I'll have to keep my expectations at nothing.

Getting up early on Saturdays is what I prefer. Although, I should probably be sleeping more. Most other days, I would be dealing with having to go to work in a couple of hours, so it's great to just relax knowing that I don't have to. Work of any kind shouldn't be on my mind today. The only thing that I have to do this morning is not get too fucked-up before Jane gets up. I need a break from the shit she's always giving me about what I do. All I ever try to do is keep myself occupied. She'll always have something to say about everything she can about me. Sometimes I think she just likes to hear herself cuss. If I get her going well enough, she'll gladly tell me exactly what she thinks about me. She makes me so proud sometimes. All the while, Jane maintains this super ability to block out her actions. She conveniently forgets everything and adamantly refuses accountability for anything.

After getting the coffee on and the kitchen picked up, I went in for a potential piss and discovered yesterday's clothes on the bathroom floor. Following a thorough inspection, I find that they're reasonably clean. At least that eliminates some of things that could have caused me to change. My phone is nowhere to be found, so finding that is a top priority for me. It's impossible not to be concerned about whom I might have called or messaged, or photos that I could have sent.

After first looking my face over in the mirror to make sure everything is as it should be, I undressed and did a full body inspection. Outside of being a little unkept, no dirt, blood, or marks anywhere. Must be I didn't piss Jane off too bad. My leg muscles are feeling sore but no mystery bruises. Making the best of a piss and shit, I once again find myself drinking and smoking naked on the toilet. It's an everyday occurrence these days and symbolizes my depression perfectly. From here, it's a quick shower to brush my teeth and wash, followed by a prolonged poaching in the lavender. Today's soaking is going to have to be extra lengthy and hot to scour the hangover I'm working with.

I still can't remember what happened last night or when exactly things went south in the memory department. It's an experience that I have all the time but never get too comfortable with. Alcohol helps. I know that Jane was bitchy at dinner, so I hung out in the garage and possibly jerked off before the night was over—that's it. It sort of feels like the more I try to figure out what's missing, the more I question what I think I know. Using what glimpses I have, I play out seemingly hundreds of potential situations in my head, usually starting with what could be the most detrimental. It can be terrifying picturing what I might have done. Sometimes I question if I could just be creating false memories by doing that. Basically, everything that I think I remember may or may not be true, and everything else, I just don't remember. The only thing I can do in situations like this is try to stay composed. Alcohol helps with that too.

Jane was filling her coffee cup just as I walked into the kitchen with mine.

"Good morning," I said, trying to be neutral in the way that I expressed it.

"Good morning."

"Happy Saturday. Do you have a lot scheduled for today?"

"Just one open house. It's a big one. Mom's determined to sell it today."

"So, not a full day?"

"No. The open house is from nine to twelve. But I have to hurry up and get going now so that I have time to catch up with her first."

"All right, I'll see you before you go." She took her coffee and began walking back to the bedroom. As she passed, we shared quick, unimpressive smiles like being forced to.

Jane claiming that she's running late is the norm. She's always behind and needs to get going five minutes ago. That just means that she doesn't want to be late for breakfast and mimosas with her mom, all before shopping for fresh flowers, refreshments, and food for the showing. They'll offer mimosas there too. They'll pour themselves a drink, check their looks, wish each other luck, and put on a proper professional face for the majority of potential buyers—families, couples, women, and the elderly. Though outside of a signed contract, the highlight of their day will be entertaining the handsome, well-dressed realtors touring the property, and outgoing single men just looking for a place that they can call home. High-end properties act as the perfect income filter for suitable fucks too. The guys that are buying big houses have big money. Add in a couple of drinks and a shit marriage and guess how some of those showings might go. One thing's for sure, Jane seems to be landing a new client every week.

Out of habit, I was going back in for wine but quickly decided that a glass of water and a real coffee would be the smarter choice. I still wanted a little wine though, so I had a few gulps out of the tap. I got lucky and walked back out to the porch just as Neighbor was running by. I couldn't help blurting out "Jesus Christ" when I noticed her. She's a different kind of pray though. Watching her jog by all sweaty and determined never fails to trigger my natural animalistic instinct to want to chase her down. She's small and dainty but still potentially hard to catch. Either way, the fun is in the hunt, and I welcome the challenge. Neighbor's alluring when she runs. I love how her bright blonde hair is always tied back and dancing around sporadically behind her as she passes by. It's like a teaser toy to a cat. She gets my attention, and in a way, I just want to jump out and grab her.

Neighbor works on her body and should be proud of her commitment. Sometimes I like to think that she knows I'm watching and enjoys my attention. Hopefully, it's her first time around. Her typically routine is to circle three or four times, and I'd hate to have missed a single lap. As she came around the second time, I was locked in hard and already wishing for a third. I would have watched her until she disappeared, but as she passed in front of my mailbox, I noticed what looked to be a ShackBrew bottle on top of its post. Knowing that I'm most likely responsible, I'm suddenly concerned again about last night's conduct. I have to remove it before Jane sees it and starts asking questions that I don't have excuses for. Neighbor likely noticed it. Something tells me if so, she got a good laugh. It was the walk down the driveway that made me recall something about possibly having the dog out. Confirming that it was the same beer I keep stocked around here backed that possibility. Plus, since that would more/less make sense of my sore legs, change of clothes, and headlamp, I'm convinced I let Warden take me for a walk last night.

I threw the morning paper and beer in the garage on my way up to inspect Burnitts. My phone was on the bar with no phone calls made or texts sent. That's always a welcomed relief. With that, and Jane at least talking to me, I was finally feeling, for the most part, okay about my behavior yesterday. From what I remember, which is essentially nothing, I'm lucky. When drinking, I always find something that I want to do. That's the part that makes me nervous.

It's still unclear to me what Jane's problem has been lately. She seems even more withdrawn and short-fused than usual. There's nothing that I can do if she wants to give up. I'm obviously on my own here. Luckily, I didn't let her get to me yesterday. With that thought, I sat at the bar and took a huge hit from a previous lit joint and held it until I couldn't any longer. It was the sigh of relief that I needed. As I looked around, the rum caught my eye. It took little convincing to chase the coffee down with a shot. It's a suitable start to a Saturday morning alone. After that, I knocked out a few reps on the bench press and left Burnitts feeling about as good as I do.

Jane was walking out just as I was about to walk in for

another coffee. She looked great as usual. She always carries herself differently when doing something that doesn't involve me. The Jane I get to be around isn't as motivated. The way I see it, she likes to flaunt a more active and interesting existence just to remind me of my relative importance. I'm not impressed. Even with that said, I'd still like to be all over her right now. But how she feels about me is out of my control. I've accepted it for the most part, now I just have to talk myself into doing something about it.

"Okay, I'm out of here. Hopefully, it won't be too exhausting. The commission will be nice though, so whatever I have to do." Jane sounded as if she was ready to take one for the team.

"I'm sure you'll draw a lot of interest. Good luck."

"Thanks, see you later."

"Have a good day." We leaned in at the same time and shared a dispassionate, quick kiss.

"Love ya," I said without thinking. I was instantly curious if she would say it back.

"Love ya," she replied without hesitation.

"Love ya" is the most we get from each other these days. It's not the most believable statement, especially with the way it's always exchanged between us. We'll say it with no embrace and no eye contact, and most of the time it's stated on the go. Saying "love ya" the way we do is closer to saying "bye" than "I love you." Either way, it's Saturday, Jane's gone, and last night seems to have gone down without a hitch. With that, it's party-on for me.

Chapter Eight

I didn't give much thought to what I was going to do today. I'd like to have anniversary plans with my wife but the occasion hasn't exactly taken precedence for Jane. Our relationship is blatantly faulty, but maybe that's all the more reason to share some laughs this weekend. I'm sure if we tried hard enough, we could find something comical about it all. Maybe we should just set differences aside and drink to what common ground we have. If anything, our anniversary should remind us that we need a break from the usual shit. Tolerating each other all year deserves proper recognition. Plus, who doesn't prefer an excuse to get drunk, dirty, and dangerous? For now, the only thing that I can think to do is get back to the porch. I'll smoke and attempt to give it better thought out there.

I was quick to rule out any kind of excessive housework. In no way will I be exerting myself for anything. I just want to take a break from all effort. Besides, the grass is good enough, and nothing inside needs cleaning up or attention. I was sure to stay on top of things throughout the week knowing that I wouldn't want to do anything but drink booze and bang. I think that I might have even walked the dog recently. However, it'll be a short, wasted day if I don't keep myself occupied in the meantime.

Before long, I found myself back at the garage to have a look around. At the very least, I should come up with a weekend list of want-to-dos. I make them in an effort to keep myself on track so that I don't end up just drinking the days away. One thing's for sure, I'm not going anywhere. Mostly, I just want to kick back. My whole week has been tense and against my will. Golfing is about the only thing that could tempt me to leave, but my legs feel like they have been climbing mountains.

As I left the porch, I quickly came up with my first to-do. Yesterday was hot, and the next few are going to be hotter. Taking care of the garden and roses this morning is something I'll gladly do. It's one of my favorite pastimes, right up there with sex, drugs, cooking, and golf. Since it's around that time to handle the monthly maintenance, I'll spread a little compost around and treat everything with Miracle Grow. That's my simple secret to the healthiest plants, courtesy of Karla.

I've been learning and enjoying gardening for many years now. How much effort is someone willing to put into something? Take a look at their garden. Good-looking, healthy gardens like mine require work. Mine are mostly products of genuine enthusiasm, not necessarily necessity. Either way, a gardener gets out what she puts in. He reaps what he sows and cares for. In that way, it's completely different than my marriage.

After Weston passed, I often helped Karla take care of the house to ease her burden. She neglected everything for a long time, even her beloved flowers. Somehow I managed to keep things alive. In time, she taught me all about roses specifically. Karla has always had a passion for gardening that I've grown to relate to more as I've aged. Jane never got into it. I think she questions her ability to be needed and fears being incapable.

Taking care of plants gives me a sense of tranquility that I just don't get much of in life anymore. When I'm working in the garden my mind stays with it. I tend not to veer off and get flooded by the relentless anxiety I typically have. It's calming taking care of something. I feel wanted, appreciated, and rewarded. Jane hasn't made me feel that way in a long time. She doesn't hide the fact that she doesn't need me and only appreciates me leaving her alone. With her, I'm only rewarded with the constant reminder.

Unfortunately, this morning's garden work hasn't been as relaxing as most, likely because of the approaching date. My difficulty understanding Jane's everyday hatred for me is already affecting my thoughts. Another day alone and dwelling is probably how it'll go for me. I have never been able to get completely used to it. Alcohol helps. I'm not sure what would be best for us as a couple. Maybe our relationship is approaching a dead end. Something drastic might have to be done to get off this path. Judging by the way Jane doesn't treat me, it's likely that she thinks the same. One thing that seems to be changing is my relatively new desire to care more about what's best for me, not so much us. I want tangible stimulation more than ever and more than anything. Something more than just minding my own cock.

Now that the day couldn't be closer, not having a gift to give Jane or a plan to get her one is on the back of my mind. My thoughts about it keep going back and forth. Not making the typical effort might be a step in the right direction for us both. I really can't decide how much I should be caring when I get almost nothing that I want from her. Every now and then, all I need is a little. A little peace and a little piece would go a long way in helping to persuade me that I'm not just chasing the dragon with Jane.

I've thought often about how our anniversary might play out over the past month or so. Would it bring us closer together, even if it's just for the weekend? So far, as I strongly suspected, it won't. This year has been as turbulent as ever. And as we've inched closer to the date, nothing has changed. My wishful thinking can only last so long. Self-preservation needs to be considered. With that, I've been trying to convince myself to stop thinking about it altogether. Jane doesn't seem to feel anything for us, and our relationship isn't close to what it should be. What we've put ourselves through is nothing to be proud of. I'm far from satisfied, but Jane considers everything else in her world more worthy of her energy.

My relationship with Jane started out as good as any. Things are much different now. Everything began to change after high school. Growing up never really sat well with her. I'm not saying Jane was immature, but all the associated life changes that came with it were exceptionally stressful and challenging for her. I assumed things would get better as we became more settled, but as the years went on, she never seemed to get completely comfortable. I miss our early dating most. She was a wildflower. We were in love, and I would have bet on our future. Back then, it was easy picturing the rest of my life with Jane, even though the vows that followed felt somewhat forced in a way. Regardless, I was hopeful. It's unfortunate that so many things back then had such long-term consequences. Looking back, we were innocent and incapable of fully comprehending how much of an impact certain situations and choices would have.

The straightforward truth about a young relationship is that the people involved haven't dealt with the same fucking shit day after day, year after year. In my case, it's been too many years with Jane. She's eaten up most of my fucking life already. In the beginning, nuances that I assumed to be short-lasting, exceptions to her norm, turned out to be her actual normal. She wasn't just "having a bad day." She didn't just "need a little space." She wasn't just "not in the mood right now," and she doesn't just want to have "a couple of drinks." Turns out, these have been unexpected but true and ongoing character traits. If I knew that back then, I'm not sure that I would have signed up.

Any reasonably sane person can only take so much of the same shit for so long. Even someone that understands and practices genuine compromise, a selfless person with the utmost respect and patience, would eventually start giving up in one way or more. The way Jane acts, the effort she puts in, the interest, and the attraction, it's not how things should be. These days, she could probably say similar things about me, but I find myself mostly just reacting to her. She, however, is constantly and naturally distant, foul, and cold. I can't keep allowing her to keep my balls in her fucking fanny pack for the rest of my days. At this point, I'd kill to get them back, even if they are busted and blue.

      The first thing that gets my attention in the garage is the grill. Immediately I decide to channel my inner Neighbor and use it for the rest of this weekend's food cooking. Charcoal grilling has always been my preferred method, but with dwindling company, it hasn't kept my interest so much. Maybe Jane would appreciate an invite to grill and drink with me. I'm not sure when the last time it was fired up, so giving it a good ash and grate cleaning can be put on the list.

      For some reason, imitating Neighbor became an idea of mine. Probably because I want to be happy and she always seems to be. Thinking of other things that I see her do, I immediately remembered one thing that I used to do all the time. After running inside for the key, I moved my humble hatchback from the driveway to the edge of the front lawn. Moving it off the pavement frees up space for basketball. The Neighbors shoot around together a lot. It's been years for me. Even though I won't have anyone to shoot around with, as usual, I'll make the best out of playing with myself. It's added to the list.

      Having the beginnings of a day plan, I head up to Burnitts to finish the joint that I have been working on. It's the kind of weekend project that I don't mind laboring over. Passing the weight bench, I decided to put workout on the list too. Neighbor got hers in already, so I should do the same. I also have to get ice and beer in the cooler and check on available food and charcoal. At this point, I should probably make an actual list. However, at the moment, what I find most important is getting some music on and the Saturday started right.

The distant sounds of small engines begin to fill the air around me. Mowers, weed-eaters, blowers, and pressure washers behind every homeowner's attempt to be better than, or at least appear better than, their neighbor. Of course, The Neighbor's already mowing his lawn. With the looks of his wife, he shouldn't have to prove anything. I noticed he always mows the last two or three strips by the road so that the clippings spray out into it. I'm assuming that's because of all the cigarette butts that find their way over there. Once his grass is perfect, it'll be straight on to washing the cars. I wish his wife would do that chore. She helps sometimes, but I never get to see her do it in a bikini as I imagine. Elevation Lane would get a lot busier if she did. In no time, it would start looking like a dog-pride parade around here. Dudes in the neighborhood would be showing up from blocks away to march their mutts around for a closer look at her. Myself not excluded.

I managed to find a decent selection of meats in the fridge. Jane's good about keeping us stocked up, likely because she's always at the store buying beer and wine anyway. I decided on dog for lunch and cow for dinner. Tomorrow, I can do homemade pizza and steak. As far as drinking goes, I determine that the appropriate ice-to-beer ratio was half a container's worth of ice to a six-pack of beer. That way, even if the freezer doesn't make much more in the next few hours, I can still get a full refill. After packing the ShackBrews and ice snugly in the soft cooler, I slung it over my shoulder and grabbed another beer to drink now. It's time to switch over because the wine has a reputation of being too much too early sometimes. There's nothing better than some cold ones in the Saturday sun anyway. I plan on coming up with some sides to grill but put the thought aside for now. Being as early as it is, I'm much more thirsty than hungry.

From the garage, I see The Neighbor moving on to washing his cars as predicted. Mine's looking like a real fucking winner on the front lawn, parallel to the road like I'm showing it off—or throwing it away, depending on who's perceiving value. I don't think it's ever been washed under my ownership. Dirt's nature's all-in-one makeup and sunblock anyway. It not only hides the blemishes but preserves the paint as well. That's what I tell Jane anyway. I love that relic of a basic car though. Scarlett's been paid off for ten years and is still reasonably reliable. And she's essentially my drinking buddy on work days. Jane hates her, but we have different dispositions. I wouldn't ever think about abandoning my drinking buddy.

Neighbor wasn't helping wash the cars so I decided to start working on the list of to-dos before the list of to-don'ts begin to dominate. The grill was the next thing I wanted to get into. I'm not exactly sure when it was used last, but it could have been last night for all I know. However, judging by how old the bratwurst remnants under the lid look, it's been a while. Whenever it was, my eyes must have been bigger than my stomach. More than likely, I expected Jane to join me. Who knows, maybe I made them and then forgot what I was doing after I ate half of one. It's practically impossible to know anything for sure when my drunk's driving.

While standing outside at the grill, I began admiring my garage. It's been good to me. It's a great size and acts as the perfect getaway from Jane. That led me to think about how this garage, with Burnitts upstairs, has almost everything I need to stay away. However, the necessity that it has lacked all of this time is a bathroom. If it had one, I could easily live up there. I'd happily make Burnitts my primary quarters if I could make it happen. It's exciting to think about because it's a way better living and entertainment space than my current accommodations, and it even includes a comfortable couch to sleep on.

Jane and I wouldn't have to cross paths as much if I

occupied my own designated area. It would be for me what the master is to her. She could have her space that she's always politely requesting, and I can have mine. Like a lot of people in a suburban development, my garage isn't used for parking. It's not for typical home overflow though either. Fuck boxes upon boxes of Christmas decor, priceless and worthless heirlooms, and other shit I don't need. Mine has been set up mostly as a workshop ever since we've lived here. The entire garage is finished, but Burnitts alone would be plenty for living. Come to think of it, I used to do a bunch of work around here and enjoyed doing it back then. It's been harder to see the point in it all in more recent years.

Looking over to specifically check, I noticed that Neighbor finally made her way outside. Every time I see her my thoughts go out on a tangent. If I were invincible, I'd be tethered to her. I just want to be in her space. I never really think about fucking Neighbor. Tasting her is another story, but I get excited enough just watching her. Hard dick comes easy seeing her body in different ways. Neighbor teases me. I masturbate to the idea of her masturbating to me masturbating. After about five minutes of her sudden invasiveness of my thoughts, I snapped myself out of it. I had to move on for the time being.

It took me a minute to remember what I was doing. I knew that I had a plan but almost forgot that the list was the plan so that I didn't forget. Exercising should help me get my shit together. Once finished, I hope to feel better about myself. If anything, it should help keep my stamina up in case that it's ever needed. With that thought, I grabbed a beer and headed back up to Burnitts. It would be best for me to redirect the sudden boost of energy that I had to something more productive than my dick.

Despite my intentions, seeing the weights was like a motivational cock block. I decide to smoke a cigarette first to help convince myself to follow through. Having grown up working in construction, I used to be stronger and in the best shape of my life. I'm sure that I'll never be at that level again. My ripped forearms, overly-jacked chest, and ladder legs have all taken a hit over the years, but so has everything else. I do make an effort to stay in decent shape though. Despite constantly fighting the desk job and beers, I wouldn't say that I was losing. There's an optimistic side of me that still believes that I could get a good portion of my better years back if I had the right incentive.

I blame most of my developed shortcomings on age, and by that, I mean marriage. In many cases, the words can be used interchangeably. It's age that causes a person to lose interest in just about everything. Age also stuffs up determination and motivation, and it has a high tendency to lead to self-hate and self-destruction. It's a fact that age kills a lot of people. Knowing what I know now, I would have loved to stay young forever.

I have a simple setup that I've had since I was younger. The old but heavy-duty weight bench and modest hundred pounds of weights have been reliable enough. Every year I attempt to get in better shape for summer. Usually, by mid-to-late summer, I'm done with a routine. By late fall, I'll be 15 pounds out of shape telling myself that I need to start working out again. Come spring, seeing half-naked girls like Neighbor trigger the actual effort. Jane used to be my drive to look good. I don't think that I've ever had the same effect on her.

As always, as soon as I get going, I start to feel the rush of adrenaline that comes with exercising hard. It's satisfying feeling my muscles flex. As I struggle, it feels like I deserve it, so I welcome it. Putting myself through pain as a punishment for self-loathe is something that I've always done. It feels better than the constant pain I endure living with it.

With exercising, I know that I should be incorporating a regular cardio routine, but I also know that I could never put miles in like I used to or like Neighbor does. With all the smoking I do, my lungs are nowhere near strong enough. These days, I'd be flirting with a heart attack if attempting to move faster than a swift stride. I can't even jerk off without running out of breath. Despite that, after an almost nonstop twenty-five minutes of pushups, curls, lifts, overheads, and toe touches, I'm feeling the burn. My exercises are often fueled by emotion. I imagine anger and lust work very much like steroids. For instance, when working out and thinking about work, Jane, or Neighbor, I can perform better and push myself to the max.

For me, beers are the best way to hydrate after a workout. My routine is to enjoy one with a smoke and some smoke as well. While opening the windows for some fresh air, I notice The Neighbors still hanging around out front. They'll likely be out there all day doing something. I wonder if they started drinking yet. Imagining myself being close enough to see led me to wish that I had a telescope. Arguably a concerning notion to come to mind, but some thoughts are hard for me to control. It would be such an opportune time to have one. I'd be able to see Neighbor like I was right next to her. All I want to be is next to her. There's no harm in just thinking about it anyway.

Thinking back to the list, I went downstairs to find my basketball and put air in it. It's been a while, but since it could be some well-needed light cardio for me, I think that I'll make the lifestyle change and start shooting around more from now on. I'd like to start now, but my arms refuse to participate. Once my muscles recover, I'll be on it. If luck's on my side, Neighbor will see me shooting around and want to stop over and do some ball handling herself. Too bad, I'd have to point her to Jane's fanny pack.

It was when I found myself having to take a rare piss that I, once again, started thinking about how much Burnitts needed a bathroom. The thought keeps making me want a solution. I have plenty of space to add a bathroom, but the money, time, and work involved to bring water and drainage out to the garage aren't feasible. Even though I need it more now than ever, I don't see how it could happen anytime soon.

I almost gave up on thinking about how I could make it work when my magic mind performed its greatest trick. I finally thought of a solution that would more/less give Burnitts the bathroom it needs. It could be done for little money and would be fast, easy work. The only problem is, if Jane isn't already mad at me, doing this would ensure it. Suddenly, treading lightly in hopes of a friction-free anniversary isn't going to be something that I can hold myself to.

Because the detached garage sits a little farther back than the house, I have to walk around the corner to get to the front porch. Inside, the entrance door opens to the foyer which opens to the living room to the right, and the kitchen to the left. The back door is visible from the front and opens to a similar layout but opposite. The guest bedroom/my room is off the back right-side corner from the front. Either way, when I come in to use any of the bathrooms, I'm likely to run into Jane if she's not in her room—what used to be our master suite. I can't avoid bumping into her when I want to. My room has a wall that faces the side of the garage where there's a door leading up to Burnitts. Not knowing for sure until I do some measuring, I might be able to install an exterior door in my room directly across. That way, my bathroom could easily serve Burnitts. Even more, with only ten feet or so between them, I could easily connect the house and garage with a roof to avoid any weather troubles. Suddenly, I'm convinced that this could be the perfect solution needed for Jane and me.

Out of nowhere, I want this to happen more than anything. After doing some quick measurements, I determine everything works out and that I should be able to do it exactly how I envision. With a door there, I would be able to walk downstairs from Burnitts, out the side garage door, and be in the bedroom's bathroom in just a few steps. Connecting the two structures with a roof would help make them function as the same space. Although this would probably fall into the category of excessive housework, that which I adamantly swore off this weekend, I decide to waste no time getting to it.

Right away, I know the extent of the project and what materials will be needed. Thankfully, I have enough stuff lying around the shop to begin my vision. With that, I retrieved the tools needed to get started and moved on with the plan. Jane will be home in a few hours, so I could have a good portion of the work done by then. I'm slightly concerned about what her reaction will be. There's a small part of me that thinks the idea could excite her right away, but a bigger part of me knows that it'll be too much at once. Of course, Jane can react any way she deems appropriate. After this is finished, she won't have to see me.

It only took an hour or so to mark and cut out the drywall from the inside location of the door, remove the insulation, and mark and cut out the siding and sheathing on the outside. All of a sudden, I had a full-on new opening in the house. There's no turning back now. I see this being perfect for Burnitts but realize right away that Jane's going to freak. She prefers that I ask her permission when wanting to do anything to the property—I don't. She's the type of person that judges art but creates none. Typically, I cross her hurdles when I get to them. Alcohol helps. Before moving on, I decide to clean up and start a garbage pile. It'll be important for me to stay on top of it. Anything that I can do to lessen the blow for Jane, lessens the blow for me. This isn't going to make sense to her, and I'm going to have to hear all about it. The neighbors will probably hear it too.

These days, Jane tries to always maintain a professional appearance outside of the house, just like her mom. When first met, she wasn't at all like Karla. She was more of a free spirit and didn't give a shit about how people looked at her. Jane's still naturally beautiful but so much different now. I guess after living and then working side by side together for years, it's no wonder they're practically the same person.

Jane cringes at my car because it's far from meeting the luxurious standards of the world around her. Scarlett's not nice enough, and Jane couldn't be more embarrassed. Of course, that's probably some of the reason why I keep driving her. She despises my frugal attire, my job, the fact I'm strongly against spending money and buying worthless shit just to keep up with current trends, and everything else about me. Jane's not going to want people to see a hole in her house. But since it's a quick job, there's a slight chance that she'll be okay with it. Hopefully, I won't be pissing her off for who knows how long. If she can look past the gap and see the bigger picture, the project will be complication-free.

With the house now punctured, I need to inventory what I have, so that I know what I need. The door's a quick job and the materials are pretty straightforward. For the roof, I have a few boards to get started but need to buy the rest. I wrote down what I lacked and went on to order everything. Within twenty minutes, I had the materials lined up from The Builds Depot. Delivery was conveniently set for sometime this afternoon. There's no doubt that today's technology caters to home drunks. I can have just about anything I need brought right to my doorstep within hours, or at worst, a couple of days. It's crazy to think that anything that I could possibly require, and most of what I might want, can be in my hands that quick without talking to someone or going anywhere. The only reason why I ever have to leave this place is work. Work fucks everything. Even so, as with Jane, I will try not to let myself think about it.

After a good start, it was time to switch gears and take a little break. I grabbed two lawn chairs from the garage so that I could sit comfortably in the driveway next to the grill and beers. For obvious reasons, chances are Jane won't be joining me first thing, but there'll be a chair waiting for her if she can keep her cool and recognize the good I'm doing here. I know our anniversary isn't until tomorrow, but tomorrow's Sunday. It's the worst day of the weekend. Today's the day to celebrate if we're going to.

With further thought, there's a fighting chance that I might have gotten a little ahead of myself. I needed to drink and smoke for a few minutes to catch up—just a little intermission to evaluate the project with a clear mind. Neighbor was sitting outside of her garage too. She makes it look fun over there. A nice little ass to look at trumps none every day. Faintly hearing their music causes me to run upstairs and put mine on a little louder for extra motivation's sake. Plus, I wanted to get a good look before getting back to it. The view of her is far better from Burnitts window. Today she has on her classic short and tight jean shorts and a light pink spaghetti strap. With an outfit like that, her body requires little imagination—though I imagine it a lot.

While heading back downstairs, I can easily see the side door and the new door hole lining up perfectly. It's looking as I hoped, and so far, no time-consuming fuck-ups. Realizing that Jane will be home anytime now, I start planning the roof. Measuring the span between the garage and house and cutting a board tightly to length enabled me to establish the height and level of the peak. Knowing that allowed me to mark and cut the siding on each side. Unless the delivery comes soon, that's as far as I can get before the boss is back home. I don't think I'll have to point out the work that I've done. Maybe she'll recognize my value and give me the proper raise I deserve.

In reality, I can only imagine what Jane's thoughts and reactions will be pulling in. With the moment soon approaching, I'm starting to shit my khakis a little. The car in the yard is what she'll first see come into view as she comes up over the hill. Jane's going to love that already. Once on the property, her eyes won't know where to begin. It looks like I'm glamping in the driveway, and being able to see directly into the house might be a little bit of a shocker. There's siding missing, boards up, and a trash pile to boot. She'll probably pull in just as I happen to be standing there stoned-faced with a ShackBrew in hand, appearing all impressed with myself.

Chapter Nine

Luckily, I was just inside the garage when I saw Jane start to pull in and was able to dart up the stairs to Burnitts without being seen. "Oh fuck," is all I could say. It was repeated several times during the ascent. Maybe I did jump the gun on this. Trepidation is what came to mind first, beer second. The cooler was downstairs, so I quickly went for a room-temperature can. I also retrieved one of the half joints in the ashtray. They're both common nervous reactions for me.

I peeked out the window just as Jane was getting out of the car. She stepped out real slow with a look that I can only describe as a mixture of fear and rage. After just standing there looking around with her jaw dangled for what seemed like forever, she finally shut the car door behind her and cautiously decided to move in. I could tell that she couldn't comprehend what was happening. It looked like Jane had to force herself to proceed. Just as she appeared to glance up toward the window, probably looking for me, I jumped out of view hoping she didn't see me watching. Regardless, with no other choice, I lit my joint, took a half-can gulp of beer, and went for it.

As I walked down the stairs, I could hear Jane calling out to me wondering where I was. I knew right then that my optimism about the project was in fact ignorance. There's nothing about it that she's going to like, and there's a good chance that I'm going to get hit for it. She's certainly not going to consider any of my reasoning. Jane likes to freak out before trying to understand anything. She's dramatic first and foremost and thinks that she has the right to be.

"What the hell is going on here, Marty?" Before I had an opportunity to answer, she continued with her next question. "What the fuck are you doing to my house?"

"I figured that it would be a good day to finally put in the door that I've been wanting." I said it like I expected her to know what I was talking about, hoping that she would think that she just didn't remember or never paid attention. I knew it was weak, but it was all I had.

"What door, Marty? What the fuck are you talking about?" Her facial expression said enough, but I have a feeling her mouth will say more.

"It's going in right there, out from the bedroom."

"What? Are you fucking kidding me? That doesn't even make any fucking sense, Marty. I don't understand what you're doing. What the... why the fuck are you doing this?"

"Jane, I've talked about installing a door there for a long time. This will be an improvement for the room. Plus, the bathroom's right there if we need it when we're outside or at Burnitts. I've been wanting to do it for years." I tried matching her look of confusion. "You've never said anything about it being a bad idea or that you didn't want me to do it." I said that with a confident but curious tone. Of course, it's all bullshit. I'm sure that I've made comments about needing a bar bathroom, but this idea came today or else it would be done already.

"This is un-fucking-believable, Marty. I don't know why you just decided to rip the house apart. How do you even think that would be okay? There's no purpose in doing any of this other than to piss me off. I don't want a fucking door there, and I don't want my house looking like this." She took a breath, but I stayed quiet. Then she kept going. "I mean look around, it's a shit-hole around here, Marty. Your piece of a shit car's on display in the yard, there's shit everywhere, and you have the driveway looking like a fucking RV park." She's pissed. I can tell by all the cussing. When Jane's at a loss for words, fuck and shit become much more prominent in her dialog. It's hard to believe she has a Bachelors in language arts.

"Jane, you might not have given it as much thought as I have, but this is exactly what Burnitts needs. We won't have to walk through the house to use the bathroom. It'll be just through the door there."

"I don't even know what to fucking say right now. I don't give a shit about Burnitts. And I'm not sure if you've noticed, but there's no fucking door there." She's telling me all about it now. Jane turned around and began tromping off. "Looks like fucking shit around here." Apparently, she did know what to say, and she made it clear.

"You're going to love it, Jane." Not that I cared. She didn't turn around or respond. After standing there for a couple of seconds hoping she would, I quickly caught up to her just as she reached the front door.

"Hey, Jane?" She stopped and turned around without saying anything. "Can I have your key?" She just stood there looking repulsed and annoyed. Eventually, I realized she wanted an explanation. "I want to move your car. I want to throw the basketball around, and it's in the way." The alcohol must have been starting to influence me because I shouldn't have said any more than I had to. This is how the truth will get me. In her eyes, she came home to her house torn apart and I just want to shoot hoops. Perhaps I should have waited on that. I didn't plan on playing until later anyway.

It wasn't until after Jane threw me the key and walked off inside that I remembered the car needed to be moved anyway because of the upcoming delivery. It probably wouldn't have made a difference with her attitude, but I should have said that instead. The drugs might be delaying me. After parking the car on the lawn next to mine, I briefly saw her turning away from the hole in the wall as I walked up. Must be she remains unimpressed because no praise was offered. Maybe I should let it soak in for a while before walking her through the plans. It'll give me some time to get some more done anyway.

I needed to sit down and have a smoke after that encounter, still shocked that I walked away unscathed. A cold beer to wash down what I deemed as a victory is also well deserved. The most stressful, potential barrier of the project has been dealt with, and I think it went over pretty smoothly. Sure, Jane's a bit irritated and didn't react the way that I was hoping, but thankfully, she didn't react the way that I was fearing either. That's a win for my age.

Moving on, I went back to the doorway to frame it in and move the wire. The work that was needed caused me to remove quite a bit of drywall around the opening, so Jane would be even more pissed if she saw the progress. I think that I have enough scraps in the garage to piece it all back together though. Before long, the opening was ready for the door. The bedroom had its electrical outlet moved and a new switch installed for the outdoor light. I wanted to stay on it and get the drywall back together, but my cooler needed topping off, and I was looking forward to getting something to eat.

I love the process of cooking with charcoal. It wouldn't take two minutes to cook these all-beef hotdogs in the microwave, but it would be nowhere near as satisfying as getting the coals going, tending the meat, and tasting the smoke and char of the grill. Having yet to see Jane since she came home, I'm hoping she's not planning on avoiding me all day. Maybe she'll join me for lunch, but I'd rather have no company at all if she's just going to bring that shitty mouth along with her. Now thinking about it, cooking grilled food with Jane was my initial intention this morning before getting sidetracked. Even though I'll likely be eating alone today, I'm used to it. That's why I'm finally doing something about it.

The concept of the door thrilled me. It's been a while since I've had a project. I wasn't necessarily looking forward to this weekend at first, but now I'm excited to get the work done and have some fun. Despite how it is, Jane and I deserve to have a good time together. We've earned it. If anything, we could look at our anniversary as a celebration of resilience, rather than a so-called marriage milestone. Either way, I'm happy and enjoying the day, so I lit the charcoals, slung the empty cooler bag over my shoulder, and headed in—through the new opening, of course.

Not to my surprise, Jane was out back with the dog and on the phone. I wish she was hanging out with me looking as happy. Anyway, it's good to see after how upset she was. I probably gave her something to talk about to her mom and friends. By the time I packed all the hotdog essentials into a grocery bag and filled my cooler with beers and ice, Jane was off the phone and walking in.

"I'm about to make lunch. Are you hungry? Warden's on the grill!"

"No thanks. I just had leftover tacos."

"Okay. Would you like to join me anyway?'

"No thanks."

"Are you still mad about the door?"

"You ask as if you expect me not to be, Marty. I mean look at this fucking house, it's trashed. And where's the fucking door anyway? Wait, let me guess, you plan on using the front door and want to close that entrance up. Who needs a front fucking door when you can just enter through a bedroom? I mean what the hell?" I don't want to jump to conclusions, but I think she's still pissed.

"Jane, I'm not taking the front door. I have one coming.

I'm also getting good work in fast. This will be mostly done by today." I said it like I expected her to be impressed.

"That's not even the point, Marty. I don't want what you're doing, and you just did it without even asking. You don't ever have any respect for my opinions and fucking wants. You just think about yourself." *You don't have any "fucking wants."*

"Well, I'm excited about it. As I said, it's going to be an improvement. It'll look great, I promise." I want to tell her to fuck off but try to keep my composure. "Come have a drink with me while I have lunch."

"Marty, I'm not going to sit in the driveway drinking and grilling like it's a fucking tailgate party. I'm pissed and just want to be left alone." Maybe I should keep trying to convince Jane to trust me and assure her that I have everything under control, but I'm aware that it would be a useless attempt. Jane won't ease up, she only knows resistance and irritability. Things between us would be so much better if she wasn't so fucking wound up all the time. My cock could probably help her with that, but there's no persuading her that my dick's good for anything. When Jane gets irate for petty reasons, it can be hard to deal with. Sometimes I become heated and need to shut myself down. Deactivating this ticking time bomb before I go off is best for everyone.

It took me a long time to learn that I get nowhere arguing with Jane. If I call her out on something, she defends herself by denying everything or claiming some bullshit reasoning or excuse. If I mention past examples of how she acted to defend a point, I just keep bringing up the past and adamantly told that it's not true. It's everything according to Jane. Even when I summarize the dialogue between us that just occurred, if it calls her out on being wrong or unreasonable, she refuses that the conversation happened the way that it did. Jane is impossibly obstinate. If I mention how I feel when she's bashing on me and running me into the ground, according to her, I'm being a pussy.

"Aw, poor Marty," she'll say. "Am I hurting your feelings?" I can't get through to her that she's causing me some irreversible trauma here. It's best if I just walk off, keep my mouth shut, and bottle it up. Burnitts is a good place to do that.

Food is now long overdue for me. I've been drinking all morning. Even though being active has been keeping my buzz down, I can feel it beginning to make its presence known. I put too much charcoal on for just three hotdogs, so I cooked them quickly and closed up the grill. If I can snuff it out before they burn all the way through, they'll still be useful for burgers later. I finished lunch within a dozen bites but wasn't ready to get up and get going right away. Having just eaten like a king on peasant options, I have to go through the usual smoke and drink routine to top myself off first. For me, it's a tradition with consuming humble food and getting royally full.

More than likely, I'll be responsible for ruining the whole weekend for Jane. That's how the anniversary will be remembered and told by her anyway. The only gift that she's getting from me is a fucking headache. I'm just a pain in the pussy to her. That's probably why I never get laid. The weekend was never going to be anything too wonderful with Jane, but I had some hope this morning that we could make the best of it. Now that I cut her house open, it might not be so easy to recover from. She was likely to get mad at me for something anyway. The odds are usually stacked against us, but I might have encouraged it this time.

Until I get the material delivery, I'm limited to what I can do with what I have available. The framing of the roof will have to wait, but I hope to get it done by day's end. There's enough drywall and mud in the garage to patch up the inside, so with that, it will be ready for paint tomorrow. It's only two-thirty now, but I'm already starting to get tired and could easily just sit here drinking, smoking, and listening to music the rest of the day. The occasional view of Neighbor makes it that much more appealing. But even my laziness doesn't top my desire to get the project done. It'll all be worth it when Burnitts is livable. I finished my smoke and moved on to knocking out the drywall, taping, and first mud coat. Within forty-five minutes, it already looks ten times better on the inside. I knew what it was going to look like, but it'll definitely help Jane see the vision. Assuming that she's capable of pulling her face out of her phone, she might end up liking what she sees.

As I was cleaning up, the buzz that I had became even more obvious to me. I recognized myself operating more/less on automatic while random thoughts ran wild. I forgot what I was doing several times and was wondering where I put shit more often than earlier. It's still early, so I consider slowing down or take a drinking break altogether. If I don't, I run the risk of losing the remainder of this fuckless day.

After convincing myself that continuing to drink as much as I have been would lead to me not completing what I could otherwise, I persuaded myself to do something practically unheard of when I'm home—I decided to drink a mid-day glass of water or two. It's not my preference, especially on a Saturday, but I realized why I might be feeling the beer come on so fast. I think that I'm dehydrated even more than usual due to all the excessive housework that I've been doing. That's why I swore it off in the first place. I didn't plan on not drinking heavily today, but for the sake of Burnitts, I suppose that I can compromise.

Out of habit, I went in through the front door despite being closer to the new opening. I was at a standstill and pretty filthy, so after chugging a couple glasses of water, I opted for a shower. It should be the hydration and rejuvenation that I need to continue strong. Inside, I didn't see Jane or the dog and assumed that they were both in the bedroom sleeping. Well, Warden probably is anyway. Jane's phone is probably keeping her occupied. It doesn't matter to him, as long as she's close. He's kind of an asshole about her. He's dependent. If she's home and he can't be right next to her at all times, he'll whine until he eventually falls asleep. It's likely a learned behavior though, Jane wines all the time. If she's gone and it's just me around, he lays in bed all day until she returns. He doesn't want to go outside. He doesn't want to drink. He won't even eat a snack if Jane's not home. If she's gone for days, I won't see him for days. When Jane's out, he's the perfect dog.

Walking into my room from the inside was a new and satisfying sight. It's going to look so much better with the door and covered pass-thru. The change is going to be more drastic than I expected. More importantly, it's going to be fully functional for Burnitts. Seeing it like this, Jane can go fuck herself off to Hell. By tomorrow, everything will be done, and she'll see how nice it is. I think we have some leftover paint from when I painted the room a few years ago, so with that and a little trim work, it'll be back to finished.

Since I installed an endless hot water system, my showering and bathing frequency and times have increased significantly. The bathroom has become a small but needed sanctuary within the walls of this *big house*. I could think of worse places to serve solitary confinement. As usual, I could have spent an hour in the shower. There was no cold water reminder telling me that it's been long enough. My body was starting to stiffen up, and part of me just wanted to lay down and call it a day. However, thinking of angry Jane, proving her wrong, and getting what I want keeps my momentum from going stale. Drying off, I caught myself in the mirror. I'm looking pretty good. It might be the beer goggles, but I could tell that I put in a good workout and have been working. My muscles were tighter than usual and more defined. Jane doesn't know what she's missing—Neighbor either.

With the plan working out so well, and me feeling like I was getting a fresh start, I'm excited to keep the ball rolling. I'm convinced that this is the right move. Jane's delusional if she thinks I needed her permission to do it. She couldn't begin to understand the practicality of it. It's not like she hangs out outside or up at the bar.

Anger is what Jane conceives in her head and births out of her mouth. She's wrong in thinking that I'm gonna let her continue getting away with raising her voice at me. She can't keep calling me a piece of shit and abandoning me anytime she feels like it, and then expect me to just forget about it.

I walked out of the bathroom, and thanks to me putting an unannounced hole in the wall, was in the garage within seconds. I'm already convinced that this will be one of the better upgrades that I've done to the house, easily in line with the bar, garden, and endless hot water system. It wasn't until I noticed Jane's car gone that I realized she wasn't home. I wonder if she left because of me? She seemed pretty mad but that's her normal. Unfortunately, it's always difficult to say just how mad she is because her emotions don't have much of an in-between. With me, if Jane's not content, she's all the way pissed off. I hope she wasn't upset with me enough to leave though. However, with the way I'm treated, I try not to care. I'm sick of being considered a fuckin subordinate. Jane couldn't care less about giving me respect, and I don't think she'll ever change. She only knows ill-temper and yelling.

I was only a few drags into a cigarette break when the delivery truck got my attention coming up the hill. It didn't sound like it was going to make it. The in-your-face, florescent orange "X" across the grill screamed to look out just as loud as its dying engine did. With the vision of completion in mind, it was well-welcomed noise pollution. Now I'll have everything I need to complete the project. Just past the driveway, the truck came to a struggling stop. From there, the driver used an attached pallet lift to bring everything up. Once finished, he stepped off to give me the paperwork.

"Hey."

"How ya doin'?"

"Good. I appreciate you getting this out to me."

"No problem. Last one of the day, easy enough."

"Nice! Good for you. It's Saturday, so I'm sure you're ready."

"Thanks, man. Glad to be done with it. Today's Friday for me. My weekend's bout to get started! Bout time," he goes.

"That's awesome. I know how that feels. Mine's already half over. I got a ShackBrew if you want one." I went for mine and the joint in the ashtray next to it.

He laughed. "Oh, I want. I better not though. I won't leave. Next guy'll be wondering where the truck's at. Maybe if we weren't down to just this one." It was a long shot but common courtesy to ask.

"Are you a subcontractor or do you work for The Builds Depot?"

"Nah, my boss is the subcontractor. I just run loads." I relit the joint as he responded and handed it his way. "Now this I can take you up on," he says.

"Yeah, I thought you might. Enjoy, happy Friday."

"Watcha got going on?"

"I'm installing a door right there and building a roof over that to the garage entrance on the other side. The garage doesn't have a bathroom but there's one just inside the house there."

"Nice. Makes sense, gotta have a garage bathroom."

"I think so, but wifey not so much. I also have a bar upstairs and not everyone's comfortable pissing in the bushes."

"I imagine, man. Roses have thorns, right? That's not the way pussy should be poked."

"That's funny! So, do you have Mondays off too?"

"Yeah, lucky to get two in a row. A lot of drivers don't."

"Man, I'd give anything to have Monday off."

"It's nice but I miss Saturdays too. Best thing about

Mondays though, my wife's at work all day, so I get a peaceful day to myself. I need it after Sundays with her."

This man just became my new fucking hero. He's on to something. If this were Monday, Jane wouldn't even be home yet. Not one time would I have been cussed at yet today. He took a second hit and handed back the joint.

"What's your name, man? I'm Marty."

"I'm Robb. Nice to meet you, Marty. Good luck with the project. I gotta hit the road but appreciate the weekend christening. You don't know how much I needed that."

"Hah, I might though. But you're welcome. Thanks again for the delivery. Actually, kinda surprised you made it here by the sounds of your truck."

"Yeah, got an asshole boss who won't fix it unless it's completely broke."

"Don't we all?" I asked, knowing exactly how asshole bosses are. "Enjoy your weekend, bro."

The only person that I had to deal with to complete the transaction was that guy? I'm tempted to write my first review ever. Robb even liked where I was going with the project. Materials delivered to my door, same day, and with a compliment too? All I want is to never have to go anywhere again.

I was looking forward to seeing the door the most. If it looks as good as it does in the picture, I know that Jane will be relieved and come to see it as I promised. I was happy to find it looked better than expected. I bought the black, fifteen-pane, insulated steel version. Since the siding was already cut to measurement, it only took me twenty minutes to hang the door and put the exterior trim on. From there I caulked the outside and insulated and trimmed the inside. I also remembered to put another coat of mud on the wall. All in all, I had a fully installed, beautiful door within an hour or so of not having one. With that, I conclude it's been a productive day's work so far. I've completed close to what I was thinking I would. Now I can enjoy a drink the right way, with certainty and redemption in mind.

Luckily, I was at Burnitts doing just that when Jane came back home. I happened to be peeking out the window at Neighbor spray-painting something outside her garage when I saw her coming up the hill. She pulled in like the swale and sidewalk didn't exist and came to an abrupt stop just after passing over them. I knew right then that I didn't dare go out to meet her. She's still not happy. Jane not having her usual parking spot because of the mess in the driveway, all from something she's hating on, is plenty enough to fuel her frustration and fury. I planned on picking up the packaging and organizing the delivery next but needed to satisfy my thirst first. Jane should understand. It took her several seconds before giving in and just parking the car back where she found it—where I wanted it. Turns out, she had bags of groceries to bring in, so it might have been most convenient anyway. It's either she walks in the grass or walks around a scattered pile of materials. Normally, I wouldn't hesitate to help carry things in, but I'll be due for an apology once she gets a good look at the door. She'll have to come to me for that. However, I wouldn't bet on seeing her anytime soon because Jane's never sorry. She truly believes that she never has anything to be sorry for. I've been intending to prove her wrong in one way or another.

With Jane now inside, I wanted to get a better look at what Neighbor was doing. It looks like a piece of furniture she's working on, maybe a plant stand or an end table. If I was a little closer I could see better. She makes me wish that I had binoculars lying around here somewhere. Would I ever leave the window though? I can't stop thinking about her and how perfect she is, even when it's my anniversary. Jane doesn't act in any way close to her. I imagine Neighbor wanting to help me today. She would be keeping me company at the very least. Regardless of what she would be doing, she would be hot and happy doing it. I can easily picture her having lunch with me, making jokes, celebrating, and drinking beer with me all day. She's as flawless as Jane is shameless. I don't think that Neighbor could be more opposite than Jane. I know the daily reveries I have of each of them couldn't be more contrasting.

I've known that, for one reason or another, Jane would find an excuse to be distant. Only true hate can drive a person to be alone by choice. This is just another typical weekend for us. The workweek will always be shit, but I've always thought that the weekends should make up for it. She never makes an exception for them. It being our anniversary isn't going to change that. Jane continues to prove that she's fine with the person she is, has been, and is becoming—I'm not.

Jane blames me for our disconnect, but she quit trying years ago. She doesn't try to make things better because she doesn't care to. Despite the ongoing torment that I endure from her, she's over it. She doesn't consider how a little self-improvement could go a long way. According to her, she's perfect as-is. There's no effort. She doesn't have any interests, hobbies, or desires that could involve me or strengthen us. I bring a lot of options to the table. Unlike me and Neighbor, she hasn't even attempted exercising in a long time. She's fine with the person she is even if it suppresses our marriage. Don't get me wrong, Jane looks phenomenal regardless. My point is that it's healthy to exercise and beneficial for any relationship. Without it means a less limber body, limited stamina, less energy and confidence, and a decreased sex drive on top of everything. All arguably important traits to possess when sharing your life with someone.

Jane believes her attitude toward me is appropriate. Even though I envy her self-satisfaction, it makes reasoning with her unbearable. She will never consider any of my concerns or the attempts that I make. With Jane, I can't get away with making a point or defending myself. I can't have an opinion, feeling, need, or desire that she would even try to compromise with if different than hers. All of our problems stem from this egotistic, self-centered, better-than-you outlook of hers. More and more, I don't want her to be my fucking problem anymore.

Before I know it, it's five o'clock. It's already been twelve hours since I first looked at the time today. I managed to get quite a bit done considering I've drank enough for two people to get drunk. Although my drinking skills are notable, there's a good chance I'm not going to remember much of this come morning. Tonight's autopilot better be well versed in transporting its shit-faced passenger. It should know not to go or do where or what I insist on.

I had to jerk off a little watching Neighbor. My dick was confined and begging for attention. Without effort, she has that effect on me. I didn't want to cum though. As I often do, I chose to save it and let it build up for later. If marriage has taught me anything, delaying pleasure is it. It's also my present self thinking about my future self again. The more I cum the better it feels for longer. That's why I make it a point to stay as hydrated as I do. No more than a minute later, I had to convince myself to put it away before I took it too far.

Once fully settled, I found my way back to the driveway chair. By the time I was halfway through a cigarette, my mind was repressed of Neighbor and I was once again lost in thought about Jane. She crushes fantasies like that. Maybe she just wants an apology from me. If that would make her want to hang out, I'm certainly capable of swallowing my pride for the greater good. It would be nice if she occasionally would. However, I'm not going to kiss her ass all night trying to get her to have a good time. She would have to at least be matching my effort. In fact, I think she should exceed it to help make up for what she's lacked all these non-fucking years.

Once I talked myself into going inside, I opted to use the

front door. It's a rare instance when I'm not trying to avoid Jane, so it made sense. We shouldn't have any more problems now that the breach in the house has been addressed. I found her at the bar hunched over her phone with a half-full glass of wine next to her. She would call it half empty or not full enough, but the truth is, it's probably too much.

"Hey."

"Hey."

I went straight for the fridge and happily found it fully restocked. Maybe it's an indication of Jane's intentions. She planned on drinking, that's for sure. Hopefully, she wants to get slutty with me while doing so. I pulled out my lighter and used it to pop the cap off my ShackBrew. It made such a loud and perfect celebratory sound that it came naturally to blurt out "Happy anniversary weekend!" At the same time, I went in for a cheers.

"Happy anniversary weekend," she replied without any believable intonation. She did return the cheers though, so I'll take it.

"What are you up to?" I asked.

She shut off her phone. "Getting ready to walk Warden." Getting ready means finishing her wine.

"Did you see the door?"

"Marty, I know what you're doing. Stop. I'm pissed off about it."

"It looks really good. Did you see it?"

"Is there an actual door there?"

"Yeah. It's nice too. Seriously, you should take a look," realizing she didn't even bother to when she pulled in. Right now, that drink of hers seemed to be her only concern.

"I'm going to walk the dog."

"All right, maybe when you get back then." I said it as if I couldn't wait. Of course, the dog's going to take fucking precedence. With that plan, she refilled her glass and leashed

Warden. I just stood there sipping my beer in restrained disbelief.

"We'll be back."

"Walk safe," is all I could think to safely say. A lot more could have be said. I watched Jane as she walked the dog down the driveway without even bothering to look back at the work. It's a bitch move that I'm sure was meant to be seen. Either way, she wasn't giving me much in terms of what her actual attitude could be. She says she's pissed off, but she's not avoiding me completely. Usually, unless we're in the middle of arguing, that's the way typical interaction between us goes, respectful enough and nothing too intense in any way. She makes it seem like she has to deal with me though, like she's being forced to. She acts like she's taken on an obligation that she can't get out from under but wants to. Even so, I still feel like the night could go either way. With that said, since it is my anniversary, I just want it to be memorable in one way or the other.

After admiring the new door for a moment from the inside, I stepped out just in time to hear Neighbor's giggly laugh. I pictured watching her as she touched her vibrator to her clit, jolted and amused by the initial sensation. Soon after, the silence around me suddenly derailed that train of thought. My radio was off. Up at Burnitts, I discovered my phone dead. After plugging it in, I found myself again at the window hoping to see her sunbathing or something. What I find is The fucking Neighbor. He's out there talking it up with his girl and Jane. Both of them aren't hiding how impressed they are with this asshole. He's out there with no fucking shirt looking like he's getting ready to fuck them both where they stand. Even the dog's acting like he wants to lick his dick. His tail's whipping around like he's found his long-lost fucking friend. Admittedly, I'm a little jealous now. Not saying that I want to lick his dick too, that's something I'd have to see first. I just wish I was in his shoes right now.

I only get to see Jane appearing interested and

presenting herself so confidently as an outsider. She doesn't offer herself to me that way anymore. It's something I miss. I think that it's the look she uncontrollably displays when altogether attracted, amused, and curious. Her gravitating smile and entrancing gaze give it away. It can't be faked. That's what I see when I think of Jane's beauty. Too bad it's directed at that fish-fucker across the street. I watched her until she eventually left, reluctantly I presume. More than likely, Warden urged her. When he gets too excited, he needs to shit.

When it comes to other opportunities, Jane has the upper hand. Women typically do. She's meeting new and different people all the time. Most would fuck her faster than The Neighbor would. She has a physical sensuality that comes naturally. Sure, Jane's a bit older and not in the shape that she could be, but she's as pretty as anyone. Jane's a definite. She's by far, not a girl that would have to be considered. I don't know anyone that would want to fuck with me. I'm never even smiled at, let alone flirted with or wanted. Jane probably has several cocks in her back pocket at her disposal. It's guaranteed that they're all bigger than mine unless they have significantly more money. Her awareness of it all shows. Not that she's narcissistic, she just doesn't care anymore about being attracted to, or interested in me.

I was back to sitting in the driveway when Jane and the dog returned. After leaving The Neighbors, they weren't gone long. I'm guessing she finished most of her wine there and kept the walk short because of it.

"Hey."

"Hey."

"How was the walk?"

"Good. I have to pee though." She passed right by without slowing. I didn't remind her that there was a bathroom just inside the new door. "Run," is all I said.

Chapter Ten

I took a longer break than I intended to thinking that Jane might come back out. After about fifteen minutes, it was obvious that she wasn't going to. I wanted to sort through the delivery anyway. It looks like I bought everything that I need despite being high when I ordered it all. Of course, I'm high now too, so who knows what the fuck. I took the lumber off the pallet and sorted it off the driveway. I also put the roofing materials, light, and various smalls just inside the garage. Getting it out of the way freed the space back up for basketball. Plus, Jane should be less pissed about it too. After doing all that and her still not returning, I had to forget about it. I don't know what she wants, and all I can do is speculate. More than likely she's rubbing a couple off while thinking of The Neighbor.

Even though my appetite was starting to sneak up on me, I decided to try to get more work done. The thought of having my own space with a killer view made it easy for me to talk myself into it. Normally, it can be hard to get shit done when the beer starts weighing me down, but since the bathroom access is going to allow me to easily get shit done from Burnitts, it's an easy sell. Plus, it's not like I have anything else better to do.

The next thing for the roof was to fasten the ridge and facia beams to the walls. To do that, I had to slip in some flashing, locate the studs, and fasten some boards on the gable ends. Once I secured some brackets, I went on to cut and hang the beams. That work took an hour to do. In the meantime, Jane was nowhere to be seen. I can't believe that she wouldn't have looked at the door by now. Since it looks amazing, this is when she'll decide to keep any new opinions of it to herself. It's obvious that she's been wrong. I could have kept going, but I couldn't ignore my hunger any longer. I've done more than I hoped for today.

I can't remember the last time I cooked on the grill twice in one day. Of course, that doesn't mean anything. Under the lid, I see there's a good pile of charcoal left, but I added more thinking that Jane might join me this time. I wouldn't mind making the best of it with her. We could grill low and slow if she's interested. I decided to bring a chair out for her just in case. The one that was originally for her is now my much-needed footrest. My feet don't want to touch the ground right now. The thought of having Jane for dinner excited me, but I'm giving up on trying if she doesn't want to. I need to remember to keep my expectations at nothing.

The next thing to do is prepare the beef and allow it to get up to temperature before cooking. I formed three burgers out of the 80/20 Angus, mixed in a little minced garlic and onion powder, then peppered them well. I won't add salt until just before searing. Jane isn't anywhere to be seen, but I noticed the bedroom door all the way shut suggesting that she's up to something. After contemplating what to drink for a moment, I decided on wine—step it up for celebration's sake. After taking a couple of beer-sized swallows, I swallowed my self-worth and submitted to seeking out Jane. My light taps on her bedroom door made me seem harmless. Without waiting for a response, I opened it just enough to peek in.

"Jane?"

"Yeah?" As she came into view, I opened it a little more.

She was lying in bed, probably resting after her recent releases.

"Just wondering if you're hungry? I'm going to cook some burgers."

"Um, I might have a burger, but I'm not that hungry."

"All right. Do you want to have a drink together or something?"

"Um... sure." I think she might have faked the hesitation. "I'll be out in a few minutes." It was kind of unexpected hearing Jane say that she was willing to hang out with me. She must have seen the door.

"Okay, I'll be outside."

"What's that?" She got up and approached the door, opening it wider once there. "Outside?"

"Yeah, I've got the grill going."

"Are you eating out there or are you bringing them in?"

"I was just going to eat outside. The music's on, and the sun's going down."

"I'm not going outside. I don't want to sit out there, Marty." The way she said it to me, with that repulsed look of hers, struck a cord. I keep trying, and this is how she always is. It's like being around me is making her nauseous. How is this fucking fair? Not only is it our anniversary in a few hours, but it's also the last real night off of the weekend.

"Are you even interested in trying to hang out? Why can't you have a fucking drink with me while I cook these burgers?" I'm still calm, but it was a question that I really want an answer to.

"I just said that I didn't want to go outside, Marty. Now you're getting mad and swearing at me." Classic Jane, doesn't take into account how she's been treating me. How dare I ask a question? And so what, I cussed out of presumably understandable frustration. It wasn't even directed at her. Either way, Jane's going to play the victim now.

"Listen, I'm not trying to get you to fucking hang out

anymore. If you would rather spend our anniversary weekend in bed with your dog dick, understood. I'm sure you've spoken to your mom more than me since being here today, even though you spent the whole morning with her. I knew that you were going to be fucking oppressive anyway. What else is new, Jane? It's fucked-up. You should just leave if you don't want to be around." The door shut louder than I intended.

"Fuck you, Marty. What's your problem?" Her yelling is slightly more tolerable when it's behind a closed door. Hopefully, she doesn't come out attacking.

Back in the kitchen, I knew that I had just blown any chance that I had for myself. That was the present me fucking the future me—very selfish of me. As far as Jane goes, there would be no company, no partying, and no crazy sex for me tonight. She was probably hoping that I'd be the first to blow, instigating it in her own fucked-up way. Looks like she'll be getting another thoughtful and loving anniversary gift from me. I'll be giving her the fuckin space she wants. The way I see it, she's being sensitive because the door came out looking phenomenal, so she needed another excuse to bail.

After pounding the rest of my wine, I refilled my glass with water while my emotions quickly went from frustrated to somewhat remorseful. Trying to justify my reaction to myself wasn't working. Now I'm wishing that I didn't say anything. Maybe the day is getting the best of me. Food is probably what I need to keep it together. I put six pieces of bacon in the microwave for five minutes, sliced some tomato and onion, and gathered the cheese, pickles, mayonnaise, ketchup, salt, and buns. With all that, I grabbed the meat and threw everything in one of Jane's grocery bags that were still left out. Then I went on to shut the blinds and look at the door again while the bacon finished and cooled. The room is going to be perfect when it's completed. How could Jane not love it? It's probably because it has nothing to do with her. The bathroom location relative to

Burnitts is undeniably as good as any. Come to think of it, I'm not sure when the last time was that I even needed a bathroom. No wonder I wake up so dehydrated all the time.

After retrieving the food, I went out to check the coals and get cooking. The oven was hot, so I shook it by the handle to spread the heat out evenly under one side, then brushed the grate free of burnt remains and ash. I salted one side of the burgers and placed them down to sear over the hot coals. Food quickly dominates my thoughts as I watch and listen to the dripping fat dissolve almost as soon as it falls. The smoke it creates is like a visual scent floating downwind and dissipating. I practically stand in it, anxiously waiting to tend to the meat.

While admiring the coals, my thoughts zoned out. It occurred to me that coal is what I could get Jane for an anniversary gift. I could get her a whole bag of the shit. It's not quite the conventional diamond jewelry she might expect, but maybe it's more appropriate for an inadequate wife. Like when a kid deserves coal for Christmas after being terrible all year. Although I've purchased diamond jewelry in the past, I'm not a big supporter. Despite their premium, they're relatively boring gemstones in my eyes. The braggarts are to blame for the demand that stimulates that kind of wonky shit. After some time, I came back to reality, but not without thinking about how coal would have been a much more fitting rock to mount on all that past jewelry that I'd given Jane—especially on the band that brought us to this point.

After a couple of minutes or so of cooking on one side, I salted the other side of the burgers and flipped them over for a couple more. Once seared, I moved them off the coals, put the slices of American cheese on, and covered the grill to let bake until melted. After that, I let the meat relax for a few minutes which allowed me time to toast some buns. Once finished, I'll put a loaded one together for Jane, but there's no way that I'm going to run it right in for her like I'm her personal fucking attendant.

Two beautiful burgers with all the fixings and a cigarette later, I no longer want to move. It getting dark is an upsetting reminder that the day's over, and Monday's coming quickly. Being thirsty, but not wanting to go inside, I checked the cooler for any remaining beer only to come up empty-fisted. I wanted more wine but instead closed up the grill and headed up to Burnitts for a warm one, and maybe a shot too. Whatever I have to do to avoid any potential meeting with Jane. I kept the lights dim and lowered the music down. I'm full, beat, buzzed, and ready to just marinate in it all. Finally feeling finished for the day and decently accomplished, I cracked open a beer, got my weed out, and welcomed myself home.

My thoughts wandered while aimlessly walking around Burnitts. I began thinking again about just how convenient the bathroom access was going to be. That led me to start thinking about Jane, and how I would never have to go inside unless there's an absolute need to. It was kind of a childish, freedom-type thought, like a teenager moving into her parents' basement and "never" having to see them again. Anyway, I challenged myself with that and immediately remembered the wine that I just wanted, not to mention anything else that I'd like chilled— the warm beer I was drinking, for example. That was the thought process that led up to me realizing that I should just plug my fridge in and keep it cold from now on. After all, with a bathroom at Burnitts, I'd be using it for more than just weekday can storage. With an available grill, bathroom, couch, and fridge, this garage will be a fully functional home. So with that idea, I plugged the fridge back in so that the beers could start getting cool. I wanted to get right to stocking it up but knew that I should let it come down to temperature first, at least for any food anyway. My next thought was that I should start sneaking some wine out.

Checking on Neighbor, I see she's still sitting outside.

The Neighbor's probably hoping Jane will walk by with the dog again. He was able to see Jane in the way that I want to. I'm sure she made a good impression. Unfortunately for me, strangers get the better Jane. I'm sure hot, younger guys get the best her. It's possible that The Neighbor didn't give her much thought, but I'm sure that Jane has been thinking about him plenty

The Neighbor's a lucky guy. His wife is what a person envisions when they're inexperienced but imagining someone that they would like to be sharing their life with, someone that's a friend and always available. She's exceptional. I can't help wanting to see her better than I can. The possibility keeps me enticed. I'm not sure why I don't own any fucking binoculars. If I order some now, maybe they could be delivered to me before her morning run. Popular opinion might be that it's a little creepy buying some just for these shenanigans, but I could justify it as harmless. I'd be on my property seeing nothing more than she voluntarily displays. It's not like I'd actually be spying on her. Sure, me watching her in secret is an orchestrated act stimulated by sexual frustration, but I don't think that it's as bad as it sounds. Either way, I'm suddenly thinking about taking up bird watching as a pastime option.

All I want to do right now is see Neighbor better. If I could get a good quality look that makes me feel close, maybe I won't need more. Maybe I can move on from her once I'm able to fill in the blanks. It was those wandering thoughts of mine that brilliantly led me to remember my old video camera. Of course! I should have thought about that a long time ago. With my camera, I'd be able to zoom in for the closest look ever and see Neighbor like I was right there next to her. Unlike binoculars, my camera just happens to be here somewhere. It would be a little creepy if I just went out and bought one specifically to feel near to her. Either way, it's another exceptional idea courtesy of me. Obviously, my brain functions on a much higher level over the weekends. It'll bottom out by Monday for sure.

I used to always have my camera out, always wanting to capture the beauty that I saw in everything. But my interests were perpetually pushed aside mid-way through my media studies. I switched majors, convincing myself that responsibilities and the associated priorities take precedence over the things that I want. I needed to get serious with money and with Jane too. Knowing that she would always want to be secure, I set aside my interests and pursued finance— something I despise. Even so, I ignorantly welcomed it as soon as possible. Apparently, I didn't learn anything too valuable with all the credits I earned. I still haven't got myself out of this hole of a marriage I'm in.

I bought a new video camera less than ten years ago, the one I have now. Just from a homeowner's standpoint alone, it was time to upgrade. At that time, I found myself reminiscing about all my old equipment and interests and suddenly had to have one. My disappointment with life was manifesting. Growing up, I always had a fascination with having a copy of my experience in this world. These days, there's not so much that I want to remember. In hindsight, I think that I bought the camera in hopes to rediscover myself. I remember Jane being impossible that weekend and resulting frustrations led me to the typical "I could hit the reset button" thoughts. I impulsively bought the best camera that I could get away with. Though I envisioned better things, it never went beyond layman-style videos. There would be no second-coming video producer for me.

The videos that I used to make avoided the ugly. In a way it was all fake, but I preferred it that way. Although far from the whole story, the manufactured moments and memories of my life are the better story. Of course, editing out the ugly doesn't mean it wasn't there. Come to think of it, not remembering things is sort of like not seeing them in that way. Just because I don't remember things doesn't mean they didn't happen. For instance, there's a good chance that I might find myself in a world of shit tomorrow for things I won't remember.

I found a full box of video cassettes and some equipment under the garage stairs but no camera though. The only thing that I can think of is that it must be in the bedroom closet. I'm committed to finding it now but need to figure out how I'm going to pull it off without suspicion from Jane. Sure, waiting until she leaves for whatever reason would be the guaranteed confrontation-free solution, but that wouldn't do anything for me right now when I really want it. I'm obsessing over seeing Neighbor better. She's right there, and I've got nothing here for me. I've had some good ideas today, but this one might trump them all.

Back upstairs, the joint was finally lit. I never did get to it. Right away, I find myself scheming a camera and wine recovery mission. Suddenly convinced that this task is an urgent matter, the operation was thoughtfully planned out. First, I needed to confirm that Target-0 (Neighbor) was still in location. The risk will be for nothing if she's evasive. Then I need to go inside and seize Asset-1 (the wine) while surveilling the premises. Locating and tracking Enemy-1 (the Jane) will help determine how and when to apprehend Asset-2 (the camera). There will likely be only a small window of opportunity and potential casualties must be understood. I will not be held a prisoner. My mind was on its typical tangent.

Being that I could be drunk, it's important that I stay focused. My thoughts have to remain on the task. With my safety taking priority, I need to stay composed and extra careful not to get caught. If Jane knew of any wine hoarding from me, her filter would fall off. I could just tell her the truth, that I wanted to restock Burnitts now that I decided to leave the fridge on, but she would see it as me taking it for myself. I sort of would be, but I'd be drinking it regardless. I just don't want to have to go inside to get it one glass at a time. There's no need for me to have to explain anything to her. Since I don't want to get cussed at, I just have to be stealthy.

The plan with the wine is to access a new box to drink from and hide the quarter-full one in the cupboard or something. Later, when the full one is no more than half emptied, providing I didn't arouse any suspicion, I'll swap the two. I'll pull the ol' switcharoo but keep drinking the fridge wine. After about a week of that, I should have a nice little stash acquired. Sure, I could go to the store and buy it myself, but I'm a supporter of home delivery. As far as I know, they don't do that with alcohol, but Jane sort of works in the same way.

Even with it being around ten now, The Neighbors were still sitting outside. I can faintly hear their music and it looks like they might be playing cards. What's the wager, I wondered? If I was him, I'd lose on purpose and give her anything she wanted. She still has that sexy spaghetti strap on, so tight that I bet I could easily see the toned definition of her chest and abdomen if I were closer. I need that camera.

On my way in, I packed up the remnants of dinner, including Jane's burger, and retrieved my wine glass. Returning these will give me a Jane-proof excuse to see what she's doing with herself. Walking up to the door, I could see through the window that she was in the living room with Warden—Enemy-1, located. This is going to be easier than I planned. As I walked in, she sat right up to look at me.

"Did you make burgers?" she asked. I made her a deluxe like mine but wasn't in a hurry to give it away just yet.

Bee-lining it toward the kitchen, "I did but they were served outside. You missed out."

"You didn't make me a burger? What the fuck? You're an asshole. You asked me if I wanted one."

Addressing Jane would be like juggling newborns—risky. I was concentrating hard on the assignment, so I stayed on course to the kitchen without a word. I'm not even sure if I heard her right. In any case, silence is my best defense. Jane tried to bait me there, but I managed to avoid her trap.

In the fridge, I find the opened wine box just as I hoped, about a third full. Once I opened a new one and peeked out to see the coast still clear, I put the emptier one in the cupboard behind the chips and filled my glass from the full one that was going in the fridge—Asset-1, more/less secured. Enemy-1 hasn't left the couch, so without hesitation, I went to the bedroom closet like it was still mine and found the camera box. Luckily, Jane didn't advance to the kitchen before I returned with the package. I quickly put the camera in the same cupboard as the wine and stood at the bar like I'd been there all along—Asset-2, more/less secured.

Before I could make an escape, Jane came in. I was cornered but knew the possibility signing up. She went directly to the fridge without so much as acknowledging me. Once her wine was refilled, that all changed.

"I can't believe you didn't make me a burger. I make you food all the time." That's not true, but if she can say it, she'll believe it. It's actually occasionally at best. "I thought you were going to bring one in for me." She didn't notice anything with the wine.

"You didn't act like you wanted one." I said it nicely but with confidence. I didn't give a fuck but was polite about it. Being in the middle of something better, I had no desire to get caught up with her—good or bad.

"You know, it's our anniversary weekend, Marty, and all you give a fuck about is yourself. All you want to do is your own thing. Fuck the house up and spend all weekend just trying to make it look better. It's fucked-up, and you're acting pathetic." Jane has a lot to say for someone that couldn't simply say that she would like a burger when I asked. Now I'm being tested. The me that I know I should be would stay quiet and leave. It's said that the bigger man walks away, but what's the sense when she makes me feel so small anyway?

"Yeah, it's our anniversary weekend, and you act like you do every other weekend, every day for that matter. I honestly don't care anymore about our anniversary. It's not like I've been expecting anything special. I don't even have a gift for you. You're just being you, so I'm being me. Can you please just leave me alone? I don't want to argue with you right now, Jane." I should be standing up for myself, but she'll just continue to put me down.

"You've told me enough about how you don't care and that you weren't going to get me anything. I don't need to fucking hear it anymore, Marty." She went walking off to the bedroom. Jane gets so mad that she can piss herself off. She slammed the door behind her but immediately opened it back up for the dog, knowing he would be there waiting to join her. Jane's relentless. She has the ability to unhinge me as no other person could. I'd appreciate a little more respect sometimes. For once, I wish she would just save some shit for someone else. I wanted more than anything to act out my anger, so I did. I switched out the wine boxes, deciding now to take the full one. After emptying the bag and putting her burger in the fridge, I shielded the wine and camera and quickly fled to Burnitts using the new exit—Asset-1 and Asset-2, fully secured.

Leave it to Jane to piss me off right when things are about to get good. At the bar, I opened the camera box like a kid on Christmas expecting their first phone, but I find it out of commission. Obviously, it was going to need to be charged. The mission was currently only partly successful. The camera was dead on arrival, and now I'm suffering from PTSD caused by the enemy. At least I have wine now, and the beers are probably getting cold too. Being somewhat eager, I only gave it a few minutes before turning the camera on while it was still plugged in. How far I could zoom is what I wanted to check. Pointing it at the bullseye on the dartboard across the room, I could fill the screen with red.

I was too wound-up to wait, so I abruptly pulled the cord from the socket and tucked myself under the window. Once in position, I tilted the viewfinder down to see while holding the camera lens just up over the sill. It was difficult to tell where I was at first, so I panned out until I eventually found Neighbor. Just as I began to zoom in on her, the battery died. It was barely a tease, but the potential excited me more than anything recently. Back at the bar, my dick needed to be pulled out. The compression in my pants proved too much to disregard, so my fly became an instant gloryhole. After a quick stretch, I had to tuck back in knowing that I would cum straightaway. With the thought of her so close, I'm uncontrollable. I'll be hard to contain by night's end. Since Jane refuses to take advantage of it, it's anyone's guess how it'll end up presenting itself.

I lit a cigarette and put the newly acquired wine in the fridge. The whereabouts of my glass stumped me for a few until I realized it was left in the kitchen. The one was sacrificed for the many. Perhaps a real wine glass is in order, it is a celebration after all. Part of me didn't want to wait any longer, but as excited as I am, letting the camera get a full charge will be best for the battery. There's an extension cord downstairs, but I was starting to feel my age. Sitting here doing nothing suddenly seemed most fitting. With Jane's hate in the back of my mind, I'm feeling kind of bummed out anyway. She does that to me. Besides, I don't think that I do much on typical nights like this. With jerking off on hold until I know that Jane's asleep, my only options are sitting on the porch, walking the dog, or taking a bath. Getting naked generally carries the most weight for me, so I shut down Burnitts, closed up the garage, and went in for the time being.

While in the kitchen filling up my wine, I couldn't tell if Jane has been out to do the same. It's hard to believe that she hasn't, but the burger still being there suggests it. Now that I think about it, she probably has a box in the bedroom so she doesn't have to come out. I wouldn't put it past her. Walking into my room, I also wonder if she has been in to see the door at all. I didn't realize it would look so nice being able to see directly outside. With its side door and light directly across, the garage and its rose-lined walls provide an added depth and view the room never had. The door looks like it's been there all along, and it's more of an upgrade than I thought it would be. There's no reason for Jane to have anything else shitty to say about it.

It'll be a while before I stop noticing the difference, both inside and out. The walls need a final coat of mud before painting, but it'll be best to do that in the morning when I'm not so crooked. After that, the inside's finished. I walked into the bathroom practically patting myself on the dick. With the door closed behind me, I started the tub water, lit a cigarette, and spent a minute lost in the mirror. My eyes look distressed and depressed. I wonder if it's officially my anniversary yet? If my reflection's any indication, it probably is. That would mean that it's Sunday. Saturday's already over, and I have to work tomorrow.

Taking off my clothes required some effort. I'm tired and drunk, and my body's aching worse with every moment. While standing there naked, it was only natural to start thinking about Neighbor again. Her body's been taking up a lot of my headspace lately. Right away, my dick went on high alert. I was hanging heavy. Not hard, but at my best not being. My balls were begging me to open the tap, but just when I was about to give in, I became distracted by the thought of trimming my body hair. For me, just maintaining my beard once a week requires effort, so you can imagine how often the rest of me gets decent attention. My body's been looking good today, and now I want to look even better. With that, a bath won't be anytime soon, so I cut it off and drained the water. Given all this hair to be hemmed, I'm definitely going to need a shower first.

The full body, royal treatment in terms of hair

management actually requires quite a bit of work. Starting with my face, I trim my beard as little as possible but generally keep it around three-quarters of an inch. While in that area, despite keeping more of a natural hairline, I clean up the neck and cheek strays. From there, I get around my ears and square up the back of my neck. Moving on, I use the three-eighths attachment over my entire chest and stomach area, with the exception of the strip under my belly button. That gets kept a little longer and becomes better defined as a happy trail. When I'm done with that, I trim my armpit hairs as short as I can without using a razor. Hairy creases have never been my thing. Then I continue down with the three-eights to trim my lower stomach and pubic region. Because I have the upper thigh hair of a man, all that hair needs to be tapered into what was shortened. Next, I get behind my balls and over the entire ass with the buzz attachment. That part can be skipped if I stay on top of it. After using hair removal cream around my nostrils and ears, I finish in the shower by razoring down and around my lower dick shaft, balls, taint, ass, and hole area. It's quite a delicate and time-consuming process with all the contours and lengths.

Trimmed through, my body was looking significantly better. Not my twenty-year-old self, but likely better than most forty-somethings. After a long, hot shower, I started the bathwater but then remembered that I ran out of wine while shaving. What's the sense without it? Once dried off, I was thinking that I might see Jane awake, so I wanted to be prepared. After a rinse and some cologne, I was ready. This is all I have to offer. If I can't turn her on like this, it's never going to happen.

Sure enough, Jane wasn't around when I came out. I was hoping that I could seduce her a little. She's usually sleeping at this time, but it would have been a good night for her to think about what she could do for me, especially considering the space that I've given her. The last time I remember her staying up this late was last New Year at her company party. Karla treated the office to a night on the town to celebrate her best year yet. There was more than enough going on there to hold Jane's attention, unlike any time when she's just with me. We didn't make it home until 3 am that night. Even with her having such a great time celebrating the year and new beginnings, I woke up on the couch alone the next day.

Not to my surprise, when I returned to the fridge, the burger was gone. I doubt I'll receive any kind of "thank you" for it. Jane probably wouldn't even believe I made it for her. Chances are, her mistaken mind assumes that she got my leftovers. From here, it's a glass of wine and some smoke for me. Given the state I'm in, the living room would be the safest place for me to indulge. As I walked past, I told the couch to fuck off and went for the chair instead. Once I lit up, my mind went right to Jane. If she were more like Neighbor, tonight could have been exceptional.

Chapter Eleven — Sunday

Out of nowhere, I began to accept that I was conscious and that I must have been sleeping. It's still dark out, so I probably should still be. My first thoughts reveal the unsettling mysteries of the night before. I think Jane was mad at me for something. Right away, something felt off, but I didn't know exactly what or why. Moving is practically impossible, so I just lay there with my eyes open not knowing anything. It's difficult to remember what I'm trying to remember. I can barely formulate a thought but soon realize what's most likely—I'm still drunk.

My mind's lost, but I can't ignore my immediate thirst. Since my body refuses to move, all I can do is blankly stare at the almost full glass in front of me. It's a real wine glass, so I assume it's not water. There are so many unknowns that I just want to ignore everything and not be aware. After sorting through some of my more broader memories, I deduce that it's Sunday. Suddenly, panic set in, and I immediately jolted up to a seating position only to fall right back down again. I'm hurt and feel like I tumbled down the fucking hill. Moaning my way back up, I find myself naked. I've got no clothes on my person, no clothes on the floor, and no clothes anywhere in sight. Fuckin hell, here we go again.

This is one of those mornings where I just need to accept

that I'm probably in a world of shit. I've lost track of seemingly everything. The only thing that I can do at this point is right as many wrongs as possible, and with that, suffer any appropriate consequences. In starting, I'll begin with some wine, allowing myself the whole glass before even attempting to face reality. Unfulfilled, I managed to mostly stand and begin moving toward the kitchen. I had to work to stay upright, and in every step, remind my muscles to move.

The microwave clock read 5:09, so I switched to my coffee cup and went for the wine. I poured a half-cup and drank it all while still standing in the fridge. I needed water. Two cups later, I filled the wine back up. The lights were all off and the blinds were down, so it was a fair start to the checks. Checking on Jane, I opened the bedroom door and found her and the dog soundly sleeping. The cock and cunt couldn't look more satisfied together. Wondering why I'm naked, I decided back on the couch would be a better spot to think about it. The attempt was barely a success. I made it no farther than I had to before setting my drink down and falling flat. The couch never felt so comfortable. At this point, I proved that I was capable of moving, but it's the last thing I want to do.

It is Sunday, right? That would mean it's my anniversary today. With that thought, I sat back up again. In trying to make sense of it all, I want a cigarette more than anything. Things are beginning to come back to me with a randomness of possibilities, and I fear the forgotten. In going to retrieve something to wear from my room, not only do I get an instant reminder of what I did yesterday, I'm thrilled about how the door looks and how great it's going to work out. I stood there for a couple of minutes running my hand over the mud work and testing the door. There was no rush on the pants, being naked complimented my new sense of freedom.

My cigarettes and phone are somewhere unknown but that always happens. After retrieving a new pack and lighter from the kitchen almost every day, I can always find leftover smokes in all the usual places. I'll have to find my phone though. Hopefully, it'll be regret free. I stepped out and immediately laughed a little seeing the cars on the front lawn. Okay, now I remember that. Burnitts looked to be all closed down, so I went right for the chair. I still don't want to stand. However, after just a few moments, my mind got the better of me. I needed to do the full walk-through inspection. There were too many unaccounted hours and pain. For all I know, I sent Karla cock shots all night and Jane kicked my ass for it. Just thinking about it makes me think I did. Suddenly, it becomes urgent for me, fingers crossed, to make sure that I didn't.

Since the panic eclipsed the hangover and aches, I was able to get up and do my rounds. While making my way to the garage, I noticed that there weren't any beer bottles on my mailbox. Maybe that means I wasn't navigating the neighborhood drunk and disorderly last night—maybe. The grill was never put away but I was probably thinking about using it today. That's right, pizza and steak are on the menu. Interesting thought considering all the potential problems I could be facing. Looking at the pass-through, I'm surprised at the amount of work that I was able to get done. It's dimly lit but looks great. Today I'll wrap up the inside and roof, and then it will be done.

Hoping to find my phone, I headed up to Burnitts. It was a drag show up the stairs. There are too many for a man in my condition. The phone was on the bar—and so was my camera. Now I remember something about that. Great idea, I thought to myself, knowing exactly what I must have been thinking. Maybe I recorded something worthwhile? Unfortunately, I found there wasn't a tape in it if I had tried. Hopefully, The Neighbors didn't catch me in the window with cock and camera out. That's not the worst that could have happened, but I try to keep my mind at bay. My phone ended up being free of any wrongdoing, so I started to feel better about my self-control. Even with that, not knowing what Jane could be mad at me for still concerns me. Waking up naked with no clothes in sight still worries me too, but at least I woke up in a familiar place this time.

Feeling somewhat satisfied with my conduct, I left Burnitts and went back to the porch thinking about what I had going on, remembering again that it was my anniversary. I've been trying to talk myself into accepting the reasons for it not being worth celebrating. The chemistry between Jane and I has been neutralized. We live together like we're being forced to. In a way, it's a mindset similar to teenage siblings having to share a room. There's no interest in each other, the space is enjoyed more when in it alone, signs of love are essentially non-existent, and time together is taken for granted. With that, what exactly would we be celebrating?

My muscles needed Aspirin. After finishing my wine and smoking another cigarette, I pulled myself up for a refill, medication, shit, and a shower. I found my clothes on the bathroom floor behind the door and water left in the tub, so I know that I've been there. That would make sense, me not wanting to get dressed after bathing. Looking in the mirror, I could tell why—somebody got a haircut. I look so much better trimmed up, less old. It took me five minutes to brush my teeth and wash. The other forty were spent just laying under the hot shower, water teasing my dick in and out of erection. I was thinking about Neighbor coming over and choosing the new door to knock on just as I came out naked to get dressed. I'd notice her approaching and turn the light on just as she stepped up.

"Hi, just a sec," I'd say, taking my time to find a pair of shorts. She would be barely dressed herself. I picture seeing her surprisingly dark nipples proudly protruding from her firm, underdeveloped titties when I came out to greet her. Her little shorts would be revealing legs so skinny that she couldn't touch her inner thighs together unless she crossed them.

"I'm sorry. I'm your neighbor. I wasn't sure what door to use." She would be smiling but somewhat blushed. I'd step out to her with my cock details heavily outlined through my shorts.

"Hi, I'm Neighbor."

"Hi, Neighbor, I'm Marty."

"Nice to meet you. Again, I apologize for this. The post office said that a package of mine was delivered, but I didn't get anything. I noticed you had a box out front and thought there could have been a mistake."

"I'd think the same. Let's check it out." The package would be hers. "Sorry for the mix-up, Neighbor. By the way, I've been meaning to introduce myself but haven't had the opportunity. I admire your commitment to running."

"Thank you! I'm obsessed with keeping my stamina up." Her body language would be saying the same. "It's been a big pleasure meeting you, Marty, and thanks for not turning your back on me."

"Same. By the way, I wouldn't do that unless you wanted me to. Either way, don't be a stranger, come anytime. Just be sure to use the same door." I'd be a second away from cumming where I stood when she would turn away knowing that I'd be watching. Her ass would be so small that I could palm it with one hand. I dare myself to cum thinking about her body and the sexual tension it produces, but again, just choose to stay on edge.

After getting dressed, I went right to putting the last coat of mud on the wall. Once this dries, I can paint and get the room back together. I wish it was ready now so that I would have something else quiet to do. Six-thirty on a Sunday in suburbia is too early for noise. Jane would fracture her filter if I woke her up working on this project. Although I've forgotten a lot about yesterday, her anger about the door stuck with me for some reason. With nothing else to do, I topped off my wine, got the coffee ready, and headed back to the porch. Out there, I find a half joint in the ashtray, so I light up and think about the day to come. My plan's simple enough: finish the roof early, cook on the grill, play some basketball, and drink all day.

Now that I'm high, I start dwelling a little about having to work tomorrow. Every Sunday's the same. They're a lot like having a view of Neighbor. I can't complain about having the day off, or the eye candy in Neighbor's case, but it's just a tease. Maybe I'll call out. Maybe the world will end today and I could part with it on a high note. The thought of Monday morning being only one day away, and Friday evening being well over a hundred hours from then makes me want to sink in a ShackBrew.

I was already getting fucked-up as the sun began to come over the horizon. With it, the day felt new and promising. As soon as I hear the first lawnmower, all noise will be fair game. Regardless, I'll keep it down for a couple of hours so that Jane can sleep. I'm ready to get moving though. If I don't, the wine will start showing. It comes in the form of drunk for me and can often lead to things not getting done. Coffee helps, and since food helps too, making myself some breakfast and drinking some coffee would combat the drunk from three sides. I could make some for Jane too. That way, even if she doesn't want to eat, I can say that I tried.

Thinking about it more wasn't necessary, so I got up to do it. Thankfully, I was still slow to move. If I was any faster, I would have missed Neighbor rounding the corner. She immediately triggered a reaction in my dick that redirected me straight back to Burnitts. Ready with the camera out, I knew she was going to be around again, and I wanted that closer look. Less than ten minutes later, I had her in view. However, I was worried about standing too close to the window and being seen, so I stood back a good five feet and began zooming in from there. Unfortunately, I was too far away. The camera couldn't get a good focus past the dirty glass and screen. I missed my opportunity. However, standing right up to the window was too much of a risk since I didn't know how well I could be seen from the outside. A better setup would be needed. The simple solution is to put a plant up to the window. That way, my camera could be close enough but still obscure. The thought of finally getting a closer look at Neighbor today makes my head active. I've waited too long for it.

Since Neighbor was done running, I went back to the coffee and breakfast plan. First, I had to finish my wine so I that could use the cup for its intended purpose. The thought of bacon made me hungry, so I put a pound and a half in the oven. At 350 degrees, it'll be twenty minutes or so. I also planned on eggs over medium and cinnamon french toast made from my homemade sourdough. With that, I'll include a sliced apple with a squirt of lemon. I downed two cups of coffee while the bacon cooked. Just as it was being pulled out, I heard Jane open the bedroom door. Warden burst out like he had been holding a piss in all night. She emerged much slower but likely pissy herself.

"Morning."

"Morning," she replied groggily. I watched her for a moment as she initially struggled with holding her two winter glasses and opening the back door at the same time. Once she figured it out, she went straight for the tap water. She drank a whole glass without stopping.

"Happy anniversary," I said approaching her. She was getting more water.

With a quick over-the-shoulder look, "happy anniversary," she responded. I leaned in and gave her a light kiss on the cheek. After standing there drinking another half-glass, this time at a more reasonable pace, she took a seat at the bar next to me.

"What are you drinking—wine already?" She leaned over to peek in my cup. She must know not to be fooled by it.

"No, just finishing a coffee, but I was thinking about

having a glass while cooking breakfast. Care to join?"

"Sure. My mom called, she's coming over in a little while." Janee didn't need to provide me with an excuse to drink.

"All right. She might want to eat, so I'll wait on breakfast." I poured wine into our coffee cups and coffee into our wine glasses. Mine was still the actual wine glass that I started using at some point yesterday. Jane laughed.

"Cheers. To mother-in-laws coming over for anniversary breakfast."

"Don't start," she said while nodding her head. With that, she stood up, tapped her cup against mine, then walked off to the living room.

Having given it no thought until now, my fingers were crossed as I noticed Jane about to turn on the TV. I knew right away that I was about to have a lapse in luck. As soon as she hit a button on the controller, the screen turned on and she had over five feet of thong aerobics in her face. It was an instructor and his two background girls. In the few seconds that it took for her to realize what was playing, the camera first went from him and his porn-sized penis growing down his gym shorts, to the one girl who lost a boob, and then to the other whose lips were peaking out the side of her string as they were all bending over doing in-sync toe touches. Just as the instructor hit the floor and started pelvic thrusting, his dick dropped out of his shorts with a heavy flop and the camera zoomed in. In that split second, I actually thought maybe Jane would like what she saw and want to do a little exercising with me. How I'm so full of hope all the time, I don't know. Without even shutting it off first, she turned around and death-starred me in the eyes as I just stood there with a smirk on my face.

"What the fuck, Marty? What the fuck are you watching on our TV?"

I get caught watching porn every once in a while, maybe a few times a year or so. After living together for so many years and being horny most of the time, it's going to happen. Jane doesn't like it. I think that she's just pissed about not being in complete control of when I get off. From magazines to late-night max movies, VHS to 4k, landline to WiFy,—porn has been enticing for me my whole life. I watch it alone but would prefer her company. There's no threat for me. Those guys are way bigger, better looking, and better performers than me—I don't care. We can watch whatever she wants. I just want her to be comfortable, horny, and having fun with it. I want it to be consistent too. Now busted, I just did what any man would do in that situation. I pulled down my pants and took a handful of my dick and balls as a piece offering.

"Sorry, wifey. I don't want to lose it." I laughed but actually felt fearful. A part of me thought that she might like to see me hanging out too. Maybe we could knock one out with these two girls in the background. "You want a piece? Leave it on, girl. Let's get our workout in."

"Your fucking disgusting," she said, shutting it off. "Fucking pervert. What is wrong with you?"

"What, no love on my anniversary? Even after all the work that I did yesterday?" I lifted my pants back up, not surprised she didn't take advantage.

"Thankfully, my mom wasn't here when I turned on the TV. You've got a problem."

"Fuckin crab apple doesn't fall far from the tree, eh? Whatever, I'll make breakfast when she gets here."

"Whatever, Marty."

Jane has always insisted that it's disturbing that I watch porn. She'll run me in the dirt for it, but at the same time, have no problem binging on any TV-MA Netflix series, and there are a lot of dicks and tits on Netflix. I have no problem admitting that horny people make me horny. I get the biggest dick, shoot the longest loads, and feel the most incredible when I get worked up and worked in the right way. Jane has orgasms but doesn't seem to crave them as I do. She's never curious about bigger or better and has no interest in trying. She has more of an occasional craving to cum at best, whereas, I have ongoing starvation. I don't want to have sex as often as I feel the need to cum, especially if I have to do all the work anyway. With that said, jerking off's doomed to come into play, but that doesn't mean that I don't want something to look at. Sure, my searches might take an occasional left turn every now and again, but that tends to happen when a person heads down that road—no judgment. I decided that it would be best for me to remove myself at that point. Jane was about to have a filter flop.

"Calm down. Want to do a shot? Maybe you should warm up that cold heart of yours before your mom gets here. Come out if you do."

Jane doesn't bother me. I've been ready to get my weed out and work plan in order anyway. Since Neighbor wasn't around to deter my thoughts, I could get right to it. Up at Burnitts, I put the music on and rolled one up. Then I went downstairs to get started. Out of nowhere, Jane came around the corner and walked up to me like she had something to say.

"Hey."

"Hey."

"Come to check out the door?"

"I came out for a shot."

"Upstairs," I said, before luckily remembering the camera was out. "I'll get it, hold on." Jane must be cooled off if she wants me to do a shot with her. Maybe that video got her thinking. Maybe she's going to want to fuck around. After hiding the camera behind the bar, I grabbed two shot glasses and one of the opened bottles of vodka. That was the quickest that I have moved in a while, suddenly excited about Jane and I possibly getting along and having a fun day.

"Please, have a seat," I insisted, directing her to one of the three chairs. Maybe someone stopped over last night? I poured us each a shot and gave her the fuller of the two.

"Cheers. To morning workouts," I said smiling.

"Cheers. To you being an even bigger dickhead than any that I've seen today."

I'm not sure if that was a compliment or not. We drank anyway. You could tell that they were hard to swallow by our expressions, but I went right to refilling. I was already buzzed and wanted Jane to catch up.

"Oh, I don't know about another one."

"All right, let's just give it a minute." I pulled out my joint and after lighting it, tried passing it to her.

"Don't. You know I don't want it, Marty. Let's just do the shot."

"Okay. Cheers. To the new door."

"Cheers," is all she said back. We drank our shots, and I promptly poured one more for Jane.

"That one's for you," I said proudly.

"Nope. I don't want it." I didn't need to pressure her, so I set it on the driveway between us for later. After returning the bottle and empty shot glass to Burnitts, Jane proved, once again, how full of shit she is. The vodka had vanished. She could have just drank it when it was offered and been grateful. Instead, she prefers to do it behind my back. What can I do?

"That didn't take much convincing."

"Never does," she said, shrugging and smiling.

With Jane being uncharacteristically friendly right now, I have to be careful not to let my guard down. With her, it's too easy for me to get deceived by her looks. I'm gullible, but aware enough to stay reserved. Her genuineness is difficult to believe, so I can't be vulnerable. I won't be resistant, but she will be tested. That said, I figured it was the perfect time to show off the door to Jane. With how good it looks, she couldn't possibly be upset.

"I have an anniversary gift."

"No, you don't."

"I do."

"I know you didn't get me anything, Marty."

"I didn't. I got myself something. It's right there behind you, see the new door?" She didn't like that, and she didn't look back at it either.

"Don't be a dick. You do know that you don't always have to be an asshole, don't you? By the way, your fucking door is stupid. Who would put a door from a bedroom to a garage?"

"The door leads outside Jane. It just happens to be easy access to the garage. Come check it out, it looks good. I'm going to build the roof today."

"Great! I'm pissed off that I didn't have a say in any of this."

"You're going to love it. Check it out."

Just when I was about to start selling her on it, her mom pulled in. Jane quickly picked up her empty shot glass and put it in the chair's cup holder. Like Karla would give a shit. It's a habit of Jane's to disguise her real self. Having Karla around, in a way, is like having two Janes; putting on face comes easy for both of them. I'm somewhat relieved that Karla's here though. Interrupting Jane probably couldn't have come at a better time.

"Hey, guys!" Karla said, appearing out of the car with a handful of roses.

"Hi, Mom," said Jane. "Good morning," we both said simultaneously.

"Why are you guys sitting in the driveway? Are you fumigating or something? Is your house broken?" She had that subtle smirk that not everyone could recognize. Karla knew what was going on around here. That's why Jane laughed and why Karla didn't expect answers. "Happy anniversary!" she went on to say, coming in for hugs. "These are from mine," handing the assortment of flowers to Jane. *Yeah, so are the ones I gave her*.

"Aw, thank you, Mom. They're beautiful as always.

Come on in, let's get a cup of coffee." Jane was suddenly happier than I've seen her all weekend, with the exception of talking to The Neighbor.

"I'm about to make breakfast if you would like to eat something." Why not throw it out there and make myself look good?

"Okay. Yes, I'll have a bite. Thank you, Marty."

I lit a cigarette, thankful they went inside. The two shots were already affecting me, so I required a minute to focus on the plan. Cook breakfast, build the roof, paint, and party—that's all it came down to. No need to overthink it. I relit the joint feeling good about the morning. Jane's still unhappy about the door, but it seems like she'll settle down eventually. Also, she wouldn't have been out here at all if things got too bad last night. I had a lot of anxiety built up about today, but it might turn out all right after all. Not getting each other gifts is probably the best thing that we could do for ourselves.

Thankfully, Jane and Karla were out back when I went in. I'm already over wanting to make breakfast, so now I just want to get it done quickly. First, I mixed up three eggs with a splash of milk and some cinnamon powder to dunk the sourdough in. No sooner than putting the bread on the pan and getting some eggs going, Jane was rounding the corner. She had their coffee cups in hand and went to refill them. One got coffee and cream right away, the other one got a little wine first.

"How are those shots treating you?" I asked Jane.

"Good."

"Are you Hungry?"

"I could probably eat. It smells good."

"All right. I'll bring it out when it's done."

I went on cooking as she went back outside. This was an obvious effort by me. Breakfast prepared by me for her and her mom, that's good husband shit right there. On a serving tray, I plated three pieces of French toast cut in half, four scrambled eggs, one lemon spritzed, sliced apple, and six pieces of bacon. That would still leave me plenty of pig. I included everything else needed and brought it all out properly.

"Oh, thank you, Marty," Karla said. "Quite the catch."

"Thank you," Jane said. "Would you mind topping off my coffee please?" I was entertained by the subliminal request. Karla was all set, so as soon as I walked in and closed the door behind me, I took off to Burnitts, poured some rum in her cup, and then ran back to fill the rest with coffee. After delivering it with a smile, I kindly parted ways.

Once the kitchen cleanup was finished, I finally returned outside. I didn't want to spend all day on this venture, so it's best to get started right away. After I had the measurement for the rafters, it took me half an hour to cut the two dozen needed and another hour or so to hang them. Karla left in the meantime, thanking me so much for breakfast and wishing me a happy anniversary and good luck on my project. I wish myself a happy anniversary and good luck too.

I assumed that Jane went back to bed, but to my surprise, she was sitting outside.

"Hey."

"Hey."

"Thanks for that refill."

"You're welcome. I thought maybe the drinks got the better of you, and you went back to bed."

"Nope. I showered."

"Yeah, how was it? Were you thinking about taking up a new aerobic routine the whole time? I saw how impressed you were with those thrusts."

"That's all you think about, Marty. Not all of us sit around playing with ourselves all fucking day."

"Tell me you didn't get one off in the shower? I call bullshit." I'm knowingly testing her but not being mean or anything.

"Fucking hell, Marty. I came out here to do a shot, and you're acting wasted and being an ass."

"Calm down, I'm just fucking with you. I just wanted a mental picture."

"Well, knock it off, and get the shots."

For whatever reason, Jane can't help coming off bitchy, bossy, and better than me. She wasn't always like that and isn't to anyone else. There was a while when she would claim that she was just having a laugh or being sarcastic when she had nothing good to say, but that just evolved into her having that attitude all the time with only the occasional dumbass excuse why. She would rather be an effortless victim of me than an active participant in us. Just in this conversation alone, but not unlike most others, I made jokes and complimented her. She cussed, called me names, and told me what to do. I'll take what I can get. She hasn't stormed off yet and wants to get a drink, so I'll gladly try to make the best of it.

"I'll tell you what, I'll pour the shots if you come up to the bar with me to drink them."

"I don't want to go up there and hang out, Marty. I'm taking the dog for a walk."

"Well, that's where the shots are, Jane. Come up if you want one." *Fuck you and your dog.*

"Fine." I led her through the side door despite the large doors being open. That way, she could get a good look at the work. Passing by it, she didn't say anything so I didn't either.

Chapter Twelve

Jane didn't comment on the work that I've done, but that's just her being full of shit again. Her coming up to Burnitts and having a drink with me makes me confident that she's had a good look and approves. She doesn't want to admit it though. Behind the bar, I lit a smoke and grabbed the bottle of vodka. I can't remember the last time that I had company up here.

"Is this what you're after?" I asked, waving the bottle at her.

"I'll take one." She was walking around, checking the place out. She probably forgot what the bar looked like.

"Oh, I see you have a good view of the neighbor up here. That's perfect. You can tell that she does aerobics." Jane found the window.

"What are you talking about?" I asked, walking over as if I didn't know what she was referring to, but more because I wanted to see. "What neighbor?" I questioned, as I stepped up to see hcr. She was still wearing her tiny running shorts and tube top. I don't think that Jane would like it if I brought up the idea of trying to get a closer look. "Oh look at that, not a bad view for you either," I remarked, as The Neighbor came into view. Of course, he had his shirt off already. Jane turned away quickly. "I bet you'll be up here more often now, won't ya?"

"Just give me the shot, Marty."

I tried toasting to marriage statistics but Jane wasn't having it. We did the shot anyway. She was quick to want to leave and passed by the work again without commenting. I thanked her for joining me and she thanked me for having her. She got what she wanted, and now it's back to the dog. That's okay with me, I want to get a better look at Neighbor anyway. Only having a few pieces of plywood to hang, I was able to sheath the roof before Jane left. She probably needed to get herself ready first.

"We'll be back."

"See ya," I said, turning around to look at her. She had a full-size water bottle with her today. Running out of wine wouldn't be happening.

After carrying up several bundles of shingles to the roof, I was ready for the long-awaited, up-close shot of Neighbor. With my camera in one hand and a plant in the other, I set myself up at the window. That's when I discovered Jane, once again, getting her up-close eyeful of The Neighbor. This must be a regular fucking thing now. I take it that they've all become friends? Jane doesn't even typically walk Warden that way. She's fucking loving it now. After about a minute, and probably half of her wine, I can't stand watching Jane get a better look than me any longer. Walking the dog to get a better look—I wish I would have thought of that.

Finding cold beer and almost a whole box of wine in the fridge was a well-welcomed change. Seeing Jane happier with another man solidifies my need to care more about myself. I need to get this project finished so that I can have my space without Jane jumping in and out when and how she pleases. From my perspective, she's drinking with me, but I'm not getting any of the benefits from it. It's our anniversary, but she would prefer to take her interest elsewhere.

Once I returned to the roof, it was time to shingle. I soon

decided that I could take my shirt off too, and threw it to the ground like I was pumped for a fight. With the nail gun allowing me to go fast, I almost finished the entire backside before Jane and Warden returned.

"Hey."

"Hey."

"I didn't think you guys were coming back, thought you might have found someplace better to hang out." It took me a second to realize why Jane's expression changed when I stood up. I don't normally have my shirt off outside, and I don't think she's seen me without one in a while. I was also well-groomed.

"What are you doing, getting sun up there?" she asked. "Nothing's different from when we left." She spoke in a "you answer to me" sort of way. I could tell she had a good buzz. Since when was she paying attention anyway?

"Go back to the neighbors if it isn't good enough. You seem a lot happier there."

"What are you talking about?"

"Jane, you had a drink with me and then essentially left to have one with the neighbors. Then you come back here and start giving me shit about something that you haven't said one thing about all weekend."

"I've said plenty. Not like it has fucking mattered anyway. Now I want it to be done. And I want the cars out of the fucking lawn too, Marty. What, I can't talk to the neighbors without you having something to say about it? It's not like I want to fuck them like you probably do, or jerk off watching them." Here it comes. Her filter foiled. Where did the Jane that left with the dog go? I knew that she was a likely imposter. After all, she did have a drink with me at Burnitts. I should have known right then, but I'm still baffled at how she's able to switch gears like that and believe that it's okay. That it's so okay, that I don't even have a right to address it.

"Where did the Jane that left with the dog go? I asked.

"She had a drink with me at Burnitts. It would have been nice if she was the one that came back."

"What are you talking about? I get back here and you have an issue with me talking to the neighbors. I mean fuck you, Marty. You always fuck shit."

"Jane, you came back asking if I was sunbathing because nothing's been done. I honestly thought that you haven't taken one look at what I've been doing. Little did I know, you've been doing fucking efficiency inspections this whole time. Your entire attitude and demeanor are different from when you left. I was thinking that we might end up having some more drinks, but you came back just wanting what I'm doing to be done."

"You can't take a joke."

"Nothing about you hints at a joke, Jane, but you conveniently claim it is when you get called out on your shit. You told me that nothing you said matters, but trust me, it does to me. It's never anything good. Try having something nice to say to me for once, or shut the fuck up.

"I don't need to be out here, Marty. Enjoy your fucking self."

Jane walked off, so I took a break. One man can only take so much wife before needing a drink. I smoked a cigarette but lit another right after. She was distracting me again. Like a pain in the ass, she is there no matter what I do. Getting out of the chair will be difficult now. I could easily just fill the cooler and sit here all day. I do plan on continuing, however, I'm filling the cooler up so that I don't have to keep going up and down the stairs for cold ones. I'm still too sore for that shit.

Getting high, drinking beer in the sun, and catching sweet peeks of Neighbor are the highlights of my week. It'll be many long days of shit before I get to this point again. Fantasizing about something different isn't much to look forward to, but I'll take what I can get for now. These days, I don't like spending so much time alone anymore. At first, I was thankful to be able to get away from Jane when she was having a tantrum. I still am, however, with it being a constant thing, there's too much solitude. I try to have what fun I can, usually meaning I get fucked-up, but something has to change. How content must I be to slowly waste my life day by dismal day? I'm disregarded but allowing it, and my life is diminishing to dark.

I tend to get myself worked up when I get to thinking like that. I sort of have to talk myself down so that I don't do anything drastic. I'm not happy but convinced that transformation can't happen in a day. Jane's never going to change, and I don't feel like I should be making any more attempts without her making moves first. I've accepted my failure for the most part. Now I just have to try to succeed at something else.

After finishing my beer, I decided to paint the room next. With Janger, it's best that I stay grounded. After a light sanding, the paint was done in no time. It's a perfect match with just one coat. Now the inside is done, and it's so much better than before. Next, I completed the electrical portion of the project by installing the walk-thru light. With those finished, I only had the front side of the roof and a small portion of the back left to shingle. It's hard to believe that I thought of this yesterday, and soon I'll have the long-awaited bar bathroom.

After avoiding it for as long as I could, I had to go in for water. The need to pound some liquid life became apparent. Inside, I was somewhat relieved to see Jane sleeping on the couch. However, there was a part of me that was hoping to see her awake. It was nice having that brief amount of company earlier. I thought about putting some porn on for her. She would love to wake up to that. Choosing to stay out of trouble, I quietly washed down some bacon with a couple of ground-cold glasses of water. A second wind is what I needed. I'm dying out, but if I get it done now, I'll have the rest of the day to fuck myself off.

Over the last few weeks, thinking of my upcoming anniversary has made me uncomfortable. I hate being forced to think through the spectrum of emotions that define my marriage. Now that the day is here, Jane being passed out and pissed as if it's just another day makes me have an "I don't care about anything" attitude. It's being reinforced by visions of her laughing with The Neighbor and calling me disgusting. With that in mind, I couldn't go back outside without changing it to my favorite site. As if I had given it thought, I went directly to the facial category, hit play on a three-hour compilation, and walked out before I was sidetracked.

I knew that I was fucking myself in a bad way with that one, but it gave me the burst of adrenaline needed to get back to work. A little more than an hour later, I was getting off the ladder for the last time. The job was done, and it was only just after three. Even so, I didn't have much more in me. I continued to pass on the beer after realizing that the shots were a little too much of a morning kick start. My roof came out straight, level, and looking good though, so I must have caught it before it got out of hand.

It's unlikely that Jane's awake yet. Even though I'd rather not put myself in the position to find out, I need to take the steaks out of the fridge and get some pepper on them before taking the bath that I'm now obsessing over. She could be standing in the way of a conflict-free effort. First, I ran up to Burnitts to check on Neighbor. She was cleaning out her garage or something. All that I can think about is coming back and having that closer look that I've been lusting for.

Peeking through the window, I could see Jane lying on the couch with the cumshots still playing in the background. Inside, I was able to get the steaks ready and rewind the video a little without her waking. There was a sense of safety when I got to the room and closed and locked the door behind me. Now protected, I wanted to be watching the performances. Those girls proudly get blasted. I was getting thirsty just thinking about it. "It's an act," you might say. "No shit," I'd say back. Most marriages are fucking productions too, except there's not a lot of fucking.

With that thought, the work paid off for the first time. Burnitts was right there through the new door. That allowed me the priceless privilege of grabbing a cold one without risk. Baths will be even longer now. There's a good chance that I'll be making this trip naked on occasion. Back at the mirror, I see that I did get some sun today, and I'm a little scuffed up from all of the work. A couple of the scratches look like they might have hurt a little too. I look noticeably better this way. After dropping my shorts and flexing my new and improved image at myself, I decided to just take a quick shower. The beer and bath could be put off. I just wanted to clean up quickly and get back outside.

Without waking Jane, I was able to sneak back through the house and grab the steaks, salt, leftover bacon, cutting board, and utensils. Maybe she's awake and faking it, creaming up over all that luscious love liquid. I doubt it. Hopefully, I'll be nowhere close when she does wake up pissed and wondering what the fuck is happening.

After lighting the grill, I thought about taking a seat, but lying down and working on my new tan was the more inviting option. I'd like to be a little more like Neighbor in that way too. Right then, the new door paid off again. Obtaining a towel wouldn't be dangerous at all. So with the towel easily acquired, laying down is exactly what I did, right there in the driveway. *Now I'm fucking sunbathing.*

Since I was dick down facing Neighbor, I didn't catch Jane coming out. I was stoned and probably zoned out to thoughts of both of them when she damn-near startled the shit out of me. Maybe I dozed off briefly.

"Why would you put that shit on the TV?"

"What? What are you talking about, Jane?"

"You think you're being funny, Marty, but you're not. You're not being disgusting, you are disgusting."

"What was on the TV? I was in there a little while ago getting food, I didn't see anything. I don't know what the fuck you're watching. What was it?"

"You know what it was."

"Should I have a look for myself?"

"Yeah, you would like that. You know what it was. I already shut it off."

I stood up to her and lit a cigarette. "What was it, some instructional video on how to treat your man or something? Did you see any good examples?"

"Fuck you."

"Bless you."

"What are you doing out here?"

"I'm celebrating. I know you don't care, but today's a special day for me. I finished my project, see?" I pointed aimlessly behind me. She didn't have a chance to respond before I asked, "what do you want, a shot?"

"I'll take one…or two."

"I bet you will. But you know that I can't deliver like those guys that you watch on TV."

"You know that I wouldn't watch that shit. I'm not anything like you."

"Thanks, Jane. That's a compliment, and believe me, I know. The vodka's upstairs if you want it." She went right for it.

I salted one side of the filets and placed them over the hot coals. After a few minutes of searing, I salted the other side and gave them a flip. My mouth was instantly salivating. Once ready, I moved the steaks off of the coals and then let them bake under the lid for additional five or six minutes. After that, they were removed from the grill and ready to rest for another five. I expected Jane to return in the meantime, but she never did. Upstairs, I found her sitting at the bar with the bottle and two shot glasses in front of her.

"Hey, what are you up to?" I asked, standing at the top of the stairs.

"I'm drinking vodka. I thought that you were going to join me."

"I've been cooking. I thought you were coming down. Tell me you're not hungry after that long, mid-day nap. Come down and pour me one."

"It's right here. Come get one."

"Jane, I'm cooking. Can't you come down? Never mind, don't worry about it. I don't want one anyway." She's always too good to meet me halfway. Since the concept of give-and-take means nothing to her, I just head back downstairs. I'm not going to suck Jane's dick if she's just going to remain fucking flaccid. She's going to have to get up and come. The weekend's almost over, and whatever enthusiasm I may have had is softening up. "Get the fuck out of my bar." She comes up one fucking time and suddenly wants to party by herself, in my home.

The food was calling to me. It's done, I'm hungry, and I didn't plan on eating with Jane anyway. She eventually found her way back after I finished the first steak. I was full but started to eat some of the other one just to give the impression that I wasn't cooking it specifically for her. Jane can have my leftovers if she wants some. I lit a cigarette as she proceeded to pour us shots. Nice of her to include me this time. She has probably had several upstairs by herself. I know how that is.

"Cheers. To Sunday shots," I proposed, just as Neighbor's laugh found its way to our ears. "Sounds like fun," I impulsively said before Jane could say cheers back. She gave me a look but didn't comment. "Sorry." I went on to revise my original cheers. "Cheers. To Sunday cumshots." She wasn't as impressed as I thought she would be.

"They mentioned having a drink together. Why don't you go over there if it sounds like so much fun?" I didn't mention to her how much I have thought about it. "To Sunday shots," she finally said. We tapped glasses and drank.

"You're the one getting to know them." She didn't say anything. "There's some extra steak there if you want it."

"Thanks, maybe."

It would be reasonable to assume Jane wouldn't be out here at all if she didn't want to get along and hang out. From experience, I know it'll just be a matter of time before she'll use something I say as an excuse to be pissed and piss off. She's not as convincing to me anymore. It's getting later, and her guilty conscience is probably getting to her. I think partly because she knows that she's been wrong to run me into the ground and disregard me all weekend, but I think mostly because she botched our anniversary doing it. Jane convincing herself that she tried is all she needs to feel justified. Soon she'll need an out, but I won't let her have it too easy. I'll let her twist and poke at me without giving her the time of day—until I won't anymore.

"I'm going to Burnitts," I said. "Do you want to come, or should I just take the bottle up for myself?"

"Sure, I'll come, but I'll be taking the bottle with me." I left the steak and remaining pieces of bacon on the grill stand. She'll know where it is if she wants it. Jane walked past the work continuing to make no mention of it. Her not bitching about it says plenty. But it would be nice to hear her directly admit to being wrong and apologize for it. Not to be acknowledged as right, just so it feels less like she's brushing it all aside as if her behavior was no big deal. Once we got to the bar, I went about my usual routine of rolling one up, even though I have partials everywhere. Jane stood eagerly waiting.

"Rack 'em up," I said. "We'll play a game."

"All right. I'll show you how to do it. Pour 'em up."

"Do you remember how to play?" She smiled but didn't respond. I lit my joint as she made a solid break. After she hit two more in, the stick came my way. I tried passing her the joint.

"Don't."

"You sure? It looks like I might have to get you high to have a chance here. How about a shotgun?"

"Nope. Keep that shit away from me. Let's just do these shots. Cheers."

"Cheers. To sticks and balls."

"To sticks and balls." Once they went down, Jane went on to pour us another. I needed a minute.

Watching Jane play pool was turning me on. We didn't talk much as we took our turns going around the table, but I was fine with it. I'm sure that it helped keep things civil. I just liked watching her anyway. Her shorts would rise that extra bit as she bent over to aim and strike. She would predictably tuck her hair behind her ear right before every shot. I liked seeing her have fun with me. To keep this going, I would have to let her win and request a rematch. The eight-ball shot needed for me to take the victory missed the corner pocket and left her with an easy opportunity. Jane agreed to the rematch.

A chaser was necessary for me to take another shot as Jane was encouraging. At this point, she was making herself at home behind my bar. Though I've imagined Neighbor bartending up here plenty, I'm not as comfortable with the idea of Jane back there. It feels like she's in my space. She won't stop curiously looking around, making comments, and asking about shit. It's a little invasive, but since she was back there anyway, I didn't think twice about requesting a beer.

"You have wine out here? Where did you get these cans of ShackBrew from?"

"I always try to keep Burnitts stocked up. Help yourself." She gave me a beer and poured herself a wine as prompt as any good server would. "Do you want to put a wager on this next game?"

"What kind of wager?"

"Um, I don't know. How confident are you that you're

going to win again?"

"Pretty confident."

"Okay, since it would obviously be considered a huge loss for you, would you be willing to put a blojob on it?"

"Sure, I'll let you blow me if I lose. And if you lose, you can blow me." The shit that comes out of her mouth is insane sometimes. She thinks she's funny. "No, no, no, no, wait," she goes. "If I win, you have to change the house back to the way that it was." She was really being funny now.

"Are you serious?"

"Yeah."

"Yeah, right. I'm not changing anything. I love it. C'mon, you're bringing up something you hate. Try to keep it fun. Come to think of it, you should be playing in your panties. What are you wearing under those shorts? Let me see."

"I'm not taking my shorts off, Marty."

"I'm half dressed, you should be too. Let me see."

"Nope."

"Actually, maybe you should put your bikini on, it is summer."

"Nope."

"Cheers. To pretty panties."

"Cheers." We did the shot. Why is she even up here? I went to the window not caring if she saw me looking out. Her resistance reminds me of my disinterest. Just when I needed it most, Neighbor wasn't out there to distract me.

"What do you want from me, Jane? Why don't you have any interest in fucking around? It's our anniversary. We're home alone, we're drinking, and we're even hanging out together. I know you're well rested. Why can't you have a little fun with it?"

"Everything that you want to do is sexual, Marty. You can't just have simple fun anymore."

"Jane, why do you consider being sexual so difficult?

How is that even close to fair? There's nothing wrong with me wanting to see your body. I could request a lot more." She insists on thinking that all I want to do is fuck. She's never going to get it no matter my attempts to explain otherwise. I don't just want to have sex.

Chapter Thirteen

The thing that I miss most that marriage takes away is being turned on. Jane and I will have occasional sex when she wants, but there's never any real buildup to it. It's always just drunken sex after a couple of months of none. It never happens as a result of helpless lust, or relentless teasing. There's no playing around, experimenting, or having fun with each other. She knows what I want but refuses my simple desires. Jane fucks up all the time but never feels the need to redeem herself in ways that I deserve. She's never sorry, so she feels no need to prove it. If anything, Jane should be taking the apologetic distraction of her anger seriously. As far as I'm concerned, nothing would say sorry more than her playing with my dick all day.

Sex with Jane is always me laying behind her so that she doesn't have to see me, or me on top of her so she doesn't have to move. That's what I assume anyway. She's always fucked differently than the way I want to. There's not much of a fun factor when it comes to our sex life. It's like she doesn't want to participate actively but still expects control. On those rare occasions when Jane lets me in, it needs to be at her pace and within her allotted time. After she cums a couple of times, I'm practically forced to. Anything more than that, then I'm overstaying my welcome.

When Jane's aware enough and consciously semi-engaged, she'll always say the same thing afterward, "Oh, I needed that." *Who fucking doesn't?* It's like she never remembers how much fun being horny and fooling around are. It's the easiest way to have the most fun if you ask me. I'm sure she's capable of enjoying herself more often, I just don't do it for her. It's not all about sex for me. Being tempted, enticed, excited, and wanting her more than anything—that's what I like to feel; that's what I need. My marriage took that away.

Not clicking with Jane intimately makes me crazy. We used to have decent sex—I think. It's difficult to say because things were different for me. Back then, I just wanted to be in her presence. I wanted to be her man more than anything. If she only wanted to make love missionary style, I was happy enough to be a part of it. Nowadays, with the way she is, I don't want to just cater to her how and when she wants. According to Jane, I'm a pervert if I ask to see her panties on our anniversary. She's never allowed us to grow sexually, but I have no desire to control my impulses. I just want to be myself.

Don't get me wrong, I definitely want to have sex with Jane. She's not horny like me though. Craving cock and cum don't come naturally to her. I can't remember the last time she couldn't take her hands off me. Jane should be wanting to enjoy me often and in different ways. We should both be allowed and willing to please each other both selflessly and selfishly. Mainly, I just like to be relaxed with sex. No hurry to start or finish, and no pressure to stay traditional and reserved. It's plain and simple —no fucking problems.

"Fine, here's the game. Every time someone misses, they take a drink. Loser takes a shot. But you have to play in your panties."

"All right, you're on. But I'm not playing in my panties."

"Seriously? Why not? If you don't want to fuck around,

Jane, I don't want to hang out."

"Oh yeah? If I don't play in my panties, you don't want to hang out anymore?"

"I just don't understand why you wouldn't. What, you can't flirt with me, remind me every once in a while why we've been doing this for so fucking long?" I was getting a little upset. Sure, it might be the alcohol starting to seep through, but it's been a long weekend of shit with her too. Maybe I'm just throwing in the towel. "Why can't you make it fun for me?"

"You got a fucking problem, Marty."

"Why, because I want my wife to have a seductive side?"

"No, Marty. I already told you, because that's all you want."

"Of all the things you do and all the time you spend doing them every single day, whether you like it or not, I'm what lives on the back-burner? You spend more time picking up dog shit than you do entertaining me. It's so hard for you to play a game in your panties in front of your husband, but you have no problem picking up dog shit twice a day. Even if that only took three or four minutes a day, that's like two hours a month, Jane. Think about it, you treat me worse than a piece of dog shit."

Jane's filter would have malfunctioned if it weren't for her phone ringing. I lit my cigarette and joint as she turned around to address it. Just when I assumed that she was on her way out, she turned back around and looked at me as she began talking.

"Hi, Wes! How are you, sweetie?" She knew that she had my attention with that. Suddenly, I felt my world change. There's so much more to me than just work and wife. It's always good to be reminded. "He's right here! I'll put you on speaker." Jane set the phone on the bar between us.

My son Wes. I've never cared for someone more. He's the only ray of sunshine in my bleak existence. My boy makes me proud of myself, and that's a beautiful feeling. He's the highlight of my life, and I'm so thankful for him.

"Hey, Wes! How are you, Son?"

"Hey, Pop, doing good! I wanted to call and wish you two a happy anniversary."

"Thanks, Son. You're more organized than I thought if our anniversary is on your calendar."

"Oh, I'm organized, but it's not on my calendar. To be honest, Grandma said something about it when she called earlier. What are you guys up to? How long has it been anyway?"

"We're just hanging out at home, playing pool at Burnitts. Um, to be honest, I have no idea how long it has been. I have tally marks etched in the wall, but I would have to count them to know for sure." Jane was shaking her head at me. "I'm just playing. It's been nineteen years to the day, Son. We waited until a couple of years after you were born because we were broke students. Try to imagine living the way you are now and raising a baby on top of it. We didn't have any money or time. There was a lot of love though."

"Yeah, I'm sure that was difficult. You did a good job Mom, it all paid off. Hey, you did all right too, Dad!"

"Thanks, man. How are classes going?"

"Really good, thanks. Katie and I are studying now. We're keeping our grades up and staying out of trouble. We were just talking about how we miss having entire summers off. Katie's right here, you guys are on speaker."

"Hi! Happy anniversary!"

"Hi, Katie! Thank you."

"Yo, Wes, guess what I did to your old room."

"Knowing you, I probably couldn't. What did you do to my room, Dad?"

"I put a door in the wall that faces Burnitts. It's right across from the side door. I figured that if I was outside and had to use the bathroom, I wouldn't have to go halfway through the house anymore."

"Yeah, he didn't even ask me, guys," chimed Jane. "I just came home to a perforated house."

"It's true, and Mommy was not happy. Let's just say, I'm still paying for the improvement."

"Sounds cool though, and it makes sense to have a door there. I would have loved having one when I lived there. Sneaking out would have been so much easier. Hey, that'll work well for Burnitts too, right? That place has always needed a bathroom."

"You're really not helping, Wes."

"You probably should have run it across Mom first, Dad."

"Maybe. You should see it though. I built a roof over it too, right to Burnitts door. It came out perfect!"

"Nice, send me a pic."

"I will!"

"Well, we're going to get back to it over here. Just wanted to say hi and congratulations."

"Okay you two, thanks for calling. Glad to hear classes are going well. We're proud of you both, and we're looking forward to seeing you soon."

"Heads up, you'll probably have to sleep on your mom's shitty couch when you guys visit. Your room is now officially part of Burnitts from now on."

"Hah! Okay! That thing is barely comfortable enough to sit on. No offense, Mom. Burnitts sounds like the place we'll be staying. All right, Pops. Try to stay out of trouble, would ya? Hey, Mom, take it easy on the old man, okay? It's only a matter of time before that door he built is going to need to be equipped with a ramp and automatic door opener. It's going to make so much more sense then. Don't be surprised if he moves Burnitts downstairs. These minor conveniences are a necessity of aging."

"I'll try, Wessy. I guess that it's good that he's trying to accommodate for his own future inabilities, like walking through one of the other two doors to come inside. We love you guys!"

"Love you guys too, talk to you soon!"

"Love you! Bye!" Jane hung up and walked off without saying anything. I wanted to cry more than the tears that built up. I love that boy.

Wes was just two years old back when we graduated. With my early focus on media, and Jane being delayed by her pregnancy and his birth, we ended up receiving our diplomas the same year. From there, we moved to suburbia and started our careers. Since the beginning, my parenting style was so much different than Jane's. Protecting Wes and demonstrating my love was my only priority every day. It never felt like a responsibility to me. I just wanted to be around him more than anything. Wes was mine, and I easily chose him. Turning my back to the world was effortless. He was what I lived for every single moment. With that said, maybe I can relate to Warden more than I like to admit.

Jane was always more disconnected than I could ever be. More often than not, she seemed burdened. She didn't resent Wes by any means, and it wasn't having him that started the change in her. However, looking back, I know it contributed. Jane began regressing during our first year of college. It was then that she started wanting her own space more and volunteering for any opportunity that would allow her a reason to leave. Later, work was her escape, and the bedroom became her hideout when home. With me diligently working to be the best influence I could be, maybe Jane just didn't have to feel the pressure. Or maybe, as with our marriage, she took the easy way out as soon as challenge presented itself.

Wes and I were the best of friends through the years. Jane used to accuse us of teaming up against her, but I always saw it as a bullshit excuse for avoiding involvement and responsibilities. I, on the other hand, was the happiest I would ever be. As Wes got older, Jane seemed to cope with the lifestyle a little better. I'm sure the alcohol helped, but Wes was developing and becoming more independent too. Maybe it was easier for her.

As Wes became a young man, we were spending less and less time together compared to the earlier years. I completely understood that, but at the same time, I missed my best friend more and more. By then, I was already feeling like I lost Jane many years before. She was my best friend too at one time. Alcohol helped. As Wes grew even older, it became mostly just Jane and me. Before I knew it, Wes was a young adult, moved out, and living off-campus with a girl he loves. Now it's just me. I don't know what to do anymore. It's been three years, and I miss him more than anything.

Hearing from Wes was the best thing for me. Jane might not give a fuck, but he does. She didn't seem to be coming back, so I grabbed my smoke and beer and made my way back to the towel. I did the shot before leaving, not at all feeling like a loser. Back at the driveway, I couldn't get myself comfortable. I just sat there over-smoking my lungs and drinking more/less unknowingly. What I was thinking about at that time, I can't say for sure. My brain was overwhelmed. I missed Wes so much that it hurt. With that, I finally pulled myself up and moved everything off of the driveway. Basketball was on the list, and it suddenly became a priority for me to shoot around. Wes and I used to play match-shot all the time. The loser of the week would have to mow. It was always his chore, but if he beat me, I would do it.

Chapter Fourteen

It wasn't long before I noticed that Jane was coming back out again. She's been relentless today. I figured that last stint with me would have been the end of her. The only thing that I could think as she came closer was that she better not fuck with me right now. My mind was starting to enter a bad space. I felt wounded and impetuous.

Contrary to all that I imagined in those few seconds, Jane came up to me with a smile. I don't know why she hasn't given up on me yet.

"Hey."

"Hey."

"Playing with all your friends?" She went right for my weakness, but what else is new?

"Fuck off, Jane. Just because you adamantly deny playing with yourself doesn't mean you don't. Matter of fact, you live your whole life in denial, but you're a fucking window. Your facade hides nothing." I know that she intended on being funny, but I don't find anything funny about my constant isolation. All I have are my crazy thoughts. "I don't have any fucking friends."

Jane constantly reminds me of my desperation. She knows I'm desperate, but would call me a pussy if I tried explaining how it's affecting me. I don't deny it. With that said, I am running out of hours until work and would prefer any company available. That's a perfect example of how desperate I am. I'm bored, and losers like me take what they can get.

Jane didn't have a chance to respond. I tossed her the ball and jolted upstairs for beers. The "Burnitts" sign caught my attention as I entered the bar. Every once in a while, it still takes me back to memories of Weston. Despite all that was going on in his world, my only recollections are of him happy and laughing. He was my age back then. I wish that I knew his secret. Jane was throwing the ball around when I returned. She missed every shot that I saw her take.

"Beer?"

"Sure, thank you."

"How about a game?" I asked.

"Yeah? What do you want to play?"

"Match-shot. Let's play 'vodka.' Loser pours one."

"Deal, you're on."

"You have to play in your panties though." I wasn't going to stop fucking with her just because she can't deal with it. I'm not that desperate. At this point, Jane's more than welcome to get pissed off and leave me for the rest of the night. She came into my world. It's the last day of the weekend, and I don't want to be around her awful, shit-serving attitude. Let her believe that I'm disgusting for being attracted to her. She should feel disgusting about herself for ruining a person's will to prosper.

"You wish," Jane said in response to my uniform request. Considering the attitude she had just a little while ago, it's hard to believe she didn't so much as cuss at me for mentioning it again. Maybe she thought about how ridiculous she's been being. Either way, she caught me off guard. I actually found her reaction kind of cute and flirtatious. Jane didn't drop her pants, but she didn't call me a pathetic fucking pervert and walk away either. I didn't let her win the first game. Her missed shots spelled out "vodka" in seven throws. She talked some shit but landed herself in debt. With that, we went to Burnitts so that she could uphold her end of the bet. Not winning could have been worse. There aren't any actual losers in the game of "vodka," not with these stakes.

My only explanation for Jane is that she's in that difficult-to-find space where she hasn't had too little, or too much to drink. She hasn't overmedicated, and the treatment is working like it's supposed to. I found it confusing and practically inconceivable that Jane was being relatively friendly. Her unceasing attempts to hang around me were beyond character. I'm sure that it has been because of our anniversary, but maybe Wes's phone call reminded her that not everything is about her.

"Cheers. Sorry about your loss. To losers."

"Cheers. I let you win."

"You lost fair and square. Here's some advice for next time though. Try playing with both of your eyes open. You keep closing one when you take a shot." We had our drinks, and Jane quickly went on to pour us another. "Not right now for me. I did the loser shot from the pool game." She poured two anyway.

"I've been wanting to talk to you," she said, suddenly sounding serious. I was was immediately nervous. Fuckin hell. Here comes the buzzkill that I've been expecting. "You've told me how you feel about giving each other anniversary gifts this year, but I have something that I've been thinking about."

"What do you mean?" Her just saying that she's been wanting to talk to me is annoying. I mean, did she have to get all the bitching out of the way first? Either way, I hope she's thinking about breaking beds with me.

"It's more like a proposal that I think you're going to like. I've been holding off so that I could mention it today, but I'm excited."

"Are you telling me right now?"

"Are you ready to be told right now?"

"I'm curious, but not sure that I do. Are you trying to encourage me to get you pregnant?"

"You wish."

"Are you proposing a divorce?"

"You wish."

"I don't know. You're confusing me a little. This is the most we've hung out and talked in a long time. Now, all of a sudden, you're excited about having something for me? I'm not sure what to think. Give me a minute, I'll try to figure you out." Maybe it has something to do with Wes. More than likely, she's just all-around fucking with me. "Are you being serious?"

"Yeah," she said. I didn't believe her.

"Is it something that you think I'm going to like, or do you know that I will?"

"I'm almost certain you will."

"It's really not a joke?"

"No joke, Marty Fields."

"Huh? Are you wanting to buy a pool?"

"No. Do you want one?"

"No, but it's probably the only way that I'll get to see you in a bikini." I relit the joint, finding myself amused, but I'm sure this will end with her saying something obnoxious. I took a long hit and held it out in her direction. "Have a hit if you're having so much fun with me." She didn't start bitching, so I knew right away that she would.

"All right, Marty. I'll take a hit, but only because it's a celebration."

"Seriously? You have to be fuckin with me. You've had a problem with me all weekend. You haven't cared, why suddenly now? Why are you being friendly? I mean, you're hanging out, playing pool and basketball, and partying up at Burnitts for like the first time ever. I'm seriously confused."

"You're the one that hasn't cared, Marty. You keep

telling me that. You've told me all about it for weeks now; you weren't looking forward to our anniversary, you weren't getting me anything, and you basically don't want anything to do with me." She's not being mean about it, but it's still frustrating that Jane can convince herself of shit that isn't true. I'm pretty sure that I would have remember that. The only things she remembers are my reactions to her fucking crazy.

Jane took the joint from me and started full-on hitting it. She doesn't smoke much, maybe a handful of times a year, but her doing so tonight makes me wonder what she has up her sleeve. Normally, when she does smoke, there's something going on in her personal world that she's excited about. This "proposal" of hers will have less to do with me than it does with her. That's how I know that she doesn't want to get pregnant. Of course, her drinking supports that conclusion too.

Jane had a second hit and handed the now blazing joint over to me as smoke rushed off the cherry. I pinched it from her and mimicked her very respectful hit. She didn't want it when I tried handing it back to her, so I set it in the ashtray as I held my smoke. I doubted that she was going to take one at all, let alone two. She should have a lot of interesting things to say now. Jane smoking is a good indication that the shots were working their magic. Once she finally exhaled, I followed suit. We both started coughing like it was our first time. I proceeded to light a cigarette as she gathered herself and had a few swallows of beer. I mimicked her with that as well.

In between giggles, Jane tried completing a sentence. It took her more than a couple of efforts to compose what she was trying to. I couldn't help but laugh at her knowing how high she must be. She had my attention though, and I liked it. With Jane determined to give me company and not so easily agitated, things suddenly started to feel more like they should. I figured that if she was going to keep acting like that, why not prolong whatever it is that she wants to tell me? Even if she is just fucking with me, or if it has little to do with me, I'm happy with her approach.

"What are you going to do when you're too fucked-up to go to work tomorrow?" she finally asked, sporting the biggest, fucked-up grin you've ever seen. Her words barely made sense.

"Are you asking me or yourself?"

"I'm asking you."

"I'm not fucked-up, but I know you are. You just hit the joint as if you do it every day."

"Maybe I do! Let me get a drag off your cigarette please."

"All right." I handed it to her. Jane smokes on super rare occasions. It's usually only when we're drinking together and she's enjoying herself. I'm not sure what she could be so excited about all of a sudden. "Why are you acting so happy? You should smoke weed every day. If it's because of your 'proposal,' then I don't even want to know right now. Let me think about what you might be scheming."

"Typical Marty, always preferring to delay. By the way, I'm not acting, I'm happy. See, only happy people smile like this!" She's so high that she wouldn't be able to stop smiling if she was pissed off. "Who knows, maybe what I have to say will make you the happiest guy in the world, or maybe it will just be a total letdown? Hmm, or maybe I'm just busting your balls altogether! You don't know. At this moment, in your world, all possibilities exist for you, Mr. Fields. Can't you see how I am like God right now? Fear not, my child, you'll realize your fate soon enough. I, on the other hand, have known it all along. I'm spooky like that." Jane's ripped. When she smokes, her inner quantum physicist comes out.

"Now that you say it like that, you're scaring me a little. You think that you're like a god?" Jane makes me laugh. Most of the time, I can't return the favor. "Tell you what, let me brew on it. Allow me an opportunity to figure you out over a ShackBrew or two. Hold off on telling me for a little bit."

"Really? You don't want to hear me out? Are you serious?"

"Let me try to guess what you're up to. Trust me, a beer will help. My brain functions better while drinking. You've made me curious, but I'm nervous too. To be honest, you're throwing me off a little by not swearing at me. Let's just throw some darts or have a vodka rematch or something. We'll see how it goes. Are you looking to take some time off and go on a vacation?"

"First of all, fuck you. How's that, better? Here's a clue for you, it's not a vacation. By the way, I'll definitely take you up on that rematch, but I'm not going to let you win so easily this time."

"All right. I'll figure it out. Don't tell me you want another fucking dog though. I want to drink this shot just thinking about it. Then you can pour me another one when you lose."

"Ooh, a puppy! That's a good idea, way better than what I got. Why stop at one?"

"Oh yeah? I'll move out right fucking now."

"Is that all it would take?"

"Fuck off, Jane. Do you want to play or not?"

"Suck my dick, Marty, unless you just want to play ball first. Of course, I'll play." Fuckin hell she has a rotten mouth.

We took our shots after saying cheers to "getting dick sucked." Jane looked as if it was the first one she's ever taken. Despite it being self-inflicted, her face read of disgust and she blamed me for the throat pain she was enduring. I didn't suffer nearly as much, but maybe I have more experience. Regardless, right now Jane's happy and in my company. The vodka's nasty, but I'll gladly torture myself if it means I can be close to her. Hope seems to never fade with me despite the typical outcomes I suffer. Fortunately for me, I'm well versed in those, so there's only potential upside.

We sat there for a couple of minutes quietly sharing high smiles as the vodka shock dissipated. Her flirtatious eyes had me fascinated. Talking at this point isn't necessary. Without a word, she's saying nothing I don't want to hear.

"Are you ready? Let's take some shots!"

"You're crazy. I'm not taking another shot right now."

"No need to start name calling, Mr. Jump To Conclusions. It's basketball time."

I was ready but my lie detector started going off. That's my dick, and Jane was activating it. When I'm excited, my blood pumps faster and it causes pressure to rise. My cock is the only thing that I have to absorb it. It's a dead giveaway and renders me unable to hide from the truth. I could be tested anytime. She's turning me on, and my dick can't lie. It's not that I don't want to show it off, but it's probably better if I don't put all my cards on the table so soon.

"Yeah, I'm ready, just a minute." I needed an opportunity to settle down. It can be difficult having a cock. Sometimes I think that I've been cursed. After all, it probably has caused more harm than good. Actually, if it weren't for Wes, I'd say no good has ever come from it. Before long, I was finally able to compose myself and lead Jane downstairs. It had been too long since we held hands.

"There's a bathroom just right there if you need one."

"Believe me, Marty, I haven't forgotten. I still can't believe you just did that."

"Same. I can't believe I got it all done this weekend either. How's it look? It's pretty convenient."

"It looks good. I was worried, but you were right. You did a good job."

"Thank you, Jane! I know it pains you to say it. Good enough to deserve a thank you or maybe even an apology?"

"Yeah! Maybe if you would apologize, I would thank you."

"How about I start with kicking your ass at vodka?"

"You would have better luck playing with yourself."

Walking out, I noticed The Neighbors outside. For the first time ever, I didn't feel jealous of what they were showcasing. The relationship I envied, I have right now with Jane. As gorgeous as Neighbor is, I ultimately prefer what's right in front of me. Even so, it's hard not to look. They're both half-naked as usual.

"What are you looking at?" I asked Jane.

"I'm not looking at anything. What are you looking at?"

"Nothing. I just noticed something over there for you."

"Yeah, I noticed her too. I better not stare though." Who is this girl? "They invited us over for a drink tomorrow."

"They did? Really?" I could feel my heart start to race. If true, I would finally have the chance to see Neighbor up close. I didn't know what to say. My excitement would have to be tamed or I'll run the risk of losing Jane this evening.

"Yeah, they're nice. It seems like they would like to get to know us."

"Are you interested?" I asked.

"Yeah, why not? Are you not?"

"I didn't say that, I'm just a little surprised. I've never met them, but they seem a little younger than us."

"Yes, you have! You've met them before. They are a little younger but, they seem fun." She said it as if they were mutually exclusive.

Jane proved to be no match on the court but managed to have a slightly better game than the last time. I think the weed allowed her to be a little more in the zone, but the alcohol left her suffering from a coordination deficiency. She was having fun.

"Do you have any guesses yet?" Jane asked.

"Not really. Let's get into it later. Right now, we're having fun. I was thinking that we could take a walk. I suppose we could even take the dog too if you want. Having a drink down at Lookout would be fun. Then we can go from there."

"Okay. Yeah, let's do it.

"I want to clean up before we go. By the way, I'm going to wait on that shot, so don't forget you owe me. I better pace myself not knowing what you might spring on me."

"Okay. I have to use the bathroom." Jane gave me an over-the-shoulder grin as she walked off toward the new door. I walked in shortly after and went straight for the wine, ready to enjoy it the way it should be—while in a good mood.

Jane met me back in the kitchen, obviously still giddy with whatever she had up her sleeve.

"Would you like a little wine before we go?" Like I had to ask. She helped herself to mine despite the box being on the counter still.

"I'm just going to pack a few ShackBrews and a snack unless you want something else."

"I do, but later would be a better time for what I'm craving." She giggled at herself.

"Excuse me?" She caught me off guard. Jane doesn't have much of a seductive side to speak of, but I think that was her attempt at trying. "Who are you?" She smiled, then took a big drink of my wine. My lie detector started going off.

"I'm your wife, don't forget it."

I can't remember the last time Jane talked to me like that. What does a man have to do for it to always be like this? I can easily put more holes in the house if that's what it takes. Jane's a rollercoaster. Every time I convince myself that I can't take any more of the uphill, she manages to make the ride fun enough for me to want to know what's next. Lately, there have been uphill struggles around every corner, so it's about time for the ride to get exciting.

"I'm not sure what you did with the real Jane, but let's get the fuck out of here before she returns. I'm going to get dressed."

"Why don't you go like that?" I just smiled and walked off, but she planted an idea that I was now forced to think about. We would be walking by Neighbor. What a way to make proper introductions, both of us half-dressed, half in the bag, and hanging out with our so-called better halves. Even with Jane starting to act like a wife, the thought of Neighbor stays with me.

It only took a minute to splash my face and put a clean shirt and deodorant on, but I spent a few more admiring my work again. Being that it was right there, a quick trip up to Burnitts took little convincing. Jane put me in a good mood, and that made me want to smoke. I would have to be quick though. If I'm gone too long, Jane will be lazy and angry by the time I return. Either way, the door couldn't agree with me more.

Back in the kitchen, I was surprised to find Jane still going strong. She caught me off-guard sitting at the bar eating toast and drinking tea. I was proud of her. Everyone knows that caffeine and calories can help combat the cunt. With that, there might be some hope for us today after all.

"Hey."

"Hey. I'm almost ready. I just needed a little energy."
Yeah, no shit.

"No rush. I'll step outside before we go. Want to join me on the porch?"

"Of course," as if she always does.

Walking out, my eyes went directly to Neighbor's house. As far as I could see, she wasn't outside. Part of me felt relieved. Maybe I was a little nervous, or maybe I just didn't need her as much anymore today.

"I guess that I should move the cars back to the driveway. I know how much you like them in the yard."

"You should get yours moved completely off the property," Jane remarked. I assume she's joking, but she didn't break face while saying it. As nice as the day has been, it suddenly started to feel like the Sunday that it is. It's the last day of the weekend and I don't want it to end.

Jane finished her tea and toast, just as I put out my smoke.

"Should we get this dog walked?"

"Yeah, let's do it. We'll grab Warden too. I'll walk you both!"

"Funny. I just remembered that you owe me a shot. And now that I think about it, I'll just leave the cars in the yard so you can keep working on your game."

We were well past the Neighbor's house before I realized it was behind us. With Jane and I talking, I paid no attention. We held hands and joked the entire way. Jane talked about her work in a way that I envied. I talked about work in the way most do. I feel like a non-player character in someone else's game. She told me that I needed to take some control and be happy. Even though I've told myself the same thing thousands of times, it was nice to hear it from her. Jane kept my mind active, and before I knew it, we arrived at Lookout.

I tied off Warden and opened a couple of beers for Jane and me. We said cheers to Lookout. It was quiet there outside of the occasional car racing down the hill. The always-present plastic shards lining the shoulder highlight the occasional consequence of that. It's nice having Jane with me. Tomorrow, I'll be sitting here alone, counting down the days until Friday.

"We should call out tomorrow," Jane suddenly said. "We didn't enjoy the full weekend as we should have. Let's take an extra day."

"Really? Can you do that?"

"For the most part. I'll need to go in for a couple of hours. After that, we should go on a date or something." Jane and I haven't gone out on an official date in forever. I feel like we're always home when we're not doing our own thing.

"I would love to stay home tomorrow," I said, unable to

hide my excitement. "I don't know though, I don't think it's been two months yet."

"Fuck 'em," she remarked without hesitation, which would be the last thing that I'd expect to hear from her. She read my thought exactly.

Every single Sunday, I consider calling out on Monday, but I prefer to skip on Fridays. However, with Jane's backing, I don't even have to think about it. Right away, I could feel the relief run through me. It feels like I can breathe again. Jane couldn't have said anything better to me. In those few words, she won me over. This is what she wanted to tell me? Now I wish that I didn't wait so long to find out.

"You know, Jane, when you're not being a total asshole you know exactly what to say to me. Look at you, knowing the way to my heart."

"I'm pretty sure that's through your dick, Marty. You know, when you're not being a total asshole it's because you're not saying anything."

"Has this been your idea all along, I play hooky on Monday, you play hooker?"

"Not exactly, but it's been something I've been thinking about." This evening's taken a turn that I would have never expected. Jane wanting to skip work and flirting with me are beyond anything that I could have imagined for today. I can't lie, and it would be obvious if I wasn't sitting down.

By the time we finished our beers, two other couples were at Lookout. Without the place to ourselves, I suggested we take a selfie and head back home. The first picture led to several more. Warden even got in on the action. We were doing the family thing, and it made me miss Wes even more. Like me at his age, he is his own man living his own way. I find comfort in his happiness and the fact that he's probably having the time of his life. The walk back home went by as fast as the walk there. I had work on my mind, but this time only positive thoughts of not having to go.

"Look at our beautiful home," Jane commented. I swear that I don't know who this girl is. Has it been so difficult for her to be like this every day? She's right though. The red front door stood out against the white siding and black windows and shutters, and matched the fully bloomed roses perfectly. The work that I did improved the exterior more than I thought it would. It tied the house and garage together and looks as if it was originally built that way. Truth be told, with Jane not having such an ugly attitude, my car really is the only eyesore on the property.

Predictable Jane had to use the bathroom as soon as she could, so I sat in the driveway with Warden. She used the front door, but I think more out of habit than resistance to the new entrance. Dog found the grill right away. I almost forgot about the steak but didn't think twice about giving it to him instead of offering it to Jane again. He'll appreciate it cold more than she would warm anyway.

Chapter Fifteen

Opposite of my brief expectation, Jane didn't appear to be coming back out to join me. Knowing her, she's passed out. The considerate man in me figured that she would like some company so I decided to let Warden in to join her. Upon entering, my suspicions were confirmed. Jane fell into the couch without so much as turning on the TV. Maybe she expected me to pick something.

Even though Jane's treating me better today than any day that I can remember recently, I still wish she could have hung in for the long one. However, I don't find myself as upset as I would usually be. Jane made me laugh today and that means everything. As she lies there unaware, without her presence to ruin it, all I see is her beauty. She attracts me with a force. Rather than attempt to wake her up or plan something obnoxious for her to discover, I'll just be here and allow her unbothered rest.

Softly resting the blanket over Jane's body made me feel like I was shielding and protecting her. With that, Wes crossed my mind again. I miss taking care of him more than anything. Back at the chair, the several cigarette butts and roaches in the plant beside it caught my attention. I'm probably responsible for that shit. Maybe I'm not taking care of my messes as I should be.

Maybe I shouldn't be creating messes in the first place. Suddenly, I started thinking that maybe it was me that needed to wake up.

Right away, I felt the overwhelming need to get my shit together, starting with the poor plant that I've been neglecting. I picked the spent smokes out of the soil, and after that, watered it with the filtered water from the fridge. Then I went through and watered the rest of the houseplants. If I could do anything for Jane today, the least I could do is clean up my act a little. My mind quickly went to developing a list of to-dos. First, I'll pour a cup of wine. After quietly picking up the kitchen, I'll move to the porch, driveway, my room, and Burnitts. Cups need to be cleaned, ashtrays need to be emptied, cars need to be moved, and bars need their booze back in place.

It didn't take long to get everything back in order. I left the grill and two chairs out thinking that's what I'll do next. Jane's likely to be out for the night, so it'll probably be another meal alone for me. Either way, I'm happy enough not to have to go to work tomorrow. I'll trade dinner company for that any day. With or without someone to eat with, I plan on feasting like it's a day that I'm supposed to be celebrating.

Back inside, I started my dough (water, flour, yeast, olive oil, sea salt, and garlic powder) and grated cheese (mozzarella, cheddar, and parmesan) for homemade pizza. The dough wasn't going to be ready to bake for an hour, so I had some time before I needed to light the grill. Jane was still curled up on the couch with Warden on the opposite side doing the same. Since I was optimistic about her waking up and being the same person that went to bed, I opted to take a quick shower. I left my shirt off when I got out and lit some candles for potential ass ambiance. Then I poured a cup of wine and a cup of water to leave out on the table for her. I know how she tends to wake up thirsty.

Back in the kitchen, I find my dough rose well enough to

give it a knockdown before its second rise. That gave me enough time to get the coals started before rolling it out and assembling the ingredients. At the grill, I noticed Neighbor back outside. Once again, she had my attention. Finding it harder to get a good look with the cars back in the driveway, I found myself running up to Burnitts for a more satisfying glimpse.

Before long, I remembered my camera behind the bar. With Jane sleeping, it was the perfect time to get that within-reach look I've been badly wanting. I went first to the window and noticed her in her usual skimpy clothes. Excitement started consuming me, so I went for a shot of rum. An alcohol-aided arousal is among my favorites.

The drink stalled me long enough to think twice about what I was doing. Not only was I in the middle of making pizza, but I also had a better chance with Jane than in a long time. Not to mention, I'd be seeing Neighbor up close, in person tomorrow anyway. With a second thought, I didn't need to be prying my lens just yet. Tomorrow, she'll literally be in my reach.

The coals wouldn't need long, so I went back in to get the dough rolled out on the parchment-lined pan, sauce spread, cheese laid, and pepperoni plotted. I decided not to try to wake Jane. Her breathing strongly indicated her body's lack of desire to function. I wasn't willing to chance anything with her attitude after getting a small but well-welcomed taste of her good side.

Outside at the grill, it was pizza on and covered. Once again finding myself without cooking company, my interest in doing anything quickly diminishes with every diminishing drink. I'm drunk and there's no reason to resist. Not only do I have tomorrow off, but I also feel more accomplished than I have in a while. My muscles are sore too. And my cock's likely to remain in involuntary intermission anyway. With all that against me, once I fill up, surrendering will be an option. Since the majority of Sunday evenings are nothing worth celebrating anyway, it's typical.

As the smell of pizza began to mask the rose-scented air around me, I knew it was almost done. Inside, Jane was still sleeping on the couch. If it wasn't for her half-filled winter glasses, I'd assume she hasn't moved at all. She was either back to sleep or trying to convince me otherwise. I didn't want to get close enough to investigate.

Once the pizza was baked perfectly, I brought it to the kitchen bar to cool and prepared some wine for the treat to come. Then I made my way around to snuff out the candles and shut the blinds. The day caught up with me quickly, and all I want to do is eat and sleep. Before going about it, I took Warden and the garbage out to complete what nightly to-do's I could remember. By then, food couldn't be put off any longer. I ate half the pie sitting at the dimly lit bar, zoned out to the homegrown flower arrangement put together by Karla. Pizza's been the best meal of the weekend from what I can remember. Even though I ate as much as I could, I leave it on the counter convinced that I'll be making a return to it. After washing it all down with an unaccustomed cup of water, I went back to the wine knowing something even stronger was imminent.

With the living room occupied, my post-meal cigarette would have to be enjoyed on the porch this evening. Out there, my mind got the best of me right away. Without knowing exactly what I was thinking, I started feeling agitated and unsettled. Working my way through my thoughts, there was nothing for me to be anxious about. I soon realized that what I was experiencing was something similar to circadian rhythm, but on a weekly scale. After being troubled by Jane and job every Sunday, week after week for so long, my brain naturally goes there. There's no reason for me not to be settled. Sure, Jane and I should be playing in each other's cum right now, but I appreciate her trying to exert herself. With tomorrow being a work-free Monday, today shouldn't feel at all like the last day of a vacation.

Thankfully, my mind went back to being in a good

place. My autopilot becomes significantly more unpredictable when it's not. It was a promising breakthrough. With that, I went back to Burnitts to celebrate cerebral control. That was accomplished by lighting my joint and taking a shot, a true tribute to self healing.

How fucking ironic is it that on the very first night after finally making Burnitts livable, I don't want to sleep here but will be anyway. I do it occasionally, but mostly prefer to be closer. The bed's Janes, and she'll ultimately find her way back to it tonight once the lack of couch comfort catches up with her. Since there's a good chance that she's going to wake up a different girl than the one that passed out happy, I'm not sure how she would react if she found me in it. From experience, I'm betting she wouldn't like it at all. With her taking up the living room for now, I'd rather just be here than in my room on the floor. It doesn't have nearly as many amenities as Burnitts, and the scenery's not even close to as good.

It came to mind that I had yet to notify my boss that I wasn't coming in. Since I was drunk, I wisely chose email over voice message. I don't stand a chance composing words verbally. As I started writing, so much of what I wanted to say was coming to mind. I typed several things before wisely deleting everything and keeping it professional. *Good morning. I will not be in the office tomorrow and will be using available sick time. I apologize for any inconvenience.* With that, it's straight to the point with only an implied excuse provided. I always make an effort never to give a direct one.

Neighbor seems to be in for the night, not that looking was intentional. I was actually relieved that she wasn't there to sidetrack me. After shutting the blinds and filling my wine, I found the couch and fell flat on it. It's been a while since I've felt physically overworked. TV's my only plan. Being as tired as I am, I don't even want to hang out with my dick. Even Neighbor couldn't spark the motivation needed for me to remain upright. With that said, my usual viewing options are off the table, Ramsey's mouth will have to do it for me this time.

The first thing that I'm aware of is my aching muscles. I'm hurting, but at the same time, I'm so comfortable. It's hard to say if I'm awake or dreaming. Jane's voice ultimately directed me to reality after hearing her relentlessly talking about something that wasn't making any sense. Eventually, I was able to put something together.

"Marty, do you want to get up and have a drink with me?" She was being nice which made me think that I was dreaming. Next, I hear her say something completely different.

"Seriously, Marty, you need to get up. You're late for work." She said that in her typical tone, the one that I could never sleep through. I didn't know what was going on at first, and I think it took me some time to realize what was. She was trying anything that she could to wake me up.

"What's going on?" I asked. It was more of an incoherent mumble than actual spoken words.

"Do you want to get up for a little while? You don't have work right now, or in the morning!"

"What? Is something wrong?" I let out a painful moan while attempting to stretch. "I need Aspirin."

"Okay. No, nothing's wrong. I'm going to grab you some Aspirin, but then I want to have a drink. I still have something for you."

Finding myself dressed was a relief. I had my pants on and knew where I was, but wasn't sure about much of anything else. Before Jane returned, I finished my leftover wine still lying down. I spilled a little, but it's my fucking couch. It was just after midnight, but the day was lost long before. With that thought, I managed to sit myself up. If Jane would have been any longer, I would have been back down again.

"Hey. Here's some Aspirin. I needed some too."

"Thanks, Jane. I'm confused. Why did you wake me up?

What are you doing right now?"

"Oh, you know, I felt bad for falling asleep. I just woke up and started looking for you."

"Yeah, what happened there?" I really didn't know, so I was hoping she would tell me.

"I don't know, basketball, I think? I suck." That's right. I convinced myself to stand and went for my smokes. Jane met me at the bar with that same suspicious smile that I remember from earlier.

"Want to do some shots?" Jane asked, apparently excited to pick up where she left off.

"Don't you have to work tomorrow?"

"I just have to leave for a couple of hours. We can still celebrate. What do you say, can you handle me?"

"It's been a tough life trying to, Jane. I don't think I can."

"What?"

"I'll do a shot but you have to pour them. I still have to pull my shit together." It would be her pleasure. We should drink to surviving our anniversary. The date's been tormenting me for weeks, and I'm relieved for it to be over. Jane probably feels the same. We deserve a drink after seeing our way through it. "I was out. Burnitts couch suits me so much better than yours."

"If you didn't like it so much, you wouldn't sleep on it every night."

"That's not true. You're the only one that enjoys that fucking thing." Jane poured and we drank to "comfortable couches." Then we went again, and drank to "Mondays off." After that, I went for cold wine. Jane wanted one as well but also poured two more shots to go with it.

"Today's going to be fun! What are you going to do when you're too fucked-up to go to work tomorrow?" she asked.

"Huh? I don't know. It literally couldn't be farther away right now. I think that I can handle myself. Plus, I'm going back to sleep. You're ensuring it with these shots." We toasted to "midnight snacks" and threw back our drinks. Both of us needed to follow it up with some wine. Three in a row is tough.

"I woke you up to give you my gift. Sorry, it's a little late. I hope you're ready for it!"

"Seriously? I thought you already did."

"Nope."

"All right."

"Mom's retiring. She's passing ABRE over to me in a month!" It took me a couple of seconds to process what I think she said.

"What? Really? Your mom's retiring?"

"Yeah!"

"She's passing the brokerage over to you?"

"Yeah! She said that she has been planning on it since before the new year and wanted to step away before the end of summer. I've known about it for a little while now. You know her. It's not surprising that she would choose to leave now when the business is doing its best. She would rather go out at her most successful than at anytime less."

"Holy shit, that's kind of unbelievable. Congratulations, Jane! I never thought anything like that would be happening soon. Good for you. Good for you both!"

That would make Jane CEO of ABRE. Not only is it an opportunity for her to make a lot more money, but she would also be in control of it all. I'm sure she has always imagined running the company. From my experience, she's the type of person that demands the final say. Now thinking about it, Jane's probably had to bite her tongue a lot through the years. I know how that feels.

"Hold on. Don't get too excited," she said. "I might just choose to be home more, I know how much you would like that."

"Okay."

"Yeah, maybe I'll have everyone else do all the work for me. I'll stay home and work on my novel."

"Nobody can tell you that you can't." Jane seemed thrilled. Maybe she's been wanting this more than I know. No wonder she's awake and wanting to liquor up. Actually, her wanting to party today makes a lot more sense to me now. I can't believe that I let myself think that she was celebrating us. This has been about her. Jane has been selfish this whole fucking time.

"Guess what, that's not all though. What I wanted to tell you is that when I take over, ABRE will be looking to fill a new video production position. All properties represented are going to have top-of-the-line video walk-throughs and outside drone footage available for marketing. I want to have the best pictures and virtual tours available for every listing. Mom has been putting off the upgrade, but I want to make the change and set a new standard as soon as possible. You're hired if you want the job."

"What? You're asking me if I want to work for you?" I laughed. "Yeah, right. You just want to be my boss, tell me what to do and have the power to fire me."

"No, you're right. I've thought about that too. I probably would have to fire you, especially knowing your history of not showing up to work. An employee calling out every other week isn't something that my company will tolerate! But think about it anyway, I know you would probably be a lot happier. In the meantime, let's celebrate!"

What I hate most in my life is my job. Still, there's no fucking way that I can see myself working for Jane. She would love to have a legit say over me. Lately, in a way, my job being so intolerable is what has kept this relationship afloat. It's been the only thing capable of making me want to be home. Jane stood up and began walking off. That's the view that I'm most familiar with. She stopped and turned around just before getting to the stairs.

"The thing is, Marty, I wouldn't be able to fire you if I wanted. Mom's signing ABRE over to us as equal partners, so congratulations on that!" She smiled. "I have to use the bathroom," then hustled her way down the stairs.

I lit another cigarette trying to sort out all that Jane has said. Karla's retiring, Jane wants to hire a video production manager, and Jane and I are now going to own ABRE equally. Partners? That's a fucked-up proposition considering we can't even manage our marriage together. It was a lot to take in, especially being half out of it. While trying to play back the conversation in my head, I thought about what Jane asked me. What am I going to do when I'm too fucked-up to go to work tomorrow?

All of a sudden, it hit me, and I can't fucking believe it. I'm not going to work tomorrow! I found myself pacing behind the bar, my heart pounding hard. Am I finally done with that fucking job? There's no way. I can't believe it. I can't believe that I'm not going to have to go to that mind-fuck anymore. That job devours so much of my head space, of my life. Every day it consumes my sanity. The relief that I should be feeling doesn't come through right away. It's too much to comprehend, and I feel a little overwhelmed. Contrary to what I would have expected, the thought is actually making me quite anxious. Alcohol will help, but what I really want to do is yell to the world. It's been so hard on me for so long that I just want to purge, but since yelling has never been my thing, I settled for refilling the shots.

Just as I was about to drink them both, I heard Jane making her way back. She shut the door a little aggressively on the way up, and it sounded like she might have tripped herself up the stairs. Her actions must be a little in front of her. She's drunk again.

Once Jane emerged from the floor, the impression that

the shots left her with was much more apparent. "Fine, the door is awesome! It looks really good. It's nice having the bathroom right there." She was having trouble walking and talking, but judging by the size of her smile, she didn't mind.

"I'm glad that you ended up liking it. I don't think I've even used it yet. I poured some shots if you want one." She found herself a stool.

"You don't think that you've used the bathroom yet?"

"What?"

"Is that what you said?" I had to think for a moment about what she was asking.

"I don't think that I've used the door specifically to use the bathroom yet. Is your mom really giving us the business?"

"Yeah! I have been waiting so that I could surprise you with it today, I mean yesterday." She laughed at herself. "By the way, she's selling it to us. She'll be taking a little off the top for a few years."

"I figured that. So, you have known about it for a while? You haven't seemed any different."

"Yeah, I don't know. It's been hard to believe. I have been wanting it for a long time. Plus, you always tell me how fed up you are with me, so I always just try to stay away. It feels real now, Marty, now that you know."

"First of all, I'm fed up with you because you always stay away. Seriously though, you and me, we're in business together?"

"Yeah!"

"I don't have to go to work tomorrow?"

"No!"

"I can quit my job?"

"Yeah!"

"I can tell my boss to mouth my fucking manhood?"

"Nooo!"

"You think that I should take over the picture and video

production side of things?"

"Yeah!"

"With a drone too?"

"Yeah, Marty! Are you saying that you're interested? It's all right if you're not. I mean, you won't be able to represent us in that piece of shit that you have showcased out front. You're going to have to get another vehicle."

"Does a shark shit in the sea, Jane? Of course, I'm interested. This is hard to believe. Is this actually happening?"

I slid a glass her way. "Cheers. To dreams coming true."

"Cheers. To dreams coming true." Jane took her shot and then found her way to the couch. "I thought you might like that." I couldn't move, stuck trying to process it all. Instead of calling out again tomorrow like I was planning to, I'll be quitting.

Time got away from me as I lost myself in blissful thought. It was all too good to be true. My mind's not used to managing so much enjoyment. It suddenly felt like Friday again, but even better. The only thing that I could think to do was fuck one off. With that, I got out of my head and called Jane over in hopes of sharing my excitement. She didn't respond. I wasn't all that surprised to find her sleeping. Burnitts' couch agrees with the drunk and tired. Jane probably had a drink or two before waking me up. After covering her up and taking a solo shot, I grabbed my cup of wine and headed into the house for water and a brief check of everything. Yesterday got away from me, and I'm not sure how I left the place.

The first thing in the kitchen that caught my attention was the pizza. Unable to help myself, I threw a piece in the microwave and moved on to the water part of the plan. I drank two full glasses before it was ready. After smashing through that slice, I threw in another one. My mind easily fell into a trance. I stood there for the full minute staring at the pizza spinning around without even realizing I strayed again. The chime brought me back to reality like a hypnotist snapping their fingers. No amount of therapy could lead to how healed I felt. Too much of my life has been revolving around a job that's been corroding me from the inside out. Even though I'll never get the years back and will likely never fully recover, I've never felt better.

The house was in great shape for the amount of drinking that went down this weekend. Considering the work I did, it's actually better than when we came into it. I've been drunk the last few days, so it all feels new still. My autopilot turns out to be surprisingly skilled with a level and saw. With Jane admitting her approval, I couldn't be more satisfied. Sure, her stubbornness wasted a couple of days, but I have to remember she came home to a punctured house with no advance notice. Not to mention, she just gave me the best gift that I could be given, with the exception of Wes.

I consciously chose not to give Jane a gift this year after being back and forth about it. Maybe my frustrations grew to be too much. More than ever, it became vital for me to stand up for myself and prove to her that I'm past my limit. It's hard for me to remember those feelings being so strong now. In hindsight, there should never have been any question as to whether or not I would be giving my wife a gift on our anniversary. The thought of questioning it, let alone my decided answer, suddenly burdened me beyond explanation. Even with trying to justify my actions by hers, it's not holding up in my mind anymore. Saying that I've been an asshole about it would be a compliment right now. It's more like I've been a good-for-nothing piece of shit. Maybe it's true but in a different way than I have meant it before —Jane doesn't deserve me.

With that, I couldn't let up on myself. I fucked-up badly. As I thought about how the bathroom project idea stemmed from evolving motivations to get away from Jane, I now wish that I wouldn't have done it at all. She's been thinking of us being closer and happier while I selfishly live in the past. That being the truth, I don't even want the space anymore. Fortunately for me, I was drunk. And with that, my mysterious mangled mind led me to the best idea that I would have all weekend. One that would, without a doubt, give me total redemption. That is, in regards to my anniversary anyway.

My vision quickly turned from self-centered to self-sacrificing. Now that I'm looking at things differently, I wouldn't have it any other way. It became obvious to me that my room has a better purpose, and that a bathroom for Burnitts would have to wait. What it should be is a dedicated and private office for Jane, something a little more functional than the living room to manage a business out of.

The room could be just as perfect for Jane as it could be for me. After all, it has its own bathroom and exit, and the bar is within reasonable walking distance. That's a good start for anything an exceptional home office needs. Now that I think about it, telling her that it had been my plan all along would be the smart thing to do. I was impressing myself with what I was formulating. The thought soon had my head spinning with furnishing and decorating ideas. I already couldn't wait to get it done. Right away, I'm looking forward to Jane realizing that I did all of it for her and hope that she feels bad about the way she reacted. It's not like her words didn't have an effect on me. More than that though, I want her to feel appreciated.

As my routine goes, I filled my wine, picked up the kitchen, shut off the lights, and found my way to the couch. Soon after, Warden made his presence known. I think he expected me to walk him or something. It only took a nod of my head for him to recognize approval to join me. He jumped up and propped himself against the opposite armrest and sat staring at me as if I was supposed to be giving him some sort of attention. After some time, it finally occurred to me that he doesn't know what the fuck is going on. Jane's not in bed and nowhere to be found. He doesn't know what to do without her.

"Where's Jane? Where is she?" He understood immediately and shot off the couch fully expecting to see her. *Fucking traitor.*

Not wanting to deal with him myself, I led Warden to Burnitts' door and then made my way back inside. Warden will be something familiar for Jane when she arises confused about everything else around her. I'll be in the company of myself, on Jane's couch as usual. Jane has her known side effects, I just never thought that losing my bar bed within the first night would be one of them.

Chapter Sixteen — Monday

Out of nowhere, I began to accept that I was conscious and that I must have been sleeping. It's still dark out, so I'm sure that I haven't been sleeping for as long as I needed to. My first concerns were born from the many unknowns of yesterday. The painful sound I inadvertently make through a long exhale and barely tolerable stretch accurately represents how I feel. My body hurts, and this shitty couch that I always find myself trying to sleep on must be the fucking reason. My mouth is severely lacking moisture, but getting up and moving won't be easy. My lips are chapped but my dried-out tongue can't even slide across them. Thankfully, there was a half-filled wine glass on the table within reasonable reach. I drank it in one swallow still lying down, being careful not to spill any on Jane's cherished sofa. I probably knew that I would wake up thirsty. After all, every morning's the same.

It didn't occur to me right away that this morning's actually not the same. I first thought of it being Monday. That bothered me right away until I remembered that I called out. My instantaneous anxiety settled quickly, and my relief alleviated my desire not to move. Without hesitation, I was on my way to the kitchen for more fluid. My eyes weren't capable of focusing yet. I had to keep them closed while standing in the fridge filling my wine. They were so dry and sensitive that the inside light seemed like a flashlight to the face. From there, I took my drink back to the couch where I belonged. An hour went by without me even knowing. Eventually, I was able to get up and head outside for a smoke. I felt discombobulated and needed that before anything. It wasn't long before everything came flooding back; Jane's up at Burnitts, I'm quitting my job, we have a business, yesterday ended up being pretty amazing, and I have an anniversary gift to give Jane.

I found it difficult at first to allow myself to be as content as I should be. It felt like my brain was searching for something to be troubled about. It's different not having anything to haunt my head. There's so much good all of a sudden that my mind needs to transition. I forgot how it felt to be excited about things. Until now, cloud-9 was always just a fantasy that helped get me through the low-lying fog that I was dying in. From now on, I expect it to be my reality.

I topped off my wine and went in to wash and pamper myself. After a healthy stint on the toilet, I eagerly got in the shower. The pressured hot water instantly massaged and soothed my sore muscles. In a way, it felt like I was rinsing away the old me. After cleaning and brushing my teeth, I drew a hot bath, ready to bathe as the new me.

My list of ideas and things to do today grew in my mind. I started by going outside to water the plants. The roses seemed exceptional this morning. They remind me of Jane in the same way that they reminded Weston of Karla, undeniably capable of both pain and beauty. Once finished, and without hesitation, I picked three gorgeous roses and brought them in to replace the wilting ones from Friday. In doing so, I swapped out the vase for a clean winter glass. In a way, the flowers represented a fresh start for Jane and me. Perhaps these won't die away so fast.

After taking care of the garden, I moved on to brew a pot of coffee. More for Jane than me. Today, I'll be partying pretty hard. After laying out a cup and some cream, I filled a glass of water to take up to Jane. With Warden by her side, she was sleeping as soundly as she normally can.

"Good morning, Jane. It's time to get up." She didn't respond, so I did what she did to me last night. "Jane, wake up! Jane, you have to go to work." Her eyes immediately opened, but I could tell she didn't know why. "Jane, you have to get up. You're late for work."

"Oh shit. What time is it?"

"Hah, I'm just messing with you. It's just after seven. I brought you some water if you want some," knowing that she likely needed it.

"Thank you." She drank the whole glass in two efforts. "Good morning," she finally said, smiling.

"Good morning."

"Thanks for waking me up. I slept really good."

"Of course you did. My couch was designed with comfort taking priority. Thanks for waking me up and partying last night. And the amazing news!"

"Can you believe it, Marty?"

"I really can't, Jane. It's still sinking in. I'm so excited."

"I knew you would be happy. I gotta pee." She stood up and gave me a peck on the lips before heading downstairs. "I'm going to get ready, come inside before I have to leave."

My eyes landed on the weight bench as I was opening Burnitts, but I wouldn't even consider it. Today's list will not include excessive work of any kind. With further thought, I decided that I would omit the list altogether. What I would like to do is hang out with Jane. That said, coffee wasn't a bad idea after all. I could make her some breakfast too. More than anything, I just want to be closer.

In my shape, getting started with the office project would require at least a couple of cups of coffee. I poured the first one after finishing my wine and decided on the porch to drink it. Just as I opened the door, Neighbor was running by. She gave me an eyeful of ass to look at before ending up at her house. I missed the laps today, left only with a tiny tease.

As I sipped on my coffee and smoked on my smoke, I was lost in euphoric thought. That combined with Neighbor's ass led me to want to cum. That's when I remembered that we planned to have a drink with her later. Today's finally the day that I'll be closer to her. Soon, reality will be knocking on fantasy's door, and I hope she's as inviting as I have imagined.

My dick doesn't lie, and I need to snap out of it. Since my only recourse is to sidetrack myself, I went in to begin cooking. The over-medium egg, ham, and cheese on a toasted and buttered everything bagel was ready just as Jane emerged ready for work.

"Hey."

"Hey. I just finished making you a breakfast bagel if you're interested."

"I definitely am, thank you! I'm going to eat it on the go though because I want to get this over with as soon as possible."

"Okay. Do you know when you'll be back?"

"I'm hoping to be home by eleven. Then you better be ready to celebrate for real!"

"Deal. I'll be ready." I wrapped up her sandwich as she filled her coffee mug. After that, it was a brisk kiss and goodbye as she made her way out the door.

"Can't wait to see you later, Mr. Boss Man."

"Bye, have a good morning. Take care of my business, please." We smiled at each other as she got in the car and shared a wave as she pulled away. I can't remember the last time I didn't want her to go.

Back inside, I put together a plan. All my shit can be thrown in the bedroom closet for now. The two bigger pieces of furniture going in the office are Jane's desk from the living room and the futon from the spare room. I'll have to get a new bed ordered and delivered here in the next day or two for when Wes and Katie visit. They're not getting my bar, that's for sure. After those two things, it'll just be a matter of decorating and personalizing. The job seemed easy enough, so after pouring myself a mouthful of wine from the tap, I went to work.

The desk is the obvious thing to start with. It will be the most time-consuming component but also the most representative of an office. There's the desk itself, a tower with two monitors, her laptop, a printer, files, accessories, and a bit more to move, set up, and organize. Once cleared, I lifted one end of the desk on an old skateboard of Wes's and drug it in from the other. Within an hour, I had it relocated and fully back together.

The room was transformed immediately. It hasn't had a piece of furniture in it since Wes left. Next, I tackled the futon. It was flipped on its back and moved in a similar fashion as the desk. Once that was positioned, the hard work was done. With that, I decided that it was smoke and beer time. Beer always tastes better to me when I'm drinking it at a time when I would otherwise be at work. Of course, I wouldn't have to call out so much if I could just drink beer at work. Too bad Karla didn't own ShackBrew.

The office really started to come together once I brought in some plants and hung a few family pictures above the desk. Since Karla's flowers were over-shadowing mine on the bar, I brought those in and displayed them on an end table that I retrieved from Burnitts. I also managed to find a sheer curtain for the door's full-length window and some feminine-colored towels for the bathroom too. For the walls, I found a mirror, tack-board, clock, and flower art to hang.

The office was finished with time to spare, so I went back to the bar. My first instinct was to go to the window until I remembered it was Monday. Unfortunately, Neighbor won't be home until later. That's reasoning enough for me to stick with

Saturdays and Sundays off, now that I'll be making my own schedule. Having Mondays off sounds good in theory, but all must be considered.

Having cold beers at Burnitts still surprises me. It would probably be wise of me to have a water option as well. I thought about me plugging the fridge in as one of the best decisions that I've made this weekend. That led me to think about the office and how that was the actual best. Then my mind put one and one together. Without needing to think twice about it, I decided that warm beer works fine enough for me and that the fridge is better suited for Jane. I brought it down with all its wine and beer. Right now, I would give her anything.

I was on the porch eating the last of the pizza when I saw Jane coming up the road. To my surprise, she pulled in and went right to parking in the yard. She got out smiling. Even with carrying a couple of bags, she practically danced her way up to me.

"Hey!"

"Hey, welcome home!"

"Thanks. Good to be home."

"New parking spot?"

"Just in case you want to try me again. Let me put this stuff away and grab a drink, I'll come out and join you."

"Okay." Fuckin hell, I didn't even have to ask.

Jane must have been focused on the wine part of her plan or else she would have noticed the missing desk. She didn't have anything to say about it. Instead, she came back commenting on the day and how pretty the flowers looked pulling in. As nice as it is, I still find her sudden and continued interest in me hard to believe. I'm a little skeptical. Jane has a reputation for flipping her switch from "it's on, let's party" to "fuck off, leave me alone." It never stays on with her. Rather, it's like her spite's on a randomized timer that can't be predicted or disabled. Sure, she's happy now, and that makes me very happy.

How long will she be able to stay energized—that's my concern.

"How's your day going?" she asked.

"My day's fantastic. How was work?"

"Easy. I couldn't wait to get back though."

"Try some pizza. You can have the rest." She began eating the last remaining slice and commented on how great it was. It made me wonder if she had any yesterday or not.

"What do you want to do today, Jane?"

"I'm up for anything! Mom talked about stopping over, and I know that I mentioned possibly having a drink with the neighbors." Fuckin hell. I didn't expect Karla to be coming over today. Always fucking unexpected. Out of habit, that was my first thought, but then I remembered how great she is. As far as The Neighbors, I wasn't going to bring that up. I haven't been sure if Jane even remembered.

"All right. What's your mom up to?"

"Honestly, I think she just wants to see you. I told her that I told you."

"Why would she want to see me?"

"I think she just wants to see how happy you are."

"I am happy." I can't remember the last time I said that and meant it. "What time?"

"She didn't say exactly but probably in a little while."

That leaves me unsure of how long I want to wait to show Jane her office. For now, I'll just lure her away the only way that I know that has worked lately.

"Want to go to Burnitts?"

"Sure. I'm not smoking though."

Jane walked into Burnitts like she owned the place. She didn't take a seat at the bar as a good patron should. She hustled her way behind it like it was her fucking job. I think she just wants me to have to ask her for whatever I want rather than help myself. In any case, I'm glad she's been enjoying herself at my establishment.

"May I have a beer, please?" I asked as I approached, already forgetting that the fridge wasn't there anymore.

"Where's the fridge?" she asked.

"Shit, I forgot. It was making a loud, funny noise this morning. I brought it downstairs to tear it apart."

"Where'd all the beer go?"

"They're down there, I wasn't thinking. Hold on, I'll go get some." I went downstairs for a few seconds and then popped my head back upstairs. "The fridge is warm. I'm going to run in for some cold bottles." After that, I retrieved four cold ones in record time and met Jane back at the bar. "To business partners."

We shot one game of pool that I claim I let her win while drinking our first beer. Back at the bar, we were into our second.

"Do you want to play again?" Jane asked.

"Yeah! You have to allow me a redemption attempt," I insisted.

"Okay, rack 'em up! I'm going to run to the bathroom." Up until then, I didn't give any thought to Jane's overactive bladder. I should have known that she was going to have to use the bathroom before long. I don't see why she wouldn't be using the most convenient one available. That said, the reveal is going to be better than planned. I thought that I was going to have to walk her into it. Her using the new door because she's at Burnitts and needs to piss is perfect considering what I was initially going for with the project.

"All right, I'll head in as well. Since your mom is probably on her way, I should put something together to eat. How about we finish this beer real quick, head inside, then get back to the game in a little while?"

"Sure, but don't forget who won the first one."

"I won't."

We finished our beers and then Jane led the way downstairs. She noticed the curtain on the door right away, but it didn't raise any questions.

"Your lucky that I'm letting you use my bathroom. You didn't even want the door."

"I know, thank you." Despite her rush, Jane stopped herself just inside the doorway and took a spanning look around without saying anything.

"Happy anniversary! Sorry, I ran a little behind with it."

"What? It looks so nice in here, an office!"

"Yeah! It's yours, I've got you all set up."

"Oh my god! I love it, Marty!" She turned around and latched on to me. From what I can remember, this is the first real embrace that we've shared in a long time. I forgot how good it felt, but I knew I was missing it.

"Check it out, let me give you the tour." I started pointing around. "Desk. Futon. Fridge. Table. Flowers. Door. Bathroom—my vision of the perfect office for you."

"All mine? Wait, what? You brought the fridge down?

"Yeah."

"Wow, this is so perfect, Marty! It looks awesome in here. Hold on, did you say the bathroom's mine too?" Of course, she could tell right away that it was. Now dancing, "Oh, Marty, this is so cool," she walked in and shut the door behind her.

I headed to the kitchen to prepare something to eat. I decided on an arugula and spinach salad. It will have feta cheese, onions, tomatoes, olives, salami, and a house dressing as well. The dressing will consist of rice vinegar, olive oil, salt, pepper, garlic, onion, and lemon juice. Jane came in as I started and offered to help. I told her that I appreciate it, but no thanks. Truth be told, I do a better job. She doesn't wield a knife with love—hate's another story.

I finished the salad as Jane went on about how much the office would be such an improvement for her, especially taking over as broker. She went back a couple of times to admire it and kept expressing her appreciation. Her gratitude was nice to hear but I haven't forgotten how much shit she dished out without hesitation. In truth, I'm lucky to have thought about it and elated that she likes it. Still, I had to keep highlighting the door. The office wouldn't be the same without it. It allows fresh air, an opportunity to step in and out quickly, and easy access to Burnitts. I kept on about it because I received so much Janger for it. By now, she probably forgot about all the cussing and ignoring she did, so I should probably just get over it.

"I love the door, Marty! Thank you so much. It makes it feel less isolated in there, and there's so much more light." I know all about feeling isolated.

"Yeah, and you can see the roses too," I replied. "It's a proper office. I really gave it some thought."

Karla was taking her sour-ass time, so I asked Jane if she wanted to do another shot. It's the preparation I need before sitting bitch between those two. She happily approved the proposition without negotiation. We did two before heading to the front porch. Karla arrived shortly after—top down on the convertible, big sunglasses, designer skirt and heels, and hair still perfect. As she approached, I took a slow, deep breath and braced myself for the Queen.

"Look at you two not working on a Monday like a couple of true business owners." Her notorious, quick-but-confident chuckle has a devious aspect to it but oddly enough comes off as honest and contagious too. It's always short-lived but at a volume louder than her words. I can't imagine her laughing in any other way.

"Hi, Mom," "Hi, Karla," we replied simultaneously. We hugged and invited her in.

I suggested we sit out back and offered to bring out some drinks. "I'll meet you guys out there." Jane led Karla to the patio as I went for a beer. I already needed a minute. I poured two waters and two wines and brought them out to the girls. Then I went back in for the salad and crockery. After that, I went back in for nothing. I was just avoiding the situation for as long as I could.

Telling myself to just get it over with, I smoked a cigarette and finished half of my ShackBrew before joining them. We talked in some detail about the business. Karla was more excited than I thought she would be. I asked what she would be doing for retirement. She said that she and the King were thinking about buying property down south to enjoy. I wasn't sure what was meant by that, but it sounded like a trafficking agenda to me. We talked about Wes, me quitting, food, and Jane. Karla asked about our anniversary, and it was nice not to have to lie this time. Jane mentioned the office, and after we finished eating and catching up, she took her mom to show it off. I got a beer and went back to the porch. It went better than anticipated. Man, wife, and wife's mom, it always sounds worse than it usually is.

We're meeting with our lawyers and signing official paperwork three Mondays from now. That's when my new role starts, and that means I have three weeks off. As an adult, I've never had three weeks off. Without any major plans, I'll probably look into new camera gear and play some golf. I'll definitely be doing a lot of cooking and drinking, and maybe Wes will have an opportunity to meet up too. I finished my beer and intended to keep myself occupied at Burnitts, but the girls were already utilizing the new office door and talking right outside of it.

"Great job, Marty. The office looks amazing!"

"Thanks, Karla. She deserves it."

"I'm a lucky wife," Jane said. "What are you up to?" she went on to ask me.

"Heading upstairs. Come on up if you guys want." I don't know why I suggested it. It just came out.

As we made our way upstairs, it occurred to me that Karla has only been up here once or twice before, and that was early on when nothing was complete. I doubt she even knows how awesome it is considering Jane just started coming up herself.

"Welcome to Burnitts." Karla didn't say anything at first. She just walked up to the "Burnitts" sign and stared at it for a moment as if she forgot what it looked like spelled out.

"You call your bar Burnitts, Marty? This place is fantastic!" She had a noticeable gleam in her eye. I gave her the tour, and she gave me her approval. "He would have loved it." I know she misses Weston. Their relationship couldn't be taken at face value. I believe that there was always a deeper love between them. Maybe, over time, they just became too comfortable with each other, and with that, grew a perceived lack of effort and interest. In a marriage, that can easily develop into feelings of vulnerability, insecurity, and doubt. Constant thoughts like that tend to make people defensive and self-protective before all else. When that happens, trust becomes impossible, and proclaimed trust can't be trusted. Sometimes, with a love so deep, it doesn't seem there at all.

"How about a shot, guys, celebrate new beginnings and old joys?" I knew Jane was in, but I didn't think Karla would be up for it. She agreed without hesitation, so I brought out my favorite "Live. Love. Liquor." shot glasses and filled them to the brim.

"To Burnitts and business," I proposed.

"To Burnitts and business," we all said. Jane and I took our shot immediately. Karla had to tap hers on the bar first. Jane laughed.

"Well versed, eh, Mom?"

"In liquor as in life and love, my child."

We enjoyed a few more laughs at Burnitts before walking Karla out. Back at the driveway, she wasn't finished displaying her sense of humor.

"You know, Marty, you can't be representing ABRE in that piece of shit," pointing to my car.

"Yeah, that was the first thing Jane told me after breaking the news, but I don't think she could do anything about it if I did. Thanks to you, of course." Her laugh almost made me mimic her in response. I told her that I would be looking into something a little more presentable, especially because I'd be able to write it off. I thanked her again for the opportunity and assured her that the business will be in good hands.

"It means nothing to me, Marty. That part of my life is over. I love you two and wish you the best of luck, but I'm retired now and want nothing to do with it. Work has taken up too much of my life as it is. I'm ready to start living every day." I can relate to that as much as anyone can, but I never expected to hear it from Karla. She always seems happy. That's how good she is at putting on face. "Thank you for showing me Burnitts, Marty. I needed that." We went on to hug and say our goodbyes.

Karla's a great friend and great family, but I am happy that she finally left so that I can get back to focusing on Jane. Also, even though I appreciate Karla, I do try to avoid getting naked in front of her, so that means that I can't get as drunk as I want to be when she's around. Now that she's gone, I can start working on it.

"Should we finish that competition?" Jane asked. Her standing there seductively rocking her hips side-to-side with her hands in her back pockets had me immediately.

"Yeah, looks like fun," I said. I like Jane requesting to go to Burnitts. These last couple of days have been epic with her. When she's joyful like that, there's nothing better.

As we entered the office to get beers, Jane remarked how she couldn't believe that it was my plan all along and how much she loved it. After that, I followed her ass the whole way up to the bar. Never have I ever wished the stairs longer. I took my eyes off of her just before she would notice, trying not to give my full interest away. It's something that I have to do when I want to be the one pursued. If Jane thinks that her being amusing is all I want, she should just leave now. I'm expecting a real effort from her today to satisfy me, however, I would prefer it if my satisfaction was effortless.

After racking up the balls, I popped some tops. That's what we toasted to. I had the urge to have a great game, so I didn't let up on Jane. After a solid break with two stripes in the pocket, I ran right through the table. She wasn't able to take a single shot. Jane wasn't happy about my display and demanded a rematch. I was all for a championship game. However, right away, I realized how much I fucked-up by winning the game like that. All I did was rob myself of opportunities to watch her bending over the table.

It's hard not to picture doing everything to Jane up and down this whole bar. What I envision most right now is coming up behind her confidently and assertively, dropping her pants and panties to her ankles, contorting her past ninety degrees, hitting it for about fifteen pumps, and leaving her there dripping, wondering where it all came from. In the mood that she's in, Jane would probably like it if I did that. She used to love it when I couldn't control myself. The problem is, if I were to do that, she would be totally satisfied. What I mean by that is, totally satisfied until who knows when. It wouldn't be today. What I want is to do the aforementioned and more. I'd like to have her now, but I'm not going to be fully satisfied with just that. If she remained willing to drink and flirt and spend some real time on each other, I would go for it. She doesn't consider that, and if it's one or the other, I prefer the latter.

To divert the possibility of ruining it for myself in ten-seconds time, I mentioned making lunch before getting into the third game. Being hungry herself, she was good with that. I went inside already knowing what was on the menu—ultimate BLTs. Ultimate BLTs are BLTs that have CPO: cheese, pickles, and onion. Mine are served on my homemade sourdough, toasted and smothered with mayonnaise and dressing. One sandwich was big enough to share, and we enjoyed it on the porch without saying much more than Mmm's and Yum's.

"Have you quit your job yet?" Jane asked.

"I will tomorrow. I'm going to go in at my normal time, clean out my desk and email my immediate resignation from there. I've been wanting to come up with something unique."

"What do you mean?"

"I don't just want to tell them that I quit, Jane. I would be missing out on a once-in-a-lifetime opportunity. I need to leave with something good. Believe me, I've been tossing around a couple of ideas."

"Sounds important. Try not to get yourself in trouble, Mr. Mouth."

Chapter Seventeen

Recently, my job has been on my mind a lot. Maybe I've been thinking about quitting too much. I haven't come up with anything yet, but my exit words should be easy to formulate. Being careful with what I say, I'll just let The Boss know how I felt while working there. I'll just say a little something about *me* and *my* feelings. It'll be wise of me to steer clear of mentioning the company or any of its people specifically; that could lead to trouble and ultimately leave me wishing I didn't. My mouth has been known to get away from me from time to time, but there's a time and place. Strong rancor can oftentimes come off as threatening. Any threat that I unknowingly make could lead to an arrest, and that arrest could very well encourage retaliating violence. Since violence can lead to deaths, and murders can lead back to arrests, it'll be best to just watch my words. I don't need to be accused of making threats. If I can stick with the quitting plan of just talking about myself, all can be avoided. This is will be one of those rare situations in which alcohol won't help.

After lunch, Jane and I went back up to Burnitts. Out of habit, I walked up to the window looking for Neighbor. It wasn't the most subtle move, so I didn't hide from it.

"What time are we having drinks with the neighbors?" I

asked.

"No time specifically. They just said that they'll be hanging outside and that we should stop over if we could. Do you want to go?" My lie detector was about to go off the fucking chart. I had to get my dick behind the bar fast. Of course, I want to go, but I can't let Jane see how excited I am.

Being sexually stimulated is addicting to me. I rarely stop thinking about it. Jane thinks I'm too much. I admit that it can be a little outrageous at times, but I'm perfectly capable of being reasonable. Jane needs to be more realistic with her spans. With that said, almost every day Neighbor does it for me, and that's at a distance. Jane's right here and doesn't. That's her doing. My dick shouldn't be faulted for its behavior. It's a natural response—think of Neighbor, get hard.

"Yeah, I'll go if you still want to. I don't think that I'll want to hang out for more than a drink or two. They might be total cunts for all I know. We'll plan an early escape, just in case." I'm so full of shit sometimes. I know that I'm not going to want to leave.

"They seem cool, but I'm good with that."

"All right, so what's the wager on this crowning game, the usual stakes?"

"Yup, loser pours the shots."

"Deal. Heads or tails for break?"

"Head of course, but tail can be good from time to time too!" She was all proud of her joke.

I didn't give her a laugh. "Whatever, just pick." She had a shit break, but I poured the shots in the end. I had fun watching her.

From there, Jane agreed to sit outside with me. We were both a little tipsy by that point. The fresh air proved nice but the sun was bright and warm. Maybe I got too much of it yesterday. I didn't make it five minutes without needing to run in for water. I filled a 32oz jug of it and grabbed us a couple of hats while in there. Having already pounded a good serving myself, I offered it right to Jane. She's always thirsty, and for once, I was proud of her for not going easy.

I threw Jane her pink ball cap and put mine on to shade my sensitive eyes. She slapped hers on backwards. I liked it.

"How about you move your car, Big Boy?"

"Why, do you want to play?"

"You bet."

"Okay, I'll bet if you want me to. If I win, you have to call out tomorrow. Your mom won't care, just tell her that you want to work a day from your new office."

"I'll think about it. What if I win?"

"I'll cook dinner," I said.

"You know that you're cooking regardless. How about you have to hang out with me next weekend? That means whatever I want to do, and I have plans to get out of here."

"Wait, I want one day, you want two?"

"Take it or leave it, buddy."

"All right, it's a bet." I figured that I had the rest of the week regardless, so I could wager the weekend. "What are you planning?"

"You'll find out when you lose!"

Finding it hard to believe that Jane just asked me to park my car in the yard, I ran in quickly for the key. While in there, I grabbed us some ShackBrews too. She has me wondering what she has planned. I'll be happy to tag along if she can behave herself from now on. However, if there's any Janger present this week, I'm staying away from her.

We opted for one-on-one, up to three games, first to seven, win by two. Hands exchanged shakes and she got first ball. Although I put up an honorable fight, she managed to take home the first two games. I didn't let her win either. Of course, I didn't play as aggressively as I could have, but at the level that I did play at, she won fair and square. I was still too sore to function normally, and just not used to moving that fast anymore.

Jane was smiling ear to ear as I sank into the chair, unable to breathe. I could tell that she was eager to rub the victory in but knew I required a couple of minutes and some water. What did I get myself into, I wondered? I wasn't ready to find out, so I needed to delay it.

"Good games, Jane." I held my hand up for a high-five. She smacked it hard, all proud of her victory. "I know you're excited to tell me about your prize, but can you hold off a bit? I just want to clean up quickly, wash this loss off my face. Afterward, we can get a glass of wine, and you can let me know what I've gotten myself into this weekend."

"Yeah, that sounds good. I'll clean up too."

"Can I use your bathroom?" I asked.

"Sure, but don't get used to it."

Knowing that it was likely going to be a while, I brought a beer and a smoke in with me to bathe. I found myself not being in a hurry to get back to Jane. It wasn't because I lost to her. I think it was because I'm not used to having all of her attention for so long. Constantly being alone seems to have grown on me a little. After my shower routine, I drew a bubble bath to immerse myself in. Thoughts of Neighbor crept up promptly, and my dick followed suit. I was imagining her body and what she would be wearing later. I thought about how close I was going to be to her and how tempting she would be. Several times, I brought myself to the point of cumming but held back. I picture an experience with her being similar. She would push me to my limit over and over again. However, with her, I wouldn't want to hold anything back.

Once my beer was finished, I was able to let up on myself. I have to start living a little more in the present. Alcohol helps. Not being sure what to wear, I settled on my usual khaki pants and a white t-shirt. With sandals being my choice footwear, business-beach is what I refer to the style as. It's the typical selection for me—relaxed with pants. For reasons similar to mine, Jane probably had to think about what to wear too. I just hope it's not something that she would wear to work. Her outfits are nice enough, they just don't come off as relaxed.

Jane was in the kitchen when I came out. She was wearing modest jean shorts and a black t-shirt. Her hair was down, and she looked great. There were two full glasses of wine sitting on the bar next to her. Either she hasn't had any without me, or she's been keeping hers topped off. More than likely she's been drinking out of the tap. She didn't waste any time with asking if I was ready to hear what we'll be doing this weekend. So much of me just wanted to ignore it for now.

"Okay, are you ready to know what you've won?"

"Sure, let's hear it."

"Just so you know, this was going to happen even if you actually won." She's always so certain of herself. I didn't know what to expect from her. It's probably going to be something fucking stupid. I know it's not going to have anything to do with playing with my dick all weekend, that's for sure. "It's already all planned out, Pops. We're driving out to meet up with Wes and Katie on Friday. We have a room for the weekend and a few fun things planned."

"What, really?" I looked at her for a second wondering if I just heard her correctly.

"Cool, right?" She smiled at me, knowing damn well how ecstatic I would be.

"Really? That's awesome! Holy shit, Jane! Are you serious? I already can't wait!" Wes is who I always want to be around. It's only with him that I've never felt like I needed to get away.

Jane and I sat in the kitchen drinking our wine just talking and laughing for a while. It reminded me of times before. We have so much going on for us suddenly. Our conversation played out as if it were natural, with no tension and no need to escape. We talked about all sorts of things like Wes and Warden and work now compared to work in a month. Even food and flowers were topics of our gabfest. Jane's company is something that I could get used to, though I expected it all along.

After our refill, I suggested we sit on the porch. I needed a cigarette after all that. I can't believe that I'm going to get to see Wes. I miss him more than my youth. Jane knew that I couldn't be happier. She looked happy too.

"Guess what," she asked.

"What?"

"In a way, you won that bet too."

"Yeah, I know. I can't wait to see him, Jane. Thank you so much."

"No, I mean outside of actually winning, you won the bet."

"I'm confused. What do you mean?"

"I'm going to stay home from work tomorrow. Actually, I have the entire week off. Mom suggested I take a vacation so that we could celebrate together!"

"What, really?"

"Yup, you got me all week, whether you like it or not. Maybe I'll teach you a few things."

"All right! Good for you. I'll love it if you keep being nice to me. Just so you know, I have been planning on being naked all week."

"Okay, I'll hold you to it. I planned on doing everything you're doing and anything you want to do, Mr. Naked!"

If Jane doesn't flip back to her usual self and actually starts putting out a little, I don't see how my life could be better right now. Good things just don't tend to happen to me very often. Now it seems like the bubble has finally burst, and it's raining wonderful things all around me. Hopefully, this is my life now. Hopefully, my life finally starts now.

With both of their cars in the driveway, I assumed that The Neighbors were home. They're likely to be outside shortly, so I'm going to need to be properly buzzed before we go. With that, I suggested we go back to Burnitts for a little bit. Jane knew that meant shots. I'm already getting used to inviting her. Upstairs, we did a shot. After that, I hit the joint and then the bench. My muscles ached, but I wanted my chest to be pumped before I left. Jane was looking impressed. She should see it when I do them naked.

After some time, Jane mentioned that the neighbors were outside. I came up to the window so that I could look too, but I was mostly curious about what Neighbor was wearing. Nothing more than I expected—just what I was wishing for.

"When do you want to go over?" she asked.

"How about we let Warden out for a little bit and then come back up for another shot? After that, we'll see if they're still out there." I was trying to be reserved. I want to go now.

Out back, Warden was being his usual self, sticking right by Jane's side as she patiently tried to sweep the patio around him. That's after she's picked up and disposed of his dog shit piles, repeatedly calling him a "good boy" while doing so. How she enjoys dealing with that dog is beyond me. He's fucking relentless. I was walking around getting a better look at the garden. I grow and take care of so much more than roses. We have a few everyday herbs, cooking herbs, a small vegetable garden, shrubs, and different varieties of colorful flowers too. It's not huge, but it's completely private. I like it because there's hardly any mowing.

After being out back for longer than expected, we finally got to the shots. Up at Burnitts, Jane confirmed that the neighbors were still outside. We planned on heading over there after the drink, but I insisted on smoking before leaving. This time, it wasn't me holding back to mask my excitement, trying to be cool and collected about Neighbor. It was me genuinely stalling. I found myself to be a little nervous suddenly. I couldn't believe what was about to happen. I hope she's as perfect as I have been imagining. Either way, I'm eager to see her. I'm not sure if alcohol would help in this situation or not.

We did another shot as I delayed. Before leaving Burnitts, I knocked out fifteen more reps. Just thinking about Neighbor, part of me wanted to get a full workout in. Both of us had to use the bathroom before we left. I looked myself over in the mirror for any fixable flaws and mouth-rinsed before pissing. On my way out, I went to the fridge and retrieved four ShackBrews for us and our new friends. Jane met me on the porch, and so began our excursion to The Neighbors.

Chapter Eighteen

I was trying not to focus hard on her as we approached. It's important that I avoid gawking at all times. They happened to notice us as we closed in, and, in my mind, she couldn't take her eyes off of me. With each step, I was getting a better and better look at her. Her body was getting closer and closer to mine. Neighbor's more than impressive, and I take in as much of her as I can before I have to reserve myself.

"Hi, guys!" They started waving and walking down to meet us at the bottom of the driveway. Both of them had friendly and welcoming smiles, but hers stood out. She was stunning. The Neighbor's probably thinking the same thing about Jane. By the time we met up, I could feel myself sweating. I had to look at her only in the eyes from here on out, and never for more than a couple of seconds unless she was talking directly to me. I was praying that my lie detector wouldn't go off.

I think that I might have made it through our introductions without being awkward. Turns out, her name is Emily, and he is Ben. They invited us up to sit and we followed. Already unable to help myself, my eyes were glued to Emily as much as possible. Her little shorts stopped right where her skinny tanned legs became her ass. As she walked, they rode a little higher. I did my best to make as many mental memories of her as possible. Emily was small and firm, and this is the closest that I've been to her. Now I want to be even closer.

I assumed that they were expecting us because there were four chairs out.

"Thanks for having us, guys. The view's a little different from over here. Sorry, you're stuck looking at that guy's piece-of-shit car over there. You can tell he never washes it." It was the perfect icebreaker for me. Emily did that laugh that I usually only hear from an envious distance. It fits her look perfectly. I followed that up by offering them a beer. "We brought you guys a beer, not sure if you drink or not." By that time, I already spotted their wine glasses. They use the real ones.

"You bet. Good man, thank you," said Ben.

"ShackBrew, all right! Thanks, you guys," remarked Emily. "I saw one on your mailbox the other morning. I'll ask how that went down another time!"

"Oh yeah, she told me about that," chimed Ben. "I told her you probably just left it there when you got the morning paper." Everyone laughed, but all I heard was Emily's.

"Me? Drink in the morning?" I looked at Jane, smiling. Smiling back, she nodded her head at me. I had to explain to her that I found a beer bottle on our mailbox the other day. I just told them all that I didn't know how it got there. There was some truth to that.

The Neighbors turned out to be pretty funny. No wonder I always hear her having such a good time. At this point, I still haven't looked long enough to take her all in. I kept my eyes mostly on Jane and Ben to avoid getting trapped in trance. Even when I had to look Emily's way, it seemed like I was looking past her. I couldn't allow my eyes to fully focus on her yet. After all that fantasizing, I'm finally close to her but still can't get a good look.

Initial conversation consisted of all the usual dialog, but we had a good time going through it. Both of ours were strongly interlaced with humor and cussing—just the way I like it. Ben said he did hotel management downtown. He loves his job. Emily said she owned a small coffee and bagel shop and that she loved her job too. I wondered if they just haven't been doing it long enough, or if liking your work just happens to be the simple secret to everything. They seemed happy enough. Of course, Jane and I probably give that impression too.

After some time, Emily excused herself and then returned with four more ShackBrews. She went down the line, handing us each one.

"All right! Thank you very much. Oh, so you're the one that put the beer on my mailbox?" I said smiling, but not exactly looking at her.

"I've been hoping it wasn't me. If it was, I'm sorry for that. Not sure what I was thinking," she remarked honestly, laughing at herself.

"No worries, just leave a full one next time." Her willingness to be accountable is different than what I'm used to.

Ben and I were left shooting the shit after Emily invited Jane inside. Jane's probably doing whatever she has to do to earn a potential client. He seemed like a decent guy. He and Emily met in college and married a few years later. Their realtor led them to HighBlue claiming it was one of the safest suburbs around. I liked him enough so far. He wasn't bitching about work, he wasn't bitching about his wife, and he wasn't bitching about life. Even though I couldn't fully relate, in a way it reinforced my hopes for a better future. With a career and wife that I love, I probably wouldn't have anything to bitch about either.

I finished my beer and Ben witnessed it. He was prompt to offer another, but I didn't want to drink a second one of his just because I came so ill-prepared. I up the ante and ask him if he would like to see my bar—dumb question. The girls weren't back out yet so we pressed on. After pointing out the roof and doorway that I built this weekend, I led him up to Burnitts to flex my liquor lounge.

Ben checked out the place while I went over to pour. He was impressed and mentioned needing one of his own. Maybe if he spent less time mowing his lawn and washing his cars, he would have time to build one. With a wife like his, he should think about trying to keep her inside. I called him over and we took our shots with a toast to being neighbors.

"Burnitts, eh? As in, burn it if you got it?" he goes.

"Oh, I'll burn it," I said. "No, it's named after Jane's Dad. He passed a while back, never got to see the place."

"Bet he would have loved it."

I lit a cigarette, knowing damn well it might bring him to think of all the butts he finds near his mailbox. He didn't say anything.

"So, do you party? Get high, Ben?"

"Yeah, that's why I live at HighBlue, high like blue sky."

"Well, pardon my delay, I'll roll us one. Better yet…" I reached under the bar and found my vape. "This is way better." I took the first hit because it's my bar, so I set the standard. I took a way bigger pull than I would normally, held it in a good moment, and then exhaled a huge cloud while finally passing it his way. He was watching the whole time and was forced to see what he was up against.

Just as Ben took a respectably long inhale, with no warning, came in the girls. He was already about the blow before they instantly startled the hit out of him. His lungs exploded with a fiery force. The girls started laughing hysterically at him. He was hurting now. I laughed, but at the same time stood fixated. I couldn't believe what was happening—Neighbor's at Burnitts. I could see her perfectly now. Jane showed her around as I watched in ecstasy. With Ben pacing around the bar trying to get his shit together, I could look hard. He had built up some tears and was barely able to get a few good breaths in. Maybe he shouldn't have hit it so hard. The girls finally giggled their fine asses up to the bar as I stood waiting. I'd be lying if I said I wasn't lucky to be standing behind it. I must be fucking dreaming. Either way, my cock doesn't discriminate.

As they stepped up, Emily's beauty couldn't be avoided. She was tiny with shiny golden skin. Her mouth and eyes mimicked each other's seducing ways with every expression. She had a light dusting of freckles on her cheekbones that seemed deliberate. I found myself captivated by her smile and teeth and had a hard time not staring at them when she spoke.

"Hey girls! Welcome to Burnitts. What can I get you?"

Emily spoke first. "I'll have what he's having," pointing at Ben.

"And, we would also like some shots, please," Jane added.

I handed Emily the pen and she proceeded to take a more civilized hit than the last guy. She passed it to Jane and she did the same. Emily turned back at me as I poured us some shots. I thought about leaving Ben out of this one but included him to play nice. I could feel her watching my actions, and all I want to do is look back at her. With the exception of learning about seeing Wes next weekend, this is the highlight of my day.

I poured four shots and lit a cigarette. The last one burned out in the ashtray as my attention turned first to the vape, then to Emily. Ben finally calmed down enough to join us. I was hoping he wouldn't. Just when I thought that Emily couldn't be more perfect, she went on to top herself.

"Cheers," I said. Everyone said cheers simultaneously.

"To Burnitts," Emily exclaimed. I couldn't believe my ears. Jane and Ben proceeded to take their shots as Emily and I tapped ours on the bar first. We caught each other's attention, and she smiled and winked at me. My dick went instant plank. Thankfully, Jane and Emily began talking, which allowed me the chance to distract myself from being so turned on. I needed to take the edge off.

Ben found the window and was now staring out toward his place. I handed him a beer knowing that the view I have might surprise him a little. Now he sees what I can see. He didn't say anything, but in a way, I still felt busted. He has to know that I check out his girl from here. Now that Ben has seen the birds-eye view that I have, I'll have to be extra careful with my window behavior from now on.

Ben thanked me for the beer, and we found our way back to the bar. Emily mentioned that she would like to play pool, but he advocated leaving soon. In his defense, it is Monday. However, I was more than okay with him going home and Emily sticking around all night. I wasn't sure if I should mention that or not. If this isn't a perfect opportunity to live out a dream, then my autopilot's leading me in the wrong direction. I quickly talked myself out of it after looking over at Jane—she's pretty.

I led Ben downstairs to give him a closer look at the work that I've done. It was a good transition to lead him out—hopefully alone. I was proud of the work and boasted about how I wanted to do something different than a vacation or jewelry this year for Jane, something that required real thought and work. I found myself bragging a little about how amazing Jane is and how much she deserved it. Our relationship was definitely exaggerated. Those are my actual feelings about her, but I've just been reminded of them yesterday. I'm not sure why I inflated my affection. Perhaps, because I'm drunk and comparing myself to this guy; the one with the perfect grass, perfect job, and perfect girl.

Ben finished his beer just as I did.

"Let me take your bottle man." That would be the last one that I'm offering him tonight. After all, he already mentioned being ready to go.

"I appreciate it. I know how you like to wander around

at night decorating mailboxes with them." At first, I thought he was joking about it again, but he sounded as if he knew a secret of mine. It's likely that he's somewhat fucked-up, but the way that he said it and looked at me caught me off guard. With that, Ben's demeanor changed. His eyes widened and his voice took a more serious tone. I wasn't sure how I wanted to react.

"Hah, that's funny. We'll probably both find one on ours in the morning. Let's just blame it on your wife."

"We could, but I was up the other night looking out the window as you stumbled up with your dog and left your bottle there. And, when I went to the store the next day, I saw a bottle on a mailbox down the road." I didn't know that I was being watched. "When Emily mentioned seeing it the next day, I wanted to mess with her a little because she got really drunk the night before and passed out early. I told her that she insisted on doing it because she thought you might be flicking cigarettes in the yard. I also told her that I thought you saw her do it, so I teased her about it all weekend. It's been a fun joke, but she needs to understand that a person can't get away with anything in a neighborhood like this. There's always someone watching."

Maybe I'm misunderstanding, but I feel like he's trying to imply something. I'm not sure if he's talking about me or him, or neither of us. Maybe I just misheard him. But, what if I didn't? Has he been seeing me looking at Emily? By the way, how often is he looking out his window in the middle of the night? What is he looking at, and what else has he seen?

I laughed. "Yeah, for some reason I thought they would look good. Just some harmless fun. I made sure to remove it before Jane saw it. But yeah, I guess there's some truth to what you're saying though. There are a lot of people in the neighborhood." I didn't bring up the butts.

Without so much as a smile or a little humor, Ben kept on about it. "Seriously, you know that there are people around here keeping an eye on you, keeping an eye on us." I could see my reflection in his now piercing eyes. "People that you haven't even met knowing more about you, your house, your life, your wife than you would ever be comfortable with. All because of an intentional effort on their part, a fixation. It's something to be concerned about. I'm always keeping an eye out to see who's watching."

"Keeping an eye on you, keeping an eye on us." "People knowing more about your wife than you would be comfortable with." What the fuck? Should I give this guy the benefit of doubt, or should I start asking questions? He's being vague with what he's saying, and I'm not sure if he's trying to insinuate something specific to me. If Ben's got something to say, then he should just come out with it directly. It's possible that he's just bitching about people being up in other people's shit. After all, I'm sure they get a lot of stares from people driving by. That comes with having a hot wife in suburbia. But, it's also possible that he just let me know that he's on to my ongoing interests in Emily and that he has been watching me. He makes me wonder about him. Has he been watching Jane?

The girls met us outside. Ben gravitated right to them and struck up a conversation with Jane about "her" roses. The way he quickly changed his attitude and look while they talked left me feeling uneasy. I let them be and started picking up the driveway. After a few minutes, he was finally ready to head out. Unfortunately, Emily was going too, but she mentioned "doing this more often." We agreed. I shook Ben's hand and gave Emily a high five, thanking them for the invite and for stopping over. After hugging Emily, Jane waved bye to Ben. It was difficult to break my gaze as I watched Neighbor walk off. I thought that a closer look would be all I needed, but it's hard not to want more.

I suggested to Jane that we move on and have a belated anniversary dinner together. She agreed, but I had something to take care of first. Everything about Emily overwhelmed my thoughts. My escape to the bathroom became unavoidable. I've had an inflated dick for the last two hours, and it was now urgently necessary to take splatters in my own hand. I barely made it across the threshold before my pants hit the floor. Just thinking about it made me full-blown and throbbing. I quickly led myself by the dick to the toilet, hardly able to lift the seat in time. It wasn't possible to hold back. I needed to cum already. Leaning forward over the toilet straddled, I braced myself against the back wall with my left hand and took aim with my right—one stroke left. I gripped my straining cock down close to my swollen balls and slowly stroked up to the top, flexing my groin at just the right time to send a thick stream of cum blasting into the water. I loosened my groin flex as it continued uninterrupted. The pressure relief valve was opened. It looked like I was pissing the cum out, and my eyes rolled back with pleasure. After a couple of seconds, my body had to flex again, briefly causing the cum torrent to pause. Then I let loose again and guided another jumbo jet airliner to its destination. After that, I flexed uncontrollably as I stroked harder, finally dying down and bringing myself to a drip tip. Within ten seconds, I lost my breath completely.

I felt immediate alleviation and remained tilted over the toilet trying to regain myself. I wasn't thinking of anything, pure bliss just took over me. Though reluctant to return vertical, Jane was waiting, and my dick needed a final squeeze and wipe-off. True to my type, I didn't so much as put my clothes on before thinking about sex again. I imagined Jane taking all that to her face and rubbing me in like lotion. I bet Neighbor would request that kind of skincare all the time.

It's interesting finally putting a name to Neighbor's body, a face to fantasy. She didn't disappoint. Emily was better than I imagined. Unfortunately, a big part of me never really wanted to meet her. Although I like flirting with erotic thoughts of her, I'm actually a little bummed-out because of what's sure to happen if we get to know each other. Emily will no longer be an unfamiliar temptation to imagine—she'll be a real person. It's guaranteed that, sooner than later, I'll see fantasy flaws that ruin the whole dream for me. I don't want to think of Neighbor as being normal. We're all ugly at times. As friends, I'm sure to see that side of her. We all experience a range of emotions, and many aren't pretty. Fantasy omits everything but beauty, and I prefer picture perfect. I am excited about the potential friendship with Emily though. She could be a good influence for Jane. Neighbor was good for the imagination while it lasted, but I prefer the real thing. That's why I like porn.

Chapter Nineteen

Jane was sitting at the bar when I came back in to join her. She looked defeated, so I suggested that we take a few minutes to relax in the living room before cooking. It's blatantly obvious that she won't be able to snap out of her exhaustion. Jane's in a shape that she could only sleep off. The last thing that I want to do right now is watch TV, but getting her away from the bar and to the couch is what has to be done. I know her look well, and she won't last long. If I don't settle her down now, things are destined to go south. She was all for it and curled into the couch with her eyes already closed. I turned on the TV and sat next to her as if I wanted to. Warden was already anxious for me to move but was patient about it. After watching no more than three minutes of kitchen rage about beef wellingtons, I could tell she was out. I'll try to wake her up in a while for a late dinner, regardless of the likely consequences.

After closing the blinds, I found myself back at the kitchen bar, struggling to decide on something to cook. Jane and I never did share a proper celebratory dinner, so I want it to be something homemade and delicious. In the end, homemade pasta and tomato sauce is what I settled on. Spaghetti is her favorite meal, and I planned to take it up a notch. I'll get the sauce started first, then move on to the noodles and garlic bread. Worst case scenario, we eat our anniversary dinner for lunch tomorrow. Neither of us has to work anyway, and the sauce is likely to be even better then.

I first started my pasta dough by bringing together eggs, flour, and oil. After ten minutes of kneading, it got wrapped up and set aside near the stove where it's warm. Caramelizing onions and garlic in olive oil came next. Then I minced beef and hot Italian sausage to sear off in the pot with them. The meats were cut fine enough to be more part of the sauce, not so much an element in it. After adding two large cans of diced tomatoes, two cans of paste, a nice splash of beef broth, and some oil, everything was combined to warm up. It was at that point, that I decided to start my water binge.

After two glasses of water myself, I brought one to Jane in case she woke up thirsty. Returning to the kitchen, I cleaned up what I could and moved on to making pasta. By far, the hardest thing about making pasta is cleanup. Flour goes everywhere when I work with it. However, other than alcohol, it's my most demanded food staple. With that, flour has permanently become part of my kitchen. After I got all the pasta through the maker and ready to cook, I set it aside and got back to the sauce. Once warm, I added a rough amount of salt, pepper, cayenne, and Italian seasonings. After that, I brought it to a boil for ten minutes, then down to a simmer to adjust flavors accordingly. At that point, I threw in some portobello mushrooms and gave it time to come together. Occasionally stirring the sauce will give me something to do for the rest of the night. I'll keep doing it even after I take it off the heat.

Outside, it was quiet. Not surprising though. Monday evenings are predictably the quietest around here. Most people have been waiting all day just for it to be fucking over. Relative to the weekends, this place seems joyless. I guess that when there are so many miserable and tired people around, that collective depression in the air can be sensed. The Neighbors are probably quiet for a different reason. The same goes for Jane.

I ran up to Burnitts quickly to hit the joint. After imagining it so many times, Neighbor being here still baffles me. She was a good fit for the bar. Jane has been looking good in here too, but she tends to come a little overdressed. Regardless, Jane likes the place more than she thought she would. I didn't want to stay at Burnitts long, but I also wasn't ready to shut it down quite yet either. If it's possible to get Jane up in a little while without problems, I'd like to bring her up and give her something special that I've been thinking about.

The sauce needed to be stirred again. Beautiful Italian aromas punched me in the nose as soon as I walked through the door. At the pot, I gave it a taste and changed nothing, so I laid us out some proper wine glasses and plate settings. After lighting some candles, I still wasn't satisfied with the setting, so I moved everything out to the back patio. The round table's far more intimate than the one-sided bar, especially with the fire lit next to it. Plus, since we rarely eat dinner outside together, it'll feel new and more date-like.

Jane could easily ruin this whole thing we've been having if she gets angry. Waking her up will be the real test of whether or not she's altered her attitude. Before changing into something more comfortable, I grabbed a quick shower to clean any residuals off. Pj pants with no boxers or shirt, that's what I choose for evening dinner attire.

Before risking a verbal lashing from Jane, I quickly ran back up to Burnitts to do a shot. The new door is fucking brilliant. When waking Jane for no other reason than asking if she would like to have fun with me, alcohol always helps. It never works in my favor. I'm only trying now because she's been different; we've been celebrating, and I made a nice meal. I took two shots so that I could be as ready as I could be. Come to find out, getting myself well prepared wasn't necessary. Jane wasn't finished surprising me. She was already up and showering. By the time I smoked and went to stir the pot, she was meeting me in the kitchen—hopefully not wanting to stir the pot.

"Hey, girl," I said, noticing her cute pajamas. They were loose cotton shorts pulled up high with a nice form-fitting t-shirt.

'   "Hey, boy! Sorry, I fell asleep on ya."

"No worries, you looked tired. I'm surprised you woke up."

"The spaghetti smells fucking amazing. I think that my stomach woke me up." She looked around, "And you have us set up outside! Is this a date?"

"It is. Happy anniversary!"

"Thank you, Marty. Happy anniversary!"

Jane coasted closer until the last possible step, never breaking eye contact. Without stopping, she came in for a kiss. This time, it wasn't the usual emotionless peck. Our lips locked softly as we genuinely embraced one another. I put my hand on her cheek, and our mouths opened wider as our kiss intensified. It was full-on. My lie detector went off. I can't remember the last time I made out with Jane, and I love it.

We pulled back from each other, both of us smiling. With that, I turned to give her a taste of the sauce. "Yum," Jane remarked, followed by "It's perfect, I can't wait to eat." I tasted it and added more salt and cayenne. Not thinking earlier, I had to run out back to grab our glasses so that we could have a drink together. Jane was excited about using a proper wine glass, admitting that hers would probably be broken by dinner's end. We toasted to spaghetti and had a laugh about her clumsiness. I suggested she take Warden out back and enjoy the fire as I plate us up. She came up and thanked me with another soft kiss before heading out.

After starting the oven and water, I went to slice some sourdough. These slices will be spread with butter, dashed with garlic, and covered in cheese. I'll leave the cheese off until the last minute of baking. In going to check on Jane and top her wine off, I noticed that she was on the phone. It wasn't until I went all the way out there that I realized that she was just taking pictures of Warden. She wanted one of the two of us, so I agreed. I squatted down and he happily sat next to me. Just as he went to lick my spaghetti breath, she snapped the picture. I was smiling, so it came out looking like I was thoroughly enjoying getting defiled by his invasive tongue—I wasn't.

Back in the kitchen, the bread went in first. Once the pot of water reached a boil, I dropped the noodles in. At that time, the bread was ready for cheese, and everything was done two minutes later. As I retrieved the plates that I thoughtlessly set up outside, I brought out the box of wine, garlic bread, and parmesan. Jane couldn't wait, so I dished up two beautiful servings of spicy homemade pasta and sauce and returned quickly to her. I was excited to please her. It's been all weekend that I've been wanting to cook and share an outside meal with her.

The spaghetti turned out amazing. So good that both of us couldn't resist attempting seconds. Neither of us fully succeeded. Jane was thankful, and it was nice hearing her appreciation. After dinner, we remained outside for a while sitting and talking around the fire. It's a gas fire, so it's not nearly as fun as a more traditional pit. Despite that, it's an ideal setting with all the foliage and flowers lit up around it. It's a tranquil spot, perfect to absorb into and rest the full away. After about two cigarettes worth of time, I was finally able to move again and could clean up. Not much later, Jane met me in the kitchen, just in time for me to be finishing. She came in with the dog following right with her.

"We want to do something, Marty." She said it in a way that indicated that she either had something specific in mind, or that it was my fault that they were not doing anything. I knew I was at fault for nothing, so I asked what she was thinking about.

"We could go for a W.A.L.K. or something."

Fuck that. No fucking way am I walking him right now. I'm tired and drunk, and the last thing I want to do is stroll around the neighborhood with those two while he shits all up and down the road. I'll have to stop and wait while Jane patiently and happily tends right to it. I don't want to listen to him getting praised for poop while she proudly transports it in bags swinging six inches from my face.

"Can you think of anything else, something that requires less movement on my part? Why don't we throw him the ball or pull on his rope?" I asked.

"I just want to do something. I haven't spent much time with him today."

Warden's a side-effect of getting along with Jane. All of a sudden, we're a threesome. It's not just Jane and me. She instantly expects me to be a happy participant in things like sharing furniture, playing, and walks with him. She has me taking pictures with him and shit. Fuckin hell, I've been here all along.

Warden's impeding. He doesn't mean to be, he's just being a dog. The problem is that he actually thinks he's one of us. He seriously thinks that we are all the same—we're not. We don't need to be sharing beds and couches. He thinks he needs to be right up his pack's ass—he doesn't. He wants to lick my face —I don't want him to. He thinks Jane is his, and that he dominates me—I say fuck-off dog. He's been a pain in my ass since we got him, and I wasn't even the one looking to fill a void.

We decided to throw the rope around, which, compared to walking, is by far the better exercise—for the dog, not me. Also, it gave him the best of both worlds compared to a ball. Not only can it be thrown just as far, but it can be wrestled back away from him too. I never gave it any previous thought. However, now that I have, rope truly is a superior dog toy. We threw it around until Warden started walking back and dropping it without a fight. I couldn't wait for him to finish. Now I can relate to how Jane feels with me. Next time, I'll keep in mind that walking would be the quicker option. As much as I enjoyed dedicating my night to entertaining the douchebag dog, I was more than ready to fuck-off somewhere else.

As Warden went to water, Jane and I went to wine. I was thinking about the surprise that I had for her. I thought about it yesterday and hoped to be able to show her today.

"Let's go to Burnitts for a few," I suggested.

Jane gave me that all-so-familiar look. "I don't know, Marty. I was kind of hoping we would settle in."

"I'm not necessarily trying to keep a party going, Jane. I just want to show you something. It's up there."

"What do you have to show me, the vodka?"

"Well, if we're there, why not? But that's not why I'm asking."

After brief consideration, "All right, you got me, Mr. Chef."

At Burnitts, I led Jane to the couch and turned on the TV. After running downstairs to grab what I wanted, I went to the bar to pour us some vodka shots. Jane got up to join me despite my intentions of serving her.

"Cheers. To surprises!" The weekend has been full of them.

"Cheers. To surprises." Jane was looking at me with curious and cautious eyes. I was excited to do this with her. After shutting the blinds, dimming the lights, and getting Jane back to sitting, I went behind the bar and grabbed the video camera.

I positioned the camera upright on the TV stand and plugged it in. Then I inserted the tape that I found in the box downstairs. Back on the couch, I covered us up, kissed Jane, and hit play. The footage was of the compilation variety—video gathered over the early years that I edited down to smaller clips and combined. It's been at least six years since we've seen it, probably closer to seven or eight.

The video was all about Wes. Jane and him at the hospital is how it began. It seems to show his first everything and more, right up to the age of ten or so. We were both mesmerized the moment it started playing. It's amazing watching him grow through the years. It all happened too fast in real life but the changes weren't as obvious. I love him at every age. Each one is different, but all are equally brilliant.

Jane was in tears for most of the footage. I was too. I thought about bringing up more tapes but decided another time would be better. I have several more like it, but waiting will give us something to look forward to the next time we're enjoying each other's company this much. Hopefully, more sooner than later. A person can only take so much pure emotion anyway. We sat there for several minutes just holding each other on the couch, both of us too involved in our own thoughts to talk. A child is literally part of its parents. That's the best way that can I describe the love between father and son. Thankfully, Wes was fortunate. He seems to have only inherited the functional aspects of us. More than anything, I can't wait to see him.

The effects of celebrating all day were catching up to me. Being that I went strong through the hours, it's not unexpected. I find myself worn out and tired, so I suggested we go in. Jane didn't jump on the proposition. Instead, she turned to me, got on my lap, held my face with both hands, and looked me dead in the eyes.

"Thank you for that, Marty," she said, then gave me a nice kiss. "I love you."

"I love you." I do. I love her so much. I love her with my whole fucking heart.

Jane claimed to have a better idea than going in. Instead, she suggested that I turn the music back on and "Live. Love. Liquor!" Her voice raised considerably when she said "liquor."

Jane was suddenly and surprisingly excited, with the energy and persuasive encouragement I prefer.

"Are you serious?" I really didn't know.

"Yeah, let's do a shot. We're on vacation! Can you keep up?"

"You're asking *me* if I can keep up with *you*? Haven't you already been sleeping today?"

"Shut up and prove it, Mr. Camera Man."

I did as Jane asked and poured us drinks. Once in hand, we toast to love. At the same time, we both tapped our glasses on the bar and took our shots. Then we did another one, that time to Burnitts.

"I've got one last surprise for you," Jane said.

"Let's have it." All of her surprises have been impressive thus far.

"You know how I said that I had to work today and then later came home with some bags?"

"Yeah."

"Well, I didn't have to work. I went shopping for your surprise!" She was impressed with herself.

"So you lied to me?"

"I guess I did. What are you going to do about it?"

"Did you eat the sandwich I made you?"

"Of course! I love it when you make me food. Thank you. Okay, hold on, I'll go get it!"

Choosing not to move, I lit a cigarette and hit the joint. This is Burnitts bar, I thought. It's a hottie-hunting, liquor-liking, music-mashing, pot-puffin, love hub. It doesn't get any better than Burnitts at a residential level. I actually prefer my home bar overall. I would rather drink at home. Unexpected obstacles don't exist because I know the place. Even when drooling drunk and sideways I can reasonably navigate with minimal destruction. Plus, I like to be naked.

Before I knew it, I heard the door shut and Jane walking

up, all the while revealing what my gift was. She picked white lingerie either because of her own liking or because she remembered it was my favorite. Her hair was down and trailed behind her as she spun around a couple of times to model her new ensemble. She posed seductively at the couch and pool table as she strutted her way over to me.

Jane's lingerie was exceptional. The fit was snug but flexible enough to move with her as she performed her amateur catwalk. The many straps were thin and contoured her body perfectly. They flawlessly accentuated all the areas that I wanted and haven't seen in a while. The parts I couldn't see were covered in a floral lace that allowed only teasing glimpses of what lay behind. Her double-strapped thong panties had one set pulled high over the hips and the other sat lower and straighter across. She also had a matching garter belt supporting her white fishnet stockings, which gave the outfit more of a "I want to fuck" feel. Her top, which included an attached neckpiece, did the same.

When Jane walked in, my jaw hit the floor and my cock hit the ceiling at the same time. I watched her with precision. This was the Jane that I hung my hat on. This was the Jane that has always done it for me, and the one that I've always wanted. She gave me every angle as she worked her approach, arms up and twirling, leg on couch with hands on hips, taking a shot at the pool table, and leaning up against it too. There were some minor hiccups with her flow, but I was more than impressed.

Jane showing up in lingerie didn't cross my mind at all. Just thinking about how the "Live. Love. Liquor." thing could have been a hint, I thought her surprise might be a set of new shot glasses or a new spirit to try. Also, since she was bringing whatever it was up to Burnitts, what else would it be? Thinking about it just before, I imagined her surprising me with something mundane, and what I might think to myself. The best that I could come up with was "next time surprise me with Neighbor." In my mind, I can be an asshole sometimes.

Jane made her way back to the bar. She was excited about my reaction.

"What do you think?"

"I'm fucking lost for words! You look incredible, I love it! And, you owned it coming in." The way she looked made me want to stay restrained, but at the same time just start taking her. I don't want to stop watching her, but at the same time, I want her right now. She put me in a beautiful, difficult position.

"I noticed you watching me play pool earlier. Do you want to watch me now?"

"Yes, I do! Rack 'em and crack 'em, girl."

I planned on making this game last as long as it could. I'll be pouring shots, missing shots, and setting her up for difficult shots as well. This is all I've been wanting. Why wouldn't she want to be here? Why wouldn't she play in her panties? I'm already having the best time ever, and this is how I want the rest of my life to be.

I could have watched Jane play all night, but we couldn't make it through a single game once the touching started. It was her that ended up losing control first. She was behind me as I was about to take a shot. Before I knew it, she had me turned around and pinned against the table. She made her way down swiftly, pulling my pants farther down as she went. I kicked a pant leg off and spread out a little to allow her restriction-free, full access. My fantasies were coming true. That's the type of bar Burnitts is.

I loved Jane loving on me. She seemed to be enjoying herself too. I've always preferred the way she plays with my dick. She has finesse like no other. I don't like anything too aggressive with blowjobs and have always favored her delicate approach. When she wants to, Jane keeps me on edge and makes me feel like she actually takes pleasure in teasing me. With that, she makes me want more.

After several minutes, Jane stood up and led me out of my pants and to the couch. I sat down and leaned back as she got on top of me. Her panties felt like silk on my dick. She slowly rubbed on me as I found the latch to her neckwear and removed her top. I went right for her. She put her hand on mine as I rubbed gently around her chest. Her tits are amazing, and the way she moves is testing. As we began making out, her sliding on me intensified. It was feeling better and better for her, and I was as hard as I could be. Her moans escalated as her grinding on my dick increased. She found her rhythm but lost control at the same time. Within moments, her movements brought her to a vigorous climax like none before. I couldn't have been more turned on. I held her as she spasmed in full orgasm, all the while trying not to cum myself. In that position, I was staring down my own barrel, but the heat that I was packing was meant for her eyes only.

Once relaxed, Jane looked at me as if I'd just given her the world. I think she forgot what sexual gratification felt like. She had my full attention now though. I urged her off and up standing as I sat at the edge of the couch. She stood in front of me and rubbed my head as I kissed around her creamy, rose-laced panties. I slowly undressed her, drew her in closer by the hips, and continued clutching her beautiful body.

I couldn't contain myself any longer. At that point, there was only one thing that I wanted to do with Jane. She's given me her full attention, and now I want to give her mine. All that I want to do is take her to bed.

"Can I take you to the bedroom?" I wasn't going to take no for an answer.

"Of course. Please." Her voice was soft and made her seem innocent, but she would do anything I wanted.

"Let me shut down Burnitts real quick." I first lit a cigarette and offered Jane one last drink. She accepted. We held off until I wrapped things up. Packing up the camera gave me an idea of what I could work on this week, making Wes copies of all the footage I have. I could have it done by the weekend if things don't get too out of hand. I should start a list of to-do's to help keep myself on track. Back at the bar, Jane stood naked, and I was ready to be of service to her.

I held my glass up to meet Jane's as we stood eye-locked. Before we brought them together, I told her that I loved her.

"I love you," she said back to me.

"Cheers to you, Miss. Jane Fields."

"Cheers to you, Mr. Marty Fields."

"To Burnitts," we both said at the same time. After toasting, we simultaneously tapped our glasses on the bar, swallowed our shots, and then slammed our empty glasses, upside down, on the bar in front of us. I took one last look around, shut off the lights, and took Jane home.

Going in, I had to point out how sneaking in and out naked is a lot easier with the new door. Jane agreed, but I don't think she's ever found herself in the position before. We went straight to the bedroom and into bed. Then I kicked Warden out so we could have it for ourselves. I got on top of her and positioned her legs where I wanted, kindly kissing and rubbing her all over as I slowly made my way in her. She felt incredible. I was as close to her as I could be, and all I wanted to do was make passionate, traditional love to her.

Jane passed out not long after we finished but not before needing her nightly wine and water. While up, I had two waters and grabbed a beer for myself. Today's been incredible and so necessary. Jane and I desperately needed to make some love. A couple can only go so long without experiencing it at that level. It worked for me. I feel euphoric and can't get enough of that Jane.

Unable to get it out of my mind, I made my way to the porch to smoke. Outside, my eyes fell on The Neighbor's place.

Maybe I read him wrong, but that guy seemed a little peculiar. I guess we all are. Either way, an idea came to mind. Once in my head, I didn't think twice about it. I cautiously made my way down the driveway and across the road. As I approached it, I finished my cigarette and flicked it at the mailbox, missing by a couple of feet. Once it was within reach, I chugged the rest of my ShackBrew and set it on top of its post. The wandering town decorator strikes again. From there, I ran back home and rejoined Jane in bed, wondering if I was being watched the whole time.

Chapter Twenty — Tuesday

Out of nowhere, I began to accept that I was conscious and that I must have been sleeping. It's not dark out so I must have had a decent night's rest. My first thoughts emerge as highlights of the night before. It's nice knowing that Jane's not mad at me for anything. I find it difficult to keep my eyes open, but I'm too comfortable to care. It's hard to wrap my head around everything that has been happening. Maybe I'm not as conscious as I think. I can't tell if I'm awake, sleeping, or going in and out of both. Am I thinking, or am I dreaming? Things are coming to me in more detail, I'm just not certain if they're real. Obviously, I must be dreaming, everything's just been too good to be true.

Being able to stretch out as far as I can without restriction is a luxury that I could get used to. A bed has never felt better. It's no wonder that the dog prefers it here. I slid out while Jane remained asleep and made my way to the kitchen for fluid. Water is essential at this point. After two glasses, I got the coffee going and filled another one to carry around with me. Of course, I'll be using my usual bathroom to freshen up. Pink towels and beauty products aren't going to stop that. Some of my happiest times have happened there. Regardless of what I told Jane, I'll always consider it my/Burnitts' bathroom.

My shower was quick. There was no need for me to try

to ignore reality today. I decided on khakis and a white t-shirt to wear to work. With that, proper footwear would have to be sandals. It's not my traditional work attire, but, as usual, it will have beer on it before the day's end. Going in looking like I do, I'll have "quitting" written all over me. Back at the porch with coffee, I notice that The Neighbor must have found the ShackBrew bottle I left for him last night. Now thinking about it, I woke up naked and probably didn't have any clothes on when I did that.

Back inside, Jane was still sleeping. She must have gotten up at some point because her glasses were empty. Warden was on the couch patiently waiting to accompany her, so I let him in knowing exactly how that feels. I also know how that fucking couch feels. I appreciate him being protective and always wanting to be with her. In this neighborhood, who knows how many people have their eyes on her, willing to do anything to get close. Anyway, good for Jane getting good rest. The last few days have been full-on. Instead of waking her, I left her with a note. *Good morning beautiful. Thank you for everything. I love you so much. -Marty.*

Getting myself in the car and driving to work today is a little easier than most. Not only will I not be staying long, but I also won't be fucking back. For the first time ever, I was actually in a hurry to get there. I couldn't wait to pack my shit up and head back home. I have some work to do while I'm there—I have a resignation letter to write. However, that's a task I look forward to and will gladly labor over.

The drive to work seemed quick. What to write occupied my thoughts. After finishing my smoke at the door, I was happy to walk in for the last time. Right away, I stood out against all the NPCs with my atypical casual wear and exposed toes. Me looking like that while carrying a black duffle bag seemed to make some people nervous. I was aware of how it all might come off but thought it would be funny to build the suspense leading up to my departure. At my desk, I could feel all eyes on me. I placed the bag on the floor next to my feet and slowly unzipped it, knowing people were watching, scared of what I might pull out. Without looking around, I sat back up and turned on my computer. There were a few sighs of relief in the background. My picture of Wes and Jane went in first. It helped get me through some gloomy times here. Outside of that and my computer, I needed nothing else. Even so, I'm taking everything that I can get away with—paper clips, folders, sticky note pads, you name it. Once the computer was up and running, I began my email.

"*This is notice of my resignation, effective immediately. My reasons and feedback are stated in the following:*

I'm done with this suck corporate dick and fuck the end user environment. I feel like the glorified middleman in this filthy threesome. As nice as a good fuck and suck sounds, not with you ass-gaps and limp-dicks. I strongly recommend that the willingness to be dirtier than a cockroach cunt in order to meet the expectations set and modeled perfectly by management be mentioned in all job descriptions provided to future company candidates. Applicants should be informed that they'll be assuming the piece of shit role to you assholes. I could slam my rock-hard dick in the door on the way out, and still come out fucking straighter than the crooked cocks leading this industry. Over the years, I've had to swallow my pride every time I walked through these doors. Now you can swallow my pride. I quit."

In an effort to avoid trouble, I think that I managed to keep the correspondence about me as planned. Perhaps some of my words got away from me—I don't care. It wasn't going to be satisfying enough to send it to The Boss only. The whole department was gonna get my status update and feelings about the place. I hit send and continued packing. Before long, the rustling around me was getting noticeably louder and people throughout the floor were starting to talk more and laugh. My laptop was the last of the things to pack up, so I eagerly shut it down and shoved it in the bag. When I stood up, it became quiet. I looked around and saw that several people were looking back at me. I think they got the memo.

It stayed relatively still as I began my walk out. As soon as the first guy shouted "yeah, Marty," the place erupted. I said what they can't, and now I'm their fucking hero for it. People were clapping as I made my way to the door. I was hearing "suck corporate dick," "rock-hard dick," and "cockroach cunt" being yelled. It was brilliant. I just put my arm up like a fucking champion and walked out without looking back.

That felt as good as anything. I wish that I could go back in and do it again. Since the cops would probably be called if I tried, I leave for the last time. Two days ago I wouldn't have believed that I'd ever be quitting my job and wanting to rush home to my wife. For the first time in too long, I'm feeling like a winner in life.

Once off the highway, I'm finally on the "high" way. Today will be the biggest celebration of the week thus far. With everything I'm imagining doing with Jane, I hope she's ready. It would be a perfect morning to stop and burn one at Lookout, but there wasn't any reason to stall today. Plus, all I have on me is my lunch liquor in the console. It's not quite the traditional ShackBrew that I prefer to enjoy there. I've also recently learned that, even though the view's perfect, I prefer Jane's company.

After just lighting my perfectly-timed cigarette, I was almost around Lookout Corner with no intention to stop when the next thing I knew, an out-of-control delivery truck was coming in for the kiss. It was moving a little too fast and aggressive for my comfort. Having no other option, I jerked to the right, barely avoiding the certain-death collision. The whole thing startled the shit out of me, and before I knew it, my going off the cliff in the next second was imminent. There was nothing I could do, I was about to die.

It all happened out of nowhere and so fast. However, once my impending fate approached, that last moment seemed to go on much longer. There was an early point in that time when I was scared. I wasn't in control and knew that it was going to be bad. I was afraid of pain, and I was afraid to suffer. I didn't plan on dying.

Not long after that, my mind blocked out the fear. I looked at it as an autopilot type of situation. Similar to when I'm drunk and letting that guy steer me around. I just have to accept that I can't do anything about it. That's my beautiful mind protecting itself as it should. I thought about a lot in that short time. Actually, my thoughts were just on their usual tangent. Wishing I had a beer definitely crossed my mind.

I couldn't believe it was happening to me. Not saying "me" as if I'm entitled or that I think the universe is against me. It's just that, out of all the things that have never happened and all the things that could happen, this is what's happening to me. There were so many potential variables that could have changed this whole outcome. I could have slept later, or called out and gone in tomorrow. Jane could have woke up and pulled me back in bed, or my car could have broken down. Not that those last two would ever happen. I don't feel "why me," I'm just amazed that everything lined up this way.

The whole thing is about as ironic as it gets. I can't remember the last time I wanted more life. Things couldn't have been better for me. Turns out, the whole thing was just another fucking tease. Now I'm finding myself edging in the wrong way. Thinking of it now, these past few days have been more like the last meal on death row. There was good food and even a Warden present. Maybe I'm lucky though, I had an opportunity to be happy again.

Luck aside, I'm somewhat pissed about this sudden and unexpected shit-show. I've been working hard all these years to ensure a heart attack. Now I'm about to be the unemployed man that dies in a car accident with a half-bottle of vodka in his car. Not just any car, an old piece of shit that appears to fit the profile perfectly. Sure, it would be a fitting description, but it would be taken out of context. I've always thought a heart attack would be the most appropriate, likely caused by Jane's neglect. That's why I'm adamant about jerking off regularly, my heart doesn't function well with any added pressure. My mind kind of goes haywire too.

In that last second, before I went hurdling over Lookout's ledge, I thought of everything. The spectrum had no boundaries, unlike the road ahead. My thoughts went from wishing I could smoke this cigarette, to how this was going to affect the people around me. I thought about my boss getting the last laugh, and how laughing was my favorite thing in the world. I thought about how this moment would look through a lens, and how I could be getting the closest look ever. I even thought about the rogue materials truck having that same orange 'X' painted on the grill as the truck that delivered my order on Saturday. Robb said that his boss was down to just the one. Today would have been his Monday—sounds like a Monday to me.

In a way, my life did flash before my eyes. By no means was it my entire life, which was nice. I'd rather not recall it all anyway. I thought of things that made me happy, things I was proud of, things I experienced, and things that I loved. I guess there wasn't any time to dwell on the negatives. My thoughts were various vivid clips of the whole adventure, just like Wes's video. There wasn't anything bad in my memories, only times of smiles and joyful tears.

My boy Wes, I love that kid so much. I love him so much that ever since the day I met him, I've wanted many more just like him. He's solely responsible for me wanting a big family, though Jane never got on board with that. He set my expectations high without even trying. I'm most proud and honored to be his dad. I've been privileged to have witnessed his life. He's a perfect person and the world is lucky to have him. I thought about Wes's future, and what might become of him. I'm confident he'll be happy. That's what I want most for Wes, but I also hope that he takes good care of my bar too.

Even Jane happened to cross my mind. Truthfully, I thought of her most. Right down to my last second, she dominates my head space as usual. It's difficult to describe what it is about her that has given me that one-of-a-kind, ineffable feeling that I've craved since first noticing her. I've never stopped being addicted to Jane and submissively dependent on her. Being without her is something I'd never choose.

Through the years, I've tried to understand what I could and have empathy for Jane. Her life, like most, hasn't been easy. Weston died within the first year of us meeting each other. After that, everything changed. A parent's death would fuck anyone's mind, and she was just a teenager—his baby girl. Jane tries to maintain good spirits on the outside, but she has always been hurting badly on the inside. This year marked the twenty-fifth year of his passing.

It was in that same year that we started university here, close to Karla. Jane always mentioned preferring to travel but I insisted on getting a degree. Thinking about it now, I'm sure she needed to get away from what was previously considered home. Her beautiful mind didn't have an opportunity to protect itself with all of the painful reminders around her. Jane's life was just flipped upside down, and what escape she could have had, she put on hold to be with Karla and me.

Jane must have been dealing with a mind that constantly occupied her in all the worst and wrong ways. I know how that can feel. Like I do now, she must have felt that so many things were out of her control. Life suddenly became more stressful than fun for her. I know how that can be too, and I am now just understanding how we all vent differently. Jane has had a lack of choice in everything. She didn't want her dad to be dead.

When Jane should have been living her best days, things were happening around her that she didn't ask for, and it was all life-altering and scary for her. Jane never had proper time to find contentment in her situation before we found out Wes would be joining us. I think that it was all too much in too little time for her. Jane's love for him is undeniable, but I do think her being unsettled and losing her dad so young affected her level of involvement and attachment. I don't think that she wanted Wes to assume that she was always going to be there.

As the years passed, Jane focused on work more and only became more easily agitated and disinterested in me. It's easy to see, now, that she probably didn't even like going to work. I think the only reason she would have chosen to work with her mom day after day was so that she could remain flexible for Wes. Her distance didn't bother me as much when he was around. Since he's been gone, I've been struggling more than I knew. In these last moments, my mind was all over the place. One thing that I am sure of, Jane has been missing her baby boy as much as I have been.

Jane's my life. She means absolutely everything to me. Without us, there would be no Wes. I love her so much that I would live my life over and over with her. She's one-hundred percent, grade-A beauty, and I'm forever hooked.

What happens after death? For me, nothing. I'm not even sure that I am dead. My life feels real but I could very well be dreaming. In this life, it's often difficult for me to tell what's actual and what's not. It's another one of those rare exceptions when alcohol doesn't help. For all I know, I could be passed out next to someone's mailbox right now with a spent cigarette in one hand and Warden's stanky leash in the other.

I suppose that if I am dead, I should pay my last respects to myself by saying a few final words. Sharing some insights that I've gained in life seems most appropriate. First, the grass will always be shorter and greener on the other side. I found it best to focus on the flowers that were right in front of me. I've learned how important it is to live every day as if it were Friday, like the first day of a lifelong vacation. Also, without question, a man should be celebrating his wife every day as if it were their anniversary. Another thing, if he's being a good boy and protects your pack as he should, show some love and throw the dog a rope every once in a while. Finally, unless you want the neighbors to see what goes on inside that dysfunctional domestic home of yours, always be sure to shut the blinds.

The EnD